"You trust ... but I still don't trust you."

"In that case, I'll do it alone."

She'd been testing him, seeing how far she could push him. Now the limits were clear. She tilted up her chin. "Not on your life."

He glanced back, a sensual smile curling his lips. "Then you'll have to take me on faith," he said, lifting a hand to graze the slope of her cheekbone.

She licked her lips. "Anything for Tucker."

"Don't say 'anything,' Callie, unless you mean it." His hand caressed her jaw, capturing it, making it a prisoner as his mouth descended, his lips rubbing lightly over hers.

"Don't read too much between the lines," she murmured a trifle breathlessly.

"Let me know when I reach 'too much.'"

Dear Reader,

Spellbinder! That's what we're striving for. The editors at Silhouette are determined to capture your imagination and win your heart with every single book we publish. Each month, six Special Editions are chosen with *you* in mind.

Our authors are our inspiration. Writers such as Nora Roberts, Tracy Sinclair, Kathleen Eagle, Carole Halson and Linda Howard—to name but a few—are masters at creating endearing characters and heartrending love stories. Their characters are everyday people—just like you and me—whose lives have been touched by love, whose dreams and desires suddenly come true!

So find a cozy, quiet place to read, and create your own special moment with a Silhouette Special Edition.

Sincerely,

The Editors
SILHOUETTE BOOKS

NATALIE BISHOP
Just a Kiss Away

Silhouette Special Edition

Published by Silhouette Books New York

America's Publisher of Contemporary Romance

SILHOUETTE BOOKS
300 East 42nd St., New York, N.Y. 10017

ISBN: 0-373-09352-7

First Silhouette Books printing December 1986

America's Publisher of Contemporary Romance

Printed in the U.S.A.

NATALIE BISHOP

lives within a stone's throw of her sister, Lisa Jackson, who is also a Silhouette author. Natalie and Lisa spend many afternoons together developing new plots and reading their best lines to each other.

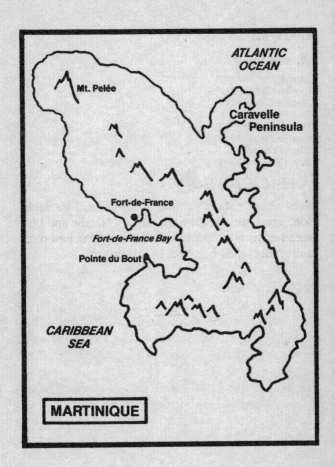

ATLANTIC
OCEAN

Mt. Pelée

Caravelle
Peninsula

Fort-de-France

Fort-de-France Bay

Pointe du Bout

CARIBBEAN
SEA

MARTINIQUE

Chapter One

Callie Cantrell slid open the door to her balcony and immediately felt the sweltering humidity of Martinique. She'd grown accustomed to it this past month, though when she'd first arrived on the Caribbean island she'd been limp and exhausted and certain she would never become acclimated. Even on its hottest days San Francisco was nothing like this!

She leaned her forearms on the wrought iron railing and gazed over the rooftops of the apartments and tenements on the hill below her, looking beyond the telltale signs of humanity toward the crystalline waters of Fort-de-France Bay. She was going to hate to leave this place; it had become a second home.

"Callie! Callie!"

Looking below her down the crooked cobblestone alley that led to the road, she saw a little boy, no more than five years old, racing around the corner waving his dust-grimed arm frantically.

Callie's heart did a curious little flip-flop. She grinned and waved back. Stephen Tucker Thomas, the only other resident of the area she knew who spoke her language, was heading in her direction full tilt.

"What are you doing up so early?" Callie called, leaning over the rail.

"I came to see you." He flashed her a huge smile and scampered up the cracked concrete steps to the apartment house's front door.

As Callie walked back inside, she wondered, not for the first time, what kind of parents Tucker had. It was barely 6:00 a.m., for Pete's sake, and the child ran loose among Martinique's narrow streets and alleys until way after dark, too. Callie rarely saw Tucker with an adult, and she'd only met his mother once. The woman had regarded Callie with suspicion and had ordered in French— Martinique's native tongue—for Tucker to leave the room. She'd then explained in broken English to Callie that she was Tucker's mother and that she had tried very hard to keep him in line but it was difficult. Tucker's father, the woman had gone on, was an American and captain of a fishing boat and he was rarely home. Aimee Thomas was basically a single parent.

Callie had privately felt she was just making excuses for being so lax, but since she hadn't wanted to alienate herself from Tucker's mother she'd kept her opinions to herself. Tucker was too important to Callie for her to object too strongly. In fact, Callie realized, ruefully wrinkling her nose, Tucker was the one reason she hadn't left Martinique earlier. She loved him—almost as much as she'd loved her own son. Joshua's death had nearly killed her, but now, almost a year later, Callie had found the road back to health; Tucker's innocent help being the last and final cure.

Her heart ached at the thought of leaving him.

Tucker impatiently rattled her apartment door and Callie hollered, "Hold on! I'm coming."

"Hurry up! I brung you something."

"That's brought, Tucker, and no, I will not accept any more gifts. You've got to take this one back," Callie said sternly, glancing toward her bedroom and the bracelet on her dresser as she made her way to the front door.

She slipped the chain off the lock and opened the door. Tucker, like the bundle of pure energy he was, hurtled himself inside and held out his hands triumphantly.

"See?" he demanded.

Cupped between his palms was a tiny, bluish-tinted starfish.

"Ahhh..." Callie put the starfish in her own palm, examining it critically as she looped an arm around Tucker's thin shoulders. "You've been beachcombing."

"Yesterday. And I go today, too."

"You're going today?"

Tucker bobbed his dark head. His eyes were a fine, clear gray and they stood out dramatically against his dark hair and skin. Callie had grown used to the way he mangled his verbs; in fact, it was amazing he spoke English as well as he did. She knew several five-year-olds back in San Francisco who didn't speak half as well as Tucker.

"I go to the pier and wait around." Tucker glanced over his shoulder as if he expected someone to materialize in the open doorway. He moved still closer to Callie. "I have to first go with *Maman*, though," he said reluctantly.

Tucker's dislike of doing anything with his mother bothered Callie. *It's none of your affair,* she reminded herself fiercely, but she hugged Tucker extra hard. "Well, I have to go out this morning, too," she said, straightening. "I'm going grocery shopping and I promise to bring you back something extra gooey and luscious from the bakery."

"Take me with you."

He begged her with his beautiful gray eyes, and Callie had to fight herself to say no. *Oh, Tucker,* she thought to herself, *you break my heart.*

"Not this morning, sweetheart," she said gently. "Your mom's waiting for you and I've got a million-and-one things to do that you'd think would be no fun.

"Now," she said briskly, before he could put forth another protest and weaken her resolve, "let's talk about that other gift you gave me. The one I have to give back."

She briskly strode into her bedroom and picked up the unusual gold and turquoise bracelet Tucker had bestowed upon her. Callie had been stunned by the gift. From all accounts Tucker lived in near squalor, and when he'd unceremoniously dropped the bracelet in her lap one afternoon Callie had done a classic double take. The bracelet was composed of blue and green triangular stones veined with, and rimmed in, gold. It was held together by dual strands of minute, forest-green beads, which looked black until exposed to brilliant sunlight, where they gleamed with a deep richness that matched the beauty of the stones.

Callie was no expert, but she knew real gold when she saw it. She'd tried to refuse but Tucker had been adamant; his eyes filling with unshed tears at her insistence that she couldn't accept it. Horrified that she'd hurt his feelings, Callie had said she would keep the bracelet for a few days. Now it was time to give it back.

She stretched out her arm to him, the bracelet hanging from her fingers. "I love it, sweetheart, but it's too expensive a gift." Callie wondered again how he'd ever come to possess it, then decided she was probably better off not knowing.

"You don't wear it," he said, hurt.

"I can't. It's too precious. I think you should give it back to your mother."

"It's mine!" he said swiftly, almost angrily. "I want you to wear it."

Callie was nonplussed. There was a mystery about Tucker's household that bothered her, but it was not her place to interfere. Tucker's mother had made it more than plain that she resented the interest her son took in Callie.

"I'll wear it today," Callie said, as a means to pacify him, "but only if you promise to take it back later."

She waited for his reply, but Tucker just stood in injured silence, his eyes on the floor. Callie squatted down to his level and tipped up his chin. "Hey, if I could, I would wear your gift every day. It's beautiful and you don't know how much it means to me that you want to give it to me. But sometimes adults can't accept certain gifts. It just wouldn't be right. What would your mother think if she knew you gave me this bracelet?"

"It's mine," Tucker insisted again, but doubt had crept into his tone.

"Promise you'll let me give it back later?"

The boy sighed heavily. "Promise," he mumbled.

"Good. I'll put it on right now." Callie slid the bracelet onto her left arm and gave Tucker a quick kiss on the top of his head. "Now scoot home before we get in hot water with your mother."

She put her palms on his shoulders and turned him in the direction of the door, but he twisted his neck to stare at Callie in puzzlement. "Hot water?" he asked.

"It's just an expression. It means 'big trouble'—the kind neither one of us wants."

He suddenly threw his arms around her neck and pressed his face into her shoulder, his thin body tense with emotion. Tears filled her eyes and she blinked quickly, fighting them back. She had to leave very soon, she realized, or it would be impossible to. It nearly was already.

Tucker ended the embrace a moment later. He was quick to display affection but also quick to sense when he needed to pull back. With a wave and slight smile he headed out the door, the clattering of his footsteps down the wooden stairs sounding more like an army than just one small boy.

"Wait a minute! Let me walk you home!"

It was already too late to catch up with him. Curbing her natural instinct to mother him, Callie let him go. He would be on his own—alone—again soon enough anyway.

She inhaled deeply and let out a slow breath. She had to keep reminding herself that Tucker belonged to his mother and father and not to her. It was difficult; he was such an endearing boy. And she'd lost her own son not so long ago.

Callie understood perfectly why she found Tucker so attractive, but she was less sure of why he had been drawn to her. She was just another tourist in a city overflowing with them, and though she had purposely moved from her hotel, stretching her meager French vocabulary to rent an apartment on the hill above the city of Fort-de-France, that was the only remarkable aspect about her.

She'd wanted to become more like one of the island residents. She'd wanted to make Martinique her home for a short while. Maybe Tucker had just needed a friend and she'd been in the right place at the right time. Or maybe, Callie mused with an inward smile, it was simply that he was intrigued with the color of her red-gold hair. Tucker had told her enough times how beautiful it was, and any time Callie held him he couldn't help fingering and playing with it.

She picked up the plastic carryall bag she used for transporting groceries, walked out and locked her door behind her. Whatever the reason, Tucker had become an integral part of her life on Martinique and she was going to have a tough time leaving him behind when her flight left at the end of the week.

The early-morning peace of the bay seeped seductively into Callie's consciousness, and her senses were lulled, attuned only to the heat, the silence, and most of all the view, as she stood on the pier and watched the ferryboat load visitors for the thirty-minute voyage from Fort-de-France to Pointe du Bout, the tourist resort on the other side of the bay.

Her carryall was loaded with groceries, and she had only one stop left to make: the bakery. But she couldn't find the energy to move. She stretched her bare arms and felt the sun soak deep into her skin, as she squinted against the blinding dazzle of light and water.

A small rubber launch at the end of another pier was being stowed with provisions, and Callie watched the two men doing the loading without really seeing them. Her thoughts were far away. She felt at peace with herself and with the world and realized with some surprise that she truly was ready to go back to the battlefield that awaited her in San Francisco.

As the small launch roared to life and pulled away from the shore, Callie's gaze followed it to the trim white and royal-blue sailboat anchored in the bay. Small waves from the wake of other boats slapped against the sailboat's gleaming hull, and a man on the sailboat moved to the rope ladder near the stern, leaning down to help load provisions from the rubber launch.

Callie's attention was miles away. She didn't notice the men and sailboat any more than she noticed the deeply tanned man about a quarter mile down the shore who held a pair of binoculars to his eyes, the binoculars trained on that particular sailboat. She didn't see those same binoculars sweep the shore, pass by her once, then abruptly return, focusing directly on her lone form.

Unaware of the close scrutiny, Callie closed her eyes and inhaled the heavy, salt-laden air. Hearing the launch rev to life once more, she slowly lifted her lids and watched the rubber craft motor back to the pier, a frothy wake fanning out behind it. To her surprise one of the men looked up, saw her, and began to wave frantically.

She glanced around. She was the only person in sight. Did she know this man? She didn't think so. He had a grizzled beard and bulky build and even from a distance she could see how dirty his clothes were.

Then he put his hands to his lips and threw her an expansive kiss, arms spread wide, his mouth split by a wide grin.

Callie laughed aloud. What was wrong with her? She'd been crazy to think she might see a familiar face so far from home. Of course the man was a stranger. Undoubtedly a native of Martinique and therefore French.

She'd just been the recipient of his romantic enthusiasm.

It felt good.

Smiling back she lifted her hand and waved a bit self-consciously, the unusual gold and turquoise bracelet on her left arm catching the light. The man in the launch waved back and then the small boat reached the pier and the two men began hauling on more provisions.

Callie looked at her watch. It was time to get moving if she planned to do anything more than hang around the piers. She turned away from the bay and walked back toward the center of Fort-de-France, Martinique's largest city.

Callie didn't feel the binoculars now trained on her retreating back. She didn't see the way the stranger peering through the lenses stiffened, the way his knuckles turned white as he watched her hurry across the street, the way he began to move after her, slowly at first, then with increasing speed and conviction. Callie was too absorbed in what she was doing to notice she was being followed.

Fort-de-France was a thriving metropolis, its streets so narrow that cars parked on the sidewalks, forcing the pedestrians to spill into the street. It was early enough, as Callie headed north, that she wasn't battling a crowd of people and cars. Her progress was rapid and she arrived at the tiny bakery within minutes.

"Bonjour," she said to the woman behind the counter.

"Bonjour." The woman smiled distractedly and waited for Callie to make a selection.

There were pastries of every kind. Flaky Neapolitans layered with custard, cone-shaped scones filled with coconut creme, pineapple tarts, croissants, crusty loaves of

French bread. Callie's French couldn't stand the test of such exotic names and she pointed to several creme-filled items, unable to resist buying several for herself.

"Thank you. *Merci*." Callie picked up the bag and stuffed it into the trusty plastic carryall she had purchased when she had first arrived on Martinique. Since she had no car she walked everywhere, and after she had found herself an apartment more than a mile from the city she'd learned to limit her purchases to what she could comfortably carry.

The sun was already hot as she headed up the hill toward her apartment. Shifting the bag from one hand to the other, she trekked along until the sidewalks of Fort-de-France gave way to a steep, narrow roadway. Traffic here was thick, and she turned at the first street that could take her away from the main thoroughfare.

A trickle of sweat ran down her back as she walked up the street. She looked back down the hill once and saw the ferry, shrunk by distance, returning across the bay from Pointe du Bout. Even from this far she could discern many of the major hotels and tourist resorts that ringed that side of the bay, their white sand beaches sloping into the sea. When Callie had first come to Martinique she'd stayed at one of those hotels, but had quickly become disenchanted with the whole tourist scene. She'd needed to live somewhere more private and had finally located a suitable apartment.

Tired now, she paused for a breath, setting down her bag and wiping perspiration from her forehead. Dear Lord, it was hot! She still hadn't learned that she couldn't travel in this heat at the same pace she did in San Francisco. The humidity was killing.

Then, resolutely straightening her shoulders, Callie pushed on again. She could have been alone on the planet, she mused, as the noise of Fort-du-France receded behind her. The only other person in view was a man walking some distance behind her. A tourist off the beaten track, she thought, reminded that this utter solitude was merely an illusion.

Cutting across a weed-choked lawn, Callie took a shortcut the rest of the way. The sun was shining brightly as she turned a corner, walked along a cracked, narrow sidewalk, then ducked into an alley between two tenement homes.

Where the hell is she going?

Gavin kept a careful distance behind the red-haired woman in the white gauze sundress. He knew who she was: he'd been sent to find her. He'd been dumbfounded when she had turned up so unexpectedly, standing boldly by the pier, her crown of auburn hair turning to fire beneath the blazing sun.

He wanted to kill her with his bare hands.

"Don't do anything rash," Victoria had warned him in her tight-lipped way. "If you have to bargain with her, okay. But don't antagonize her any further!"

Gavin's face was grim. Antagonize her? Hell, he wanted to shake her until she fell into pieces. He wanted to shatter her self-indulgent world and leave her in the rubble. There would be no bargaining as far as he was concerned. Victoria would have to get used to the idea that the only way to deal with *her* was by bringing things down to a level she could understand.

Bargaining was for beggars as far as Gavin was concerned. The days of bargaining were long past. Now was the time for action.

* * *

Callie stopped again, halfway through the alley, arms aching. She swept back her hair, making a face at its long, untamed style. When she got back to San Francisco she was going to cut it. She wasn't the same person who had left in such a quailing panic over a month before, and she was determined to let the members of her late husband's family know it. She'd loved Jonathan, but she'd lost him in the same accident that had taken Joshua. She didn't feel the same emotion for any of the other Cantrells.

Picking up her bag Callie continued on the sun-cracked dirt path between the tenements. She met no one and the silence was unbroken as she walked on. The sun reflected off the white walls and prickled her scalp. The air was heavy and hot. Tiredly she blew on straggles of hair that fell into her eyes and thought about the pitcher of iced lemonade that awaited her in her tiny refrigerator.

A pebble lodged itself in her thong and she stopped, lifting her foot and wiggling her toes. Lemonade and a croissant on the little table on her balcony, she told herself. Maybe she would even splurge and try one of the gooey pastries she'd gotten for—

"Somehow we all knew you'd come back here," an angry male voice ground out.

Callie nearly jumped from her skin. He'd made no sound and she'd thought she was alone. Before she could respond a hand grabbed her upper arm and twisted her back until she was pressed against the hot wall of the tenement.

"Wh-a-at?" Callie gasped, the air rushing from her lungs as she turned startled blue eyes on her attacker.

"Are you surprised someone found you?" he asked sardonically, and Callie's pulse began to race as her surprise turned to fear. "Don't tell me you don't know who I am," he went on, his eyes narrowed on her face. "Somehow I thought you'd be expecting one of us."

With a feeling of unreality Callie stared at the man. There was a grimness of purpose around his mouth that chilled her blood. She tried to capture her scattered wits. "There must be some mistake," she managed shakily. "I don't know who you are."

"Really. Take a good, hard look and make an educated guess."

Callie could do little else. His face, tanned to the color of teak, was within inches of hers. His eyes were blue, bluer than her own, with thick, dark lashes and tiny white lines edging from the corners where the sun never reached. Dark hair framed a lean, savage face; she was certain his nose had been broken more than once. His mouth was wide and sensual and she thought a bit cruel; his jaw, firm and jutting, sported a dark growth of beard. He looked handsome and dangerous and determined.

Callie swallowed. "I don't know you. I'm sure I don't. What—what do you want?"

"Oh, I think you know."

His hand still held her left wrist and Callie felt faint. The grip was tight and hurting, and only the sunbaked wall of the tenement kept her on her feet. "Money?" she suggested faintly.

His laugh had an edge to it that scraped Callie's nerves. "We don't all think like you do, y'know. If you'd figured that out earlier maybe none of this would have happened."

"I don't know who you think I am, but believe me, I've never seen you before."

His fingers flexed and tightened on her wrist. "Or anyone like me either, hmmm?" Then with an abrupt change of tone he muttered savagely, "That's not going to save you. My God, I'd like to strangle you!"

Callie believed him.

"Please…" She hated begging but fear was making her weak. She realized belatedly that her hand was still gripped around her plastic carryall, gripped in fact as if her very life depended on it. Slowly she dropped it to the ground. "I have some cash with me—not much—but maybe enough…"

"Goddammit, Teresa, quit with the games. I don't have time for all this drama! Are you going to take me to the boy or do I have to choke it out of you? So help me I will," he said through his teeth, "just give me a little more provocation."

Teresa? Callie seized on this piece of information like a lifeline. "I'm not Teresa. My name's Callie. You've got me mixed up with—"

He swore violently and grabbed her right wrist, too. She was pinned, wide-eyed, against the wall. Then he twisted up her left arm until the bracelet Tucker had given her was at eye level between them.

"You're a liar and a bad one at that. What more proof do I need?"

Callie didn't know what he meant and she didn't care. All she could think about was Tucker and the bracelet. It was a valuable piece of jewelry. It was perhaps the only item of value Tucker's family possessed. And now this man with the blue, blue eyes was staring at it, assessing its value. Damn him, if he tried to steal Tucker's beautiful bracelet he'd be in for the fight of his life! She'd rather die than let him take it from her!

"Let go of me," she said tautly, jerking her arm. But his grip was too strong, his long fingers easily holding her victim. She glared at him, matching his savagery with her own determination and anger.

"Looks like I struck a nerve," he said with a smugness that infuriated Callie. "We both know where you got the bracelet, don't we?"

"If you know how I got it, you're a mind reader."

He smiled coldly. "Stephen gave it to you."

Callie's swift intake of breath gave her away. *Stephen? Stephen Tucker Thomas? How had he known?*

She stared at him blankly, wondering what kind of strange trap she'd wandered into. How could he know? What did he want?

"Who *are* you?" she asked, her voice quavering with real fear.

"I'm the man who's going to make you pay for what you've done, Teresa. That's who I am. And if you give the idea some real thought, you'll put all the pieces together."

She couldn't tell him there was no way for her to understand; he wouldn't listen to her if she tried. It was insane and she felt panicked inside.

Her next move was pure reflex. She kicked him as hard as she could and connected with his shin. He cursed viciously but didn't release her. Callie tried to kick again but suddenly she was slammed against the wall with his full weight pressing against her.

"I'm not Teresa," Callie gasped. "I'm not. In my wallet ... my identification ... you'll see."

"I'm not letting you go no matter what you say," he growled furiously. "I *know* you. And so help me, before this is over you're going to know me. You're going to know I mean what I say."

"It's a mistake." Callie's knees threatened to collapse. "It's a mistake."

She could hear the hard pounding of his heart as if it were in her own ears. Her own pulse beat in rapid tandem. She hadn't been this close to a man since Jonathan, and the bizarre events that had led to this encounter only added to the intensity. She was literally pinned beneath him.

A scream rose in her throat, but as if he sensed it his grip changed and one hand circled her throat.

"Don't," he said softly.

"You're scaring me." Callie felt tears building behind her eyes.

"That's the idea," he muttered grimly.

A sound caught their attention. At the north end of the alleyway, two young men were just entering.

Thank God! Callie could have wept with joy. Salvation was at hand!

But then she met the eyes of her captor and they read each other's mind at the same moment, Callie gauging just when to cry for help, her attacker wondering how to silence her.

She opened her mouth, but her cry was extinguished as his mouth suddenly descended on hers, cutting off her breath. As a kiss it left a lot to be desired but as a means of keeping her quiet it was an effective as a gag. She made choking sounds that could have meant anything, and though she tried to push him away she was helpless against his weight and the surprise of his unexpected maneuver.

She pounded on his back but he was impervious to the action, and his fingers held her face a prisoner. There was no passion in the kiss, just a steely determination that Callie found more frightening than anything he'd done so far. She prepared herself for the wave of revulsion that was sure to follow, but instead she felt a kind of horrified curiosity. He loathed what he was doing; she could feel it in the tight, unyielding contours of his lips, the tense hostility that radiated from every pore. If this was the way he felt about the mysterious Teresa, Callie found herself glad she wasn't in the other woman's shoes.

Except that she was—sort of. At least *he* thought she was.

One of his hands was wound in her hair and her head was trapped. The two youths sniggered as they walked by, and Callie's heart sank as she realized how much like an act of passion it looked.

As soon as the two youths were out of earshot, Callie's captor released her.

"We both enjoyed that about the same amount, so don't get any bright ideas about why I did it," he said scathingly. "I think it was pretty obvious anyway."

Catching her breath, Callie just glared at him. She actually thought about slapping him and letting loose a bloodcurdling scream at the same time. But instinct warned her against antagonizing him further. This man was no ordinary hoodlum; he was too polished, too sure. And he was obviously American like herself. If he would just give her the chance to explain that she wasn't Teresa maybe he would leave her alone.

"Where's the boy?" he asked again. "Tell me."

She knew with bone-deep certainty that he was after Tucker. Her stomach sickeningly dipped as Callie wondered if Tucker, or this Teresa person, had stolen the bracelet from him. Not that she cared; she wouldn't reveal anything to him that might put Tucker in danger.

She heaved a deep sigh. "Listen to me. I'm not Teresa. I'm Callie, Callie Cant—" She cut herself off at the last minute, realizing it wasn't beyond probability that he knew exactly who she was and that the whole scenario was an act. She was, after all, a very wealthy woman now; the Cantrell fortune had fallen to her after Jonathan's death. She just still had trouble remembering that fact. "It doesn't matter. What does matter, is I'm not Teresa. I don't know who you are, or anything about any boy. I'm on vacation. I'm a tourist. That's all."

His eyes swept over her face. "You're really quite good. If I didn't have the evidence that said otherwise, I might be inclined to believe you."

Callie made a frustrated sound. "Look at my identification, for God's sake!" she urged, throwing caution to the winds. If he was really after Callie Cantrell, he'd already found her; no amount of lying could save her now. "My wallet's in my bag. You'll see I'm who I say I am."

"Fake identification's not beyond your capabilities," he said flatly.

"Oh, God, just look at it!"

He shook his head. "When we get to your place, maybe."

"My... place?"

He'd been looking in the direction the youths had taken, as if considering where to go from there. Now his dark head turned back to her and he regarded her impatiently. "Did you really think I'd leave you now that I've found you?"

"I'm not who you think I am," she whispered.

"Yes, you are. You're all that and more."

For the first time Callie really assessed the situation. This stranger thought she was someone else. He truly believed she was this Teresa person. He wouldn't listen to reason and there was nothing she could do to prove to him she was who she said she was.

And he wanted to follow her to her apartment. *What if Tucker was back there, waiting for her?*

"You're crazy," she whispered, and then, since in the aftermath of the kiss his grip had weakened, Callie twisted from his grasp and jumped away in one swift movement, running for the end of the alley with all her might.

He tackled her so neatly that she didn't feel it until it was all over. Her face hit the dirt and her chin jarred with the impact. For a wild moment she wished she could be hurt, at least rendered unconscious. Then maybe he would leave her for someone else to find.

But she wasn't hurt and she couldn't just pass out by willing it to happen. Instead, she felt hands, incredibly gentle hands, turning her over, and she saw a stranger's concerned face bending close to hers, his cerulean eyes peering deep into her soul.

"Oh, damn, Teresa," he said with a heavy sigh. "I don't like this any better than you do, but I'm going to stick to you like a lover until you give me the boy, so you might as well stop fighting now. Where is he? Tell me, and I'll let you go."

Chapter Two

Callie was unable to answer him. She was fast losing her fear of him, though she couldn't say why, yet she wasn't about to reveal anything about Tucker. She didn't know who this man was and she didn't trust him. She just stared at him through resolute eyes, warning him wordlessly that he had picked on the wrong type of woman.

"So that's the way it is," he said, his mouth tightening. Callie stiffened as one of his hands slipped beneath her head, but he just began to gently explore her scalp. She suffered the perusal of strong fingers until he'd assured himself that her only injury was the small bruise beneath her jaw. This he touched carefully, but Callie twisted her head away.

"Are you all right, Teresa?" he asked.

Callie refused to answer *Teresa*. Good Lord, what did it take to convince him he'd made a mistake?

"How does your jaw feel?"

"Terrible."

The faintest gleam of humor entered his eyes, but then it was gone. "Can you get to your feet?" he asked, holding out a hand, but Callie struggled up without his help.

She had actually been toying with the idea of making another break for it but all thoughts of escape swiftly receded as the blood rushed from her head. She was seized by a wave of dizziness. Dimly she realized he had found her thongs and was holding them out to her, but a second later his arm was around her waist.

"You okay?" he asked, brows drawn in concern.

She was hanging on to him as if her life depended on it, her fingers clenched into the fabric of his shirt.

"No... I feel..."

"It's reaction," he said when she couldn't continue. "You took a nasty bump on the jaw. Just stand here a minute and don't talk. You'll be all right."

All right? Who was he kidding? She didn't think she'd ever be all right again.

After several moments her head cleared and she abruptly let go of his support. His arms dropped away from her with such undisguised relief that Callie felt a prickle of annoyance. She hadn't asked for this; he'd forced it on her. And if he found touching her so offensive he shouldn't have accosted her in the first place.

Reaction was indeed setting in—only it wasn't reaction from the fall, it was reaction to the whole situation—to him! Callie leaned a trembling palm against the wall of the tenement, swallowing hard. "Could you just leave me alone, please?" she asked in an unsteady voice.

For the first time she witnessed some uncertainty in his expression, even some regret. But if she'd expected him to believe her declarations of innocence she was rudely disillusioned when a moment later he said, "Just don't try to run away again and we'll get along fine."

"Who are you?" Callie asked tremulously.

"I'm Gavin."

He was watching her closely, as if expecting the name to mean something to her. Callie sighed and asked, "Gavin, who?"

"Rutledge," he said evenly. "As if you hadn't guessed."

"I am not Teresa, and I've never heard of you in my life."

"I don't believe you."

He'd dropped her thongs on the ground in front of her and Callie wiggled her toes inside them. "Then it's your problem," she said testily.

"Our problem," he pointed out as he headed back in the direction of her carryall. As she watched him walk away Callie tried to get her legs in gear but she was too limp-muscled to run. What was the point anyway? she concluded gloomily. He would catch her even if she was at her best form; he already had once.

She realized the only way of dealing with him was talking to him reasonably. Even the most stubborn person would lose conviction if faced with overwhelming evidence, and she had the overwhelming evidence. He couldn't believe she was Teresa forever.

Callie hadn't noticed what kind of condition she was in until that moment. Her white dress was filthy, her arms and legs streaked with dust and sweat. She could just imagine what kind of state her hair was in and only the bracelet on her arm appeared as clean and beautiful as it had been when she'd put it on that morning.

Gingerly she took a step, realized she wasn't going to fall apart, then took another, straightening her shoulders as Gavin returned with her carryall. He prudently didn't hand it to her, aware of her teetering self-control.

"Do you need some help?" he asked.

Belatedly Callie remembered he'd said he wanted to go to her place. Her place. Tucker. Fear swept over her anew and she realized she would have to delay him somehow.

"No, I'll be fine as soon as you let me go."

"I can't do that," he said softly.

"I don't have any boy. I'm not who you think I am."

"Prove it by showing me your apartment."

Calling upon talents she hadn't known she possessed, Callie tilted up her chin and regarded him coolly. "I'm not in the habit of showing any strange man my apartment. If you want to talk, we'll talk, but let it be somewhere else."

Gavin raised his brows. "Where?"

"I don't care." She carefully touched her chin. "I'm not feeling the best," she said, using her small injury as an excuse, "and I'd like something cool to drink."

Gavin inhaled between his teeth, his glance skating over her dishabille. He wanted to argue but he was conscious of her pale cheeks and couldn't help feeling regret for hurting her. He considered for a moment then said, "Well, that suits me just fine. But we're going to go somewhere where we can talk privately."

"Fine."

"There's nowhere near that's quiet enough. We'll take a taxi to my hotel."

"Forget it." Callie was willing to be reasonable, but after the rough way he'd just treated her she wasn't about to venture onto his turf.

Still, it was imperative that she get Gavin as far away from Tucker as possible. As she tried to think of somewhere else to go the ferry horn blasted twice, as if signaling her.

The Pointe du Bout hotels.

"I'd like to go to the Bakoua Beach Hotel," Callie said, seeing Gavin's head swivel sharply to stare at her. "I've stayed there," she explained a trifle defensively. "There's an outdoor restaurant where we can talk privately. I realize it's on the other side of the bay but I would—feel comfortable there."

And it's miles away from Tucker.

Gavin considered a moment, then shrugged. "Bakoua it is."

The Bakoua Beach Hotel was renowned, a bit exclusive, and the perfect place to dissuade Gavin from making any more threatening moves. She could even check in for the night if she had to, Callie reasoned. *Anything* to keep Gavin from Tucker.

She tried to dust herself off as they walked back toward the main road.

"Wouldn't you like to change first?" Gavin suggested, but Callie shook her head.

"All I want to do is sit. If you get that taxi...?"

He probably thought it was odd that she wasn't concerned with vanity but he didn't argue. Instead he persuaded Callie to sit on the curb as he tried to signal a taxi. Eventually one of the taxi drivers spied Gavin and Callie and motioned that he would pick them up after he dropped off his passengers.

A few minutes later the taxi pulled up beside them. Gavin tucked a hand under Callie's upper arm and helped her to her feet. She wanted to jerk her arm away but forced herself to comply. Inside, her temper was burning. She couldn't wait to hear his apology when he found out she really was Callie Cantrell.

"Bakoua Beach, *s'il vous plaît*," Callie said before Gavin could give any other instructions. She trusted him only so far.

He slid her a sardonic look but said nothing as he climbed in the back seat beside her.

Callie let her muscles go limp, and leaned her head back against the cushion. The drive was a little more than thirty minutes, and she was glad for the respite. Gavin remained silent while she watched the landscape flicker by outside the window. The road curved around the bay and she could see snatches of blue-green water between the stretches of hills, palms and buildings.

Her wallet was inside her carryall. She thought about pulling it out and showing it to Gavin, but decided it would be better to wait until they could speak privately. Besides, she needed some time to think first.

The taxi pulled into the sweeping drive in front of the Bakoua Beach. Gavin paid the fare then guided Callie inside, his hand at her elbow. This time she did pull away as they walked through the open-air lobby, past the woman at the reception desk, around the circular, outdoor bar and to the steps that led to the beach.

The Bakoua Beach Hotel was built onto a hillside, the main reception area a level above the pool, the pool above the cabanas, the cabanas above the beach. Gavin took Callie to the restaurant near the beach, but the amount of stairs she had to climb down took their toll on her shattered nerves and by the time he pulled back her chair her knees were trembling.

"*Thé glacé*," he said to the waitress as he sat down across from Callie. He raised two fingers. "*Deux*."

Iced tea. Callie was glad he'd remembered her request for a drink, but she was too tired to comment. She wondered just how good his command of the French language was. Maybe better than her own? Just who *was* he?

"You look like you're going to faint," Gavin said, his gaze moving over her pale face.

"I never faint."

"Congratulations," he said mockingly to her challenging tone.

"You think I'm someone else. You don't know anything about me."

"I know a helluva lot more about you than I'd like to," he ground out.

"I'm not Teresa," Callie repeated tiredly. "My name is Callie Cantrell. If you'd just look in my wallet . . . it's in my bag . . ."

He stared at her for several moments and she stared back. Then, taking her own fate into her hands Callie dug through her groceries and pulled out her wallet, flipping it open triumphantly.

"See?" she said, pointing to the picture on her California driver's license.

The iced tea came as he was looking at her picture. Callie reached for her glass and sat back, her gaze centered on the dark, silky hair at his crown. When she felt as if an eternity had come and gone and still he didn't speak, she lost patience and asked, "Well? Now do you believe me?"

His dark brows were knit in concentration, his lips pressed together and a thin trickle of sweat ran down the curve of his jaw.

"Just look at the name," Callie urged, "and the picture. I'm who I say I am. You've made a mistake, but I'm willing to forget the whole thing if you'll just leave me alone."

He lifted his eyes and glanced at her bracelet. Callie had to fight the urge to hide her arm beneath the table's edge.

"I can't," he said simply and looked again at her identification.

Callie's lips parted in dismay. How could he not believe her? What was it about her that had convinced him so positively that she was Teresa? Good Lord! He didn't even believe her with her own picture staring him right in the face.

"The way I see it," she said dryly, "if my license is good enough for the state of California, it ought to be good enough for you."

He didn't answer.

Callie sighed. She saw her credit cards and the crinkled edges of the odd-size hundred-franc bills that wouldn't fit neatly into her wallet. Gavin studied her picture intently but his expression gave no clue to his thoughts. At long last he said, "You applied for this driver's license less than a year ago."

"It's a renewal." At his silence she added with a trace of anger, "It is. I've lived in California all my life and before I was Callie Cantrell I was Callie Shipley."

"You're married?"

As this was the first question that indicated he gave any credence to her story at all, Callie answered readily. "I was. I'm a widow now."

He scowled and instantly his behavior changed. Once more she was confronted with the surly stranger who'd accosted her in the alley. "That, I know," he said, violence in his tone. "I know what you did."

No one could have missed the hate in his voice and Callie, her nerves scraped raw, was super sensitive as it was. Tears began to pool in her eyes, and at his look of disgust she turned away. Damn him! She was trying so very, very hard to play it his way when she owed him absolutely nothing! The least he could be was civil.

"Why won't you believe me?" she demanded, her voice catching against her will.

His sigh was filled with impatience. "It's time you dropped the act. I want answers, Teresa. No more game playing."

"I don't have answers. I'm not Teresa."

"God, you're good!"

Callie's look was troubled at this sudden display of emotion, and he made a sharp movement with his arm. "I could almost believe you if I didn't know better," he went on. "That lost and miserable act is hard to resist."

"It's no act."

"Oh, hell."

"Even you're finding it hard to believe your own impossible ideas." Callie half expected some angry retort, and she reached for her iced tea again with a trembling hand.

"I find you hard to believe," he said cryptically. "Where's the boy? Just tell me that."

"What boy?"

"Your *son*," he whispered harshly. "Or have you forgotten what motherhood's all about?"

Callie's throat went dry. He'd touched a very sensitive issue, though she knew it was pure coincidence. Still, the pain that refused to die throbbed in her chest. "The only son I ever had is dead," she said after a pause. "He's dead."

Gavin's lips slackened in disbelief. "My God," he whispered, shocked. "He's dead?"

"Don't worry. He wasn't the boy you're looking for. He was my son. He has nothing to do with you and this Teresa person. He only mattered to me."

Her voice broke then. This was the worst kind of torture. If she'd felt weak before, she felt doubly so now. She just wished the earth would open up and swallow her.

He was watching her with a mixture of fascination and horror. "Lady," he growled, "you're the worst kind of liar, mixing the truth with your own sick lies."

"You don't know anything about me!" Callie flashed. "Nothing! Who *are* you?"

"You ought to know," he drawled dangerously, "since you married my brother."

"I don't know you, and I'm certain I don't know your brother. The only man I've ever been married to was Jonathan Cantrell and as Jonathan has only one brother, Derek Cantrell, whom I've met many times, I'd say you just made another mistake."

His eyes narrowed. "You were married to Stephen for over three years."

"No."

"You left him about a year and a half ago and you took your son with you."

Callie shook her head. "You're wrong—again."

"Did you know Stephen's dead? He got himself killed trying to find you. He said he'd find you or die trying. How ironic that he was right."

His voice had lowered to a whisper, but that took nothing away from its intensity. On the contrary, every syllable seemed to hammer into her brain. Callie wondered how much more of this she could take.

"What's the matter?" he asked suddenly.

"Nothing."

"Don't give me that. You look terrible."

Was that a news bulletin? Of course she looked terrible! He'd frightened her—*terrorized* her—chased her down and manhandled her. She couldn't look any other way.

"Is it your jaw?" he asked, tiny lines forming between his brows.

Inadvertently he'd given her the means to salvage her ragged self-control. "Yes, it's my jaw," she lied, gingerly cupping her chin and wincing. Let him believe her weakness was from pain, not fear.

Gavin made an impatient sound with his teeth.

"It's killing me," Callie embellished, closing her eyes.

"It's your own damn fault."

"No, it's not." Callie let her chin tremble. "You tackled me and I went face down."

"I never meant to hurt you," he said tautly.

Callie squinted at him, achieving a measure of enjoyment from her small revenge. "As I recall it, you wanted to kill me." She shifted in her chair and sighed. "Maybe some more tea . . . would help . . ."

"You need to lie down," he said, as if speaking to himself.

"I'm not going to your hotel room."

He smiled faintly, then sobered as he witnessed her flash of spirit give way to what he thought was pain. He looked down at the table and she sensed he was indecisive about what to do with her. She had a mental image of what he was seeing and understood his doubts. She probably looked like death itself.

He pinched the bridge of his nose. "If you're not Teresa, you look enough like her to be her double. And the bracelet . . ." he said, trailing off as the waitress approached their table again. Gavin ordered more tea, then asked Callie if she would like anything to eat. Before she could answer he told the waitress, in English, to bring the continental breakfast tray for two. The waitress nodded her understanding and Callie realized with faint surprise that she was indeed hungry.

"If I can do anything to convince you that I'm who I say I am, I'll do it," Callie said eagerly, once they were alone again. "If you want to ask me questions, ask. You'll realize I really am Callie Cantrell."

"I would like to believe you," he said. Then as if hearing how that sounded, he frowned. "All right. We'll play it your way. Where are you from?"

"San Francisco."

"And you're just vacationing here, on Martinique?"

"That's right."

"You weren't married to my brother, Stephen?"

"No."

Gavin paused. It was painfully apparent he didn't believe her. His jaw worked for a moment and he said, "You're Teresa. You've got to be."

The tray of croissants, jellies, butter and fresh pineapple rings arrived at that moment. Two more tall glasses of iced tea were put down in front of them and Callie felt her sinking spirits revive at the sight of food.

Gavin didn't touch the tray. He was distant and remote, staring moodily across the water toward Fort-de-France. "Stephen didn't tell you about me? Even in passing?" he asked.

"I don't know Stephen." Callie buttered a croissant.

"Stephen was my half brother," Gavin said with an effort.

"I don't know him."

"Damn it, Teresa. Cut the charade."

"It's no charade," Callie answered evenly, dropping her knife. "I don't know how many times I have to say it. *I'm not Teresa*. I don't know your brother—Stephen—and I've never heard of you until today. You've got me mixed up with someone else and that's all there is to it. My identification proves it, but you just can't admit that you're wrong! If I could prove who I was to you, I would, but—" Callie cut herself off with a sharp breath. What was she thinking of? Of course there was a way! She could have Gavin call William Lister, the attorney for the Cantrell estate and a man Callie trusted implicitly. William was the one person she'd told where she was going.

Gavin leaned forward. "What?" he asked softly.

Callie shook her head. "Listen," she said eagerly. "You can call my friends and family in San Francisco. I'll give you the number. William Lister is my attorney and he's also a personal friend."

Gavin stared at her. "You're really going to take this all the way, aren't you?"

"I'm not Teresa Rutledge," Callie said firmly.

"Teresa Thomas."

Callie blinked. "Teresa Thomas? I thought you said she was married to your brother."

"My half brother."

"But . . . ?"

Gavin waited but Callie didn't say anything more. Gavin's brother was Stephen Thomas. Tucker's name was Stephen Tucker Thomas. Could it be that Gavin's brother was Tucker's father? Was it true? How could it be?

Callie thought hard. Gavin had said that *Stephen* had given her the bracelet and she'd just assumed he meant Tucker. But maybe he'd meant his brother. . . .

"You said Stephen, your brother, gave Teresa the bracelet?" Callie asked, testing her theory.

Gavin's lips compressed, but he nodded curtly.

Callie was completely confused. So he hadn't meant
Tucker! Then was Tucker the boy Gavin was after? How
had he come by the bracelet, if he wasn't? Gavin had led
Callie to believe that his brother, Stephen, was Tucker's
father but how could that be? Tucker's father, though an
American, was presumably alive and well and off on another long-term fishing expedition. And the woman
Callie had been introduced to as Tucker's mother was
certainly not the mysterious Teresa; she had dark skin
and hair, spoke French like a native, and looked nothing
like Callie.

And Tucker's family was very poor. If Gavin was some
kind of shirttail relative of Tucker's, how come he wore
expensive clothes, rode in taxis, and seemed completely
at ease at a renowned hotel like the Bakoua Beach?

"You really don't know who I am?" Gavin asked,
drawing out each word.

Callie shook her head in confusion.

"Well, I'll admit the Rutledge's aren't proud of me but
I thought my name might have cropped up sometime.
Bad pennies invariably turn up. Or are called upon dur-
ing a family crisis," he added wryly.

"Mr. Rutledge," Callie said faintly, realizing she was
way out of her depth. "What is it about me that has you
totally convinced I'm this Teresa?"

He scowled and for a moment Callie was certain he
wouldn't answer. But then he caught himself, stamped
out his impatience and decided, Callie could plainly see,
to humor her.

"Lots of reasons. I followed you here to Martinique."
He lifted one finger. "You were on the pier this morning, wearing the bracelet." He lifted a second finger.
"And the last should be self-evident—your looks. You
didn't even try to change the color of your hair."

"I take it you've never actually met Teresa," she said slowly. The woman Tucker called *Maman* was obviously not Teresa.

"That's right. But I've got a picture."

"May I see it?"

Gavin shot her a look but dutifully pulled out a well-worn snapshot. Callie's fingers trembled slightly as she took it from him.

"It was taken not long after the wedding, when you and Stephen stopped to visit Victoria. Victoria gave it to me when she asked me to find you and the boy."

Callie was only half listening. The young girl in the picture was not the woman Callie knew as Tucker's mother. She did, however, bear a striking resemblance to Callie but her face was into the sun and she was squinting against the glare. Callie estimated her age to be around twenty and as Callie herself was twenty-seven, she asked, "How old is this photograph?"

"It was taken eight years ago."

Callie shook her head. "It's not me. I don't know how to convince you, but it's not me." She turned her attention to the man standing next to Teresa, his arm wrapped protectively around her waist. He was dark, like Gavin, with a serious face, but otherwise there was little resemblance.

"Who's Victoria?" Callie asked.

"The Rutledge matriarch—my grandmother. The woman you're extorting money from," he added softly.

Callie shoved the picture back to him. "I don't think I want to know any more. I'm not who you think I am. What do I have to do to convince you that you've made a mistake?"

Gavin's eyes held hers for several moments then he frowned down at the picture. "Give me some background on Callie Cantrell—her husband, her family, her life—then I'll call this William friend of yours, see what he says. Then you can tell me how you got the bracelet. After that..." He lifted his shoulders. "I don't know. Maybe you can convince me. It's just that I've got this gut feeling about you. And I'm a man who usually follows his instincts."

Far across the bay a flock of gulls swooped down, crying plaintively. Callie silently wondered what good it would do to bare her soul to this man, but she found she really had no choice. He'd embroiled her in his affairs against her will and now all she could do was try to work her way back out.

"Okay," she said, reaching for her iced tea. "I'll tell you all there is to know about Callie Cantrell. But tell me something first: what if, after I've told my story, you still don't believe me? What then?"

Gavin's jaw tensed. "We'll just have to cross that bridge when we come to it. Go ahead. I'm listening...."

It had never been easy for Callie to talk about the accident that had deprived her of her husband and son, yet for some reason, it seemed the best place to start.

"My husband and son were killed in an automobile accident a little over a year ago. A drunk driver going the wrong way on the freeway ran into them. I was devastated. Jonathan and I were married while we were both still in college and after we'd been married three years, we had Joshua. I loved my life. It was perfect. I loved Jonathan and Joshua."

Gavin was silent and Callie continued, "It's taken me a long time to get some perspective back in my life. This past year has been—terrible. If it hadn't been for William I think I would have gone crazy. He loved Jonathan and Joshua, too.''

"This is William Lister, your attorney?''

Gavin was diffident and Callie understood. If and when he found her revelations to be true he was going to have an awful lot to apologize for.

"William is the attorney for the Cantrell estate.'' A trace of steel entered Callie's voice that she was unaware of, but which Gavin heard. "I should explain that the Cantrell's are a wealthy and prestigious San Francisco family. When Jonathan died, I inherited practically everything. There are—others—in his family who feel they've been cheated.'' Callie paused, reliving some of the horrible infighting and accusations she'd endured ever since she'd ended up with the Cantrell fortune.

"Have they been cheated?'' Gavin asked.

"Of course not!'' Callie was indignant. Her cheeks flushed as she recalled the way she'd been treated by Jonathan's family. "Let me explain. The Cantrells have never liked me. I wasn't rich enough, or sophisticated enough, to fit into their plan for Jonathan. But Jonathan was—'' Callie smiled wistfully "—the kind of man you couldn't intimidate. He loved me and married me anyway.''

Gavin lifted one brow. He didn't really believe this woman, yet there was a ring of truth to her words he couldn't ignore. What he did accept as fact was that she'd loved someone once—this man Jonathan—and that she probably loved him still. It couldn't be Stephen she was recalling; Teresa had treated him too badly. But *was* she Teresa? Or was she really who she said she was, this Callie Cantrell?

Whoever she was, she was lost to her story, and he listened quietly as she went on.

"By the terms of Jonathan's grandfather's will, the Cantrell fortune was to be passed in its entirety to his firstborn. Jonathan's father, Robert Cantrell, apparently saw no reason to change that dictate so, much to the despair of his other two children, the fortune passed to Jonathan. Following tradition, Jonathan left everything to Joshua but as they died together, the money ended up in my lap."

The gleam of humor she had seen once before showed in Gavin's eyes. "My God," he said with silent laughter. "I bet that stirred up a hornet's nest."

"It's been nothing to laugh about," Callie answered a trifle tartly, but she could have cheered at the realization that Gavin was finally believing her. "I think I can honestly say that Jonathan's brother and sister hate me. Naturally, they're contesting the will."

"Naturally."

Gavin seemed to understand an awful lot about what was happening with the Cantrells, Callie thought, but she was determined to make him see she was telling the truth. "I don't even care about the money, but I'm furious with the way they've handled Jonathan's death. It's as if the man didn't matter. All that matters is the money."

Gavin's blue eyes studied her wordlessly. Callie grew uncomfortable under his scrutiny and said, "So if you're really looking for an heiress, instead of a little boy, you've found yourself one. Only she's not for sale."

His lips curved. "That's quite a story."

"It's the truth," Callie said levelly.

"Oh, I can believe the family jealousy and rivalry. I've had a taste of it myself. Is that why you came to Martinique, to escape?"

"Yes." Callie leaned forward on her elbows. "Just for a little while. You do believe me then, don't you?"

"Maybe. Tell me more about Callie Cantrell."

There wasn't a whole lot more to tell. She'd just finished relating the most important part of her life. But she was willing to continue and she backtracked some, explaining exactly how and when she met Jonathan, what her hard-working parents had been like, what having Joshua had meant to her, how she'd dealt with the loneliness of the past year.

She concluded by giving Gavin William Lister's office number and urging him to call and verify her story. Gavin tucked the scrap of paper she'd written William's number on in the breast pocket of his shirt. She could see that her story had made a marked impression on him; he'd stopped calling her Teresa and had dropped the long-suffering attitude he'd adopted when he'd thought she was deliberately being obtuse and lying to him.

It was late afternoon by the time Callie was finished talking, and shadows from the thatched shade umbrellas dotting the beach had lengthened into gray ribbons across the sand.

Gavin was rubbing a hand through the stubble on his jaw, his gaze turning from Callie, to the sea, then back to Callie. Several times he'd asked questions that were meant to be traps, but since Callie was speaking the truth he had been unable to trip her up.

"You couldn't have made up that entire story," he said at length. "Every detail is filled in; there were no mistakes."

"Thank you." Callie didn't know what else to say.

"You are either Callie Cantrell or else you know her intimately. There's no other answer."

Callie didn't like the sound of that but she kept her silence.

"There's still something you haven't told me though."

His eyes were on the bracelet. For most of the afternoon he'd paid little or no attention to it and Callie had pushed its relevance to a distant part of her mind. But now his eyes were studying it with a concentration she found mildly alarming.

"Where did you get the bracelet?" Gavin asked, and before Callie really realized what she was doing, she answered, "I picked up the bracelet at a small, exclusive jewelry store in Barbados. I flew there first, for a couple of days, and the bracelet was on display in the window."

"Barbados?" Gavin was disbelieving.

"Yes. I don't know what it means to you, but I imagine it's probably one of dozens found in the islands. I fell in love with it on sight."

Lies, lies, and more lies. After giving him a straightforward and credible story about her past she was lying! But she couldn't bring Tucker into this bizarre discussion. She didn't trust Gavin enough to give away his whereabouts—at least not right away, until she'd done some research on him herself.

"Stephen gave you that bracelet," Gavin said in a low voice. "I saw how you looked when I mentioned his name."

"I have never met your brother," Callie reminded him. "I think you're giving this bracelet far too much importance."

"It's a one of a kind, Callie. It's worth a small fortune. Stephen had it specially made for Teresa as a wedding gift. The stones were from an original Rutledge necklace that had been in the family for centuries before Stephen had it dismantled and redesigned. No—" Gavin slowly shook his head from side to side "—even a noaccount Rutledge like myself could recognize that bracelet."

Callie felt as if a cold hand had traced a line down her back. Could Tucker's absent father really be Stephen Thomas? How else could Tucker have gained possession of the bracelet? But who, and where, was this Teresa person?

"Teresa must have pawned it in Barbados," Gavin was musing to himself, "though from all accounts, she sounds like the type of woman who wouldn't give up a beautiful piece of jewelry unless she absolutely had to, which, according to Victoria, she didn't have to."

"Gavin?"

His dark head swiveled in her direction. "Hmm?"

"You keep asking about a boy—Teresa's son. What about him?"

He actually smiled and Callie was surprised at how it transformed his face. Gone was the grim stranger and in his place was a man who under other circumstances Callie could have found very appealing. "I guess I do owe you some kind of explanation."

"You mean you believe I'm Callie Cantrell?"

"I believe your story," he countered, "and I believe I've made some mistakes. Let's leave the rest for now until I can do some thinking." At her look, he added quickly, "Oh, don't worry. I'm not going to keep you hostage all night. You can go back to Fort-de-France as soon as you like." His expression sobered again. "I'd like to come with you, however."

Callie felt tension return. "Why?"

"Because I need to set some things straight in my mind. And I need to repay you for all the trouble I've caused."

"Don't worry about it," Callie dismissed quickly. She didn't want Gavin anywhere near her apartment or Tucker.

Gavin didn't say anything but Callie could feel his suspicions beginning to grow again. She changed the subject by prodding gently, "You were going to tell me about Teresa's son."

"If he exists," Gavin said flatly.

"*If?*"

Gavin laughed shortly. "The Rutledge's are known for having skeletons in every closet and Teresa, though she just married into the family, turned out to run true to color. She bled Stephen dry for every penny of his inheritance then took off—never to be heard from again, until she ran out of cash. At least this is the way I heard it all secondhand," he added with a touch of mockery. "Stephen went wild looking for her but she was gone without a trace. They'd had some kind of fight right before she left and he somehow blamed himself for her disappearance. The rest of the Rutledges thought it was just good riddance when Teresa left."

"Yourself included?" Callie couldn't help interjecting.

"I wasn't around," Gavin answered shortly. "I had no real opinion about Teresa one way or the other."

"Please, go on," Callie urged when it became apparent that he was wondering about the advisability of explaining his situation to her.

Gavin grimaced. "There isn't a lot more to tell. Stephen died in a small-plane crash and shortly thereafter Victoria began receiving letters from Teresa, begging for money. It seemed she'd had a son—Stephen's son—and she needed help providing for him."

Gavin wasn't watching Callie, but she could practically feel the way he was trying to probe her feelings, to assure himself that she wasn't the scheming Teresa. Callie was holding her breath. She'd thought Jonathan's family was rife with jealousy, anger, and avarice but the Rutledges sounded as if they'd written the book.

"Victoria didn't believe her at first, so Teresa started sending photographs of the boy as an infant. She even sent a birth certificate, and that's when Victoria began to believe. She tried to talk Teresa into coming back to Denver and when that failed, she tried to pinpoint her whereabouts. But Teresa wrote from all over: Europe, the U.S., Mexico, the Caribbean.... She was never in one place long. All she wanted was money and Victoria sent it to her. The last place Teresa wrote from was Martin‹ ique."

Callie lifted her glass of tea, found it empty, and set it down again. She felt some kind of remark was called for but had no idea in the world what to say. Finally she asked, "And how did you get involved?"

"I was drafted. My grandmother is not the type of woman to allow herself to be emotionally blackmailed forever. She wrote to Teresa and said she wanted to meet her great-grandson and Teresa dropped a postcard back that said if Victoria sent more money—substantially more money—she would disclose the boy's where-abouts. Of course, it didn't happen. That's when I was called upon to help and *voila!*—" Gavin smiled humor-lessly "—here I am."

Callie exhaled slowly. No wonder Gavin had felt like strangling her when he thought she was Teresa. "And the boy?" *Tucker?*

"Who knows if he exists or not?" Gavin shrugged with grim acceptance. "I don't think it's beyond my ex-sister-in-law to invent him."

Callie realized that all through their discussion Gavin had never called Tucker by name. She'd thought he had once, but he'd been referring to his brother.

"What's the boy's name?" Callie asked, her throat dry.

"Stephen," Gavin said, unknowingly crystallizing all of Callie's fears. "Just like his father. Why?"

Callie shook her head and wiped her sweating palms in the folds of her dress. Stephen Thomas. Stephen Tucker Thomas. It wasn't coincidence.

Should she tell Gavin? she wondered, then knew instantly that she wouldn't. He'd just spun a fantastic tale of family intrigue—one that she would have to accept on faith. What if it wasn't true? What if Gavin were the villian, not the white knight? What if she, Callie, was just a pawn in an elaborate scheme where a child's welfare was at stake?

Callie immediately got a grip on herself. She was getting fanciful. There was a simple explanation, she was sure of it, and she just needed to get Tucker and his mother alone and find out what it was.

In the meantime she had to clear up a few things with Gavin. "I don't understand the relationship between you and your half brother. His name was Stephen Thomas?" At Gavin's nod she said, "And yours is Rutledge. You obviously had different fathers since your last names are different."

"That's right. My mother was Stephen's mother."

"Then . . . your mother was a Rutledge?"

Gavin nodded.

"Then you should have a different last name, your father's last name. It doesn't make sense unless . . ." Callie trailed off, coming to the right conclusion a heartbeat too late.

"Unless I was a bastard," Gavin put in helpfully.

Callie looked at him in distress.

Gavin laughed, a deeply amused rumble in his chest that sounded low and attractive. "Didn't you guess? I'm a member of the family the Rutledges would just as soon forget."

"I don't believe that's true." Callie felt her cheeks warm with embarrassment. "You're here, aren't you? Helping them?"

"Look, Callie, you just spent the greater part of the afternoon telling me about the Cantrells. Family love and honor go right out the window when there's money involved—especially a great deal of money—and no one wants to lessen their share of the pie. The Rutledges would just as soon I wasn't in line for an inheritance— which I'm not. And I'd venture to guess that, apart from Victoria, they don't want to share with any son of Stephen's either."

Callie regarded him helplessly, as confused by the lack of love in his family as she'd been by Jonathan's. Her own parents, while they were still living, had been loving and kind and it was beyond Callie to imagine that other families could be so hateful and avaricious. But she'd seen it with the Cantrells, and she was hearing about it with the Rutledges.

"So why do you care?" she asked Gavin. "Why are you so involved with Teresa?"

Gavin's smile was cold. "I don't give a damn about many of the Rutledges, but my brother was a good man. If Stephen had a son, I'm going to find him for him. And if Teresa's the bitch she seems to be, I'm going to take care of her too.

"I'm going to find Teresa, Callie. I'm going to find her for my brother and for the boy."

Dusk settled dark shadows on Gavin's face and Callie couldn't help the shiver of apprehension that slid down her spine. He sounded so positive. What if he found out about her lies regarding the bracelet? She doubted he would continue to believe in her innocence, yet she was still afraid to tell him about Tucker. Whether it was because she automatically distrusted wealthy families or because she felt a deep maternal instinct where Tucker was concerned she didn't know, but in either case, Callie couldn't divulge the truth.

Then suddenly Gavin forced her into taking another step in deception.

"Callie," he said casually, "what's the name of the shop where you purchased the bracelet?"

Chapter Three

The trouble with a lie was that one always begat another. Like a snowball, Callie's one tiny deception was turning into an avalanche as she spun another lie and another and yet another.

"I can't remember the name of the shop. It was on the main street in Bridgetown, Barbados's largest city."

Callie had never been to Bridgetown in her life. She hoped to God Gavin hadn't either.

"What's the name of the street?"

Callie frowned. Inside, she was a mass of nerves. The trust she'd built with Gavin was small and if he believed she was lying it would disappear entirely. She needed him to trust her. If he didn't, he wouldn't let her leave and she wouldn't be able to get back to Tucker.

"I can't remember. But it was a very exclusive store. It had black-and-gray striped awnings above the windows and the windows were etched with silver lettering." Callie stole from her memory, describing one of San Francisco's most elegant jewelry stores to make her lie sound more authentic.

"But you can't remember the name?" Gavin asked, frowning.

Callie frantically tried to come up with a name. What did she know about Barbados! Barbados was a British island, wasn't it? Or at least it had been once.

"I think it was something like Weatherby's, or Weatherstone, or something..." Callie lifted her palms and gave him a crooked smile. "I'm sorry."

He shook his head. "It doesn't matter. Bridgetown isn't that big. I'll be able to find it."

Callie's smile fell from her lips. "You plan on going to Barbados?"

"If that's what it takes." Gavin sighed and leaned back in his chair, his eyes meeting hers. Callie's heart gave an odd little jerk as he said, "I've got to find Teresa. She must have pawned that bracelet on Barbados...maybe she's even on that island."

"You're certain this is your bracelet?"

"Teresa's bracelet. I doubt there are two of them. If so, one's a reproduction of another. May I see it?"

Callie was reluctant to let him have it, but she couldn't really refuse. She slipped it from her arm and tried to control her tension as Gavin turned it over and over in his palms.

"This is real gold," he said. "It's got to have been Teresa's." He handed it back to her and Callie breathed an inner sigh of relief.

Silence settled between them. The sun was an orange globe sinking into a pink sea and Callie watched it unseeingly, her mind imprinted with the picture of Gavin's brooding face. She waited as long as she could stand it before asking a trifle diffidently, "You do believe me then?"

"Yes. I think I do."

Hallelujah! It had taken over half a day but she'd convinced him of the truth—at least part of the truth.

"I owe you a tremendous apology," he said in a voice pitched a tone or two lower than normal. "My God, what you must think of me."

"It doesn't matter," Callie assured him lightly. All she wanted to do now was escape before he learned of her deception over Tucker.

"I'm not usually quite so barbaric."

"Look, I understand. Really. From what you've told me you have every right to want to strangle this Teresa person."

Gavin made a self-deprecating sound and said, "For God's sake, Callie, I've been the worst kind of monster. Don't be nice about it. I don't deserve it." He drew in a long breath. "How's your chin?"

"I'll survive the bruise."

"Oh, Callie..."

Her throat felt hot and tight. Reaction, she told herself. She had looked forward to his apology but now his sensitivity took her by surprise. It made her like him more than she wanted to.

"I should be going," she murmured, reaching for her bag.

"I'm sorry about everything. Very, very sorry."

"Forget it." She had to get away soon or she would be tempted to break down and tell him everything. But she couldn't play that kind of game with Tucker's welfare. She had to talk to the boy first.

To Callie's amazement Gavin signed the tab to his room. "You're staying here?" she asked, her softening feelings taking an abrupt turn. Gavin was a guest of the hotel and he hadn't even told her!

He nodded, then saw her expression. "There didn't seem to be any reason to tell you," he explained. "Would it have made a difference?"

Callie couldn't find an answer. Yes, it would have made a difference! She distrusted the fact that he'd held back on that piece of information. It seemed indicative of the kind of man he was.

Yet, did it *really* make a difference? She would have probably chosen the Bakoua Beach Hotel anyway; she felt safe here.

"I'll take you home to your apartment," Gavin said, scraping back his chair and moving toward the stairs.

"No...really, er, thanks. There's no point. I'll just catch a taxi."

"I'd feel better if I came with you. Let me do something to make up for this afternoon."

"I appreciate the gesture, Gavin, but it's really not necessary." Callie laughed softly, stepping away from the table toward the stairs. She had to convince him there was no reason to be so solicitous. "To be perfectly honest, I'd like to be alone."

She couldn't *wait* to be alone. As she stood at the bottom of the stairway, her face turned toward the evening breeze off the bay, she saw the ferryboat chugging across the water. Within fifteen minutes it would be docking on this side of the bay, at the Pointe du Bout marina. Suddenly she wanted to be on that ferry with the sea wind whipping her hair, cooling her heated flesh, easing her troubled thoughts.

She held out her hand to Gavin. "You've got William Lister's number. You can verify everything with him if you still need more proof that I'm Callie Cantrell. I appreciate your problems and hope you work them out, but I don't see how I can help you further.''

Gavin accepted her hand, closing it within his callused palm. Callie was surprised. She hadn't expected him to have weathered hands; his tale of the Rutledge fortunes had led her to believe he would never have to work another day in his life. But then he was the bastard son, she remembered. Out of favor with the family through no fault of his own. She felt an unusual kinship with him at that moment.

Gavin leaned against a post, reluctantly dropping her hand. He shoved his fists into the pockets of his tan slacks. ''I don't want you to leave,'' he said softly.

''I have to.'' Callie turned away. It was madness to even feel this longing that had somehow crept over her.

''Give me your address here, at least. I'd like to talk to you when I get back from Barbados.''

''I'm sorry. I'm leaving for San Francisco at the end of the week. I don't think we'll have time to see each other again.''

''I see.''

He didn't. Callie knew he thought he would never be able to make up for how he'd treated her, but that wasn't really the case. She was attracted to him. Under different circumstances she might even consider getting involved.

She shook her head. How odd! The first man that had piqued her interest since Jonathan and he'd frightened her out of her wits.

''Goodbye, Gavin.''

She left before he could make her change her mind. For some reason she walked toward reception, as if she did truly intend to call a taxi. But then she circled around, going out the main building by a side door that led to the path to the marina.

A useless deception, but Callie was taking no chances.

Gavin watched Callie walk away, aware of how her dress brushed her legs, the way her hair swung around her shoulders. He was totally baffled by her. He had the sensation that he'd just been expertly conned.

Without knowing or understanding why, he followed her. She intrigued him. She tantalized him. She dazzled him.

He couldn't remember ever feeling this way before.

He'd been so certain she was Teresa. And he was so utterly relieved that she wasn't.

Or was she?

A cold hand seemed to squeeze his heart as he witnessed her double back to one of the Bakoua's side doors. He waited, then followed. He saw her white dress disappear into the gathering gloom as she hurried down the path toward the tourist shops and other hotels of Pointe du Bout.

With a sharp intake of breath and a string of unvoiced curses, Gavin went after her.

Callie's heart was beating unevenly, and she had to repress the urge to look over her shoulder.

Hurry. Hurry. Hurry.

She was not a superstitious person but she couldn't control the feeling of urgency that assailed her. She had to get back to Tucker. Immediately. Without Gavin Rutledge.

An idea had begun to form that she couldn't get out of her mind. What if Tucker was being cared for by people other than his parents? That would certainly explain why he spoke such excellent English when his mother, with whom he lived alone, was French. It would also explain his mother's wariness where Callie was concerned; she wouldn't want Tucker to become too attached to anyone.

What if Teresa had stowed Tucker with people she knew on Martinique. What if Teresa—of the red hair and blue eyes, so much like Callie's own—were Tucker's own mother? What if Tucker had seen the resemblance and had chosen Callie as a kind of surrogate mother...?

She couldn't stop herself from looking over her shoulder. By now she was in the hub of the tourist shops that were scattered along the periphery of the Pointe du Bout marina's docks. There were people behind her but none that she recognized. She glanced both left and right. The narrow white spires and rigging of the sailboats created a mesh against the darkening sky.

Tucker. Stephen Tucker Thomas. Whose child was he?

The ferry horn blasted twice and Callie hurried down the pier. Once more she glanced nervously behind her, then chided herself. Who could be following her? No one. Only Gavin, and she'd convinced him she knew nothing about Teresa's son.

It seemed to take forever for the people to empty the ferry. Callie stood in the crush of tourists eager to visit Fort-de-France by night. The ferry's evening lights came on, sending streaks of moving illumination across the dark waters of the bay.

She stepped onto the boat, hazarding one more glance at the pier. Nothing. The ghosts were all in her own mind.

When the engines changed and the ferry began to pull back into the bay, Callie was on the aft deck, one hand gripped tightly around the wide white railing. She breathed a sigh of relief. It was over. Now all she had to do was get back to Fort-de-France and try to drag the truth from Tucker.

Gavin stayed in the interior of the ferry, propped against the wall in a dimly lit corner. He'd waited until Callie had appeared on deck before he'd boarded, being careful to keep out of her line of vision. Now he could see her legs and the lower half of her dress through the window to the aft deck. The wind was brisk and she had to keep one hand firmly planted on her thigh to hold her billowing skirt in place. Every so often he would get a tantalizing glimpse of tanned skin and curved, healthy muscles before she would clamp down on the capricious fabric. Even in his anger Gavin felt a tug on his senses and he took a long breath to clear his head.

If she wasn't Teresa, she knew where Teresa was. No other answer made sense.

"Damn. Damn, damn, damn."

He wished he could start the day—his whole miserable life!—over again. He couldn't believe it, but it was true: he was becoming infatuated with this woman. And the hell of it was she might turn out to be his brother's conniving ex-wife.

Chapter Four

The breeze off the bay lifted Callie's already wind-whipped hair as she hurriedly stepped from the ferry to the dock. She weaved her way through the sauntering crowd, chafing at the snail's pace. A string of yellow lights swung gently from the overhead shelter, making her feel exposed and vulnerable. There was no reason to feel so paranoid, she reminded herself. Tucker was safe and well and very possibly loitering impatiently around her apartment. She'd promised him a treat from the bakery and he was unlikely to forget.

Finally she reached the sidewalk and tried signaling a taxi. It was a hopeless gesture. The traffic whizzing down the four-lane street wouldn't slow down for anything short of a ten-car pileup. Callie bit her lip and waited for the traffic light to change. She wasn't near a crosswalk, but if she could make her way to the median in the center, then across the other lanes, she could save precious minutes by getting to the taxi station.

Hurry. Hurry. Hurry.

The light changed from green to yellow, then to red. She dug her fingernails into her palms, waiting for the traffic to slow. It seemed to take an eternity. Finally she dared to step off the curb, only to be blasted by a dozen horns, the driver nearest her shaking his fist outside the window and yelling at her in rapid-fire French.

Ignoring him, Callie darted between the cars, reached the median, glanced toward the traffic light and saw it change to green again.

"Hey! You!"

The hairs on the back of her neck rose. She whipped around, certain it had been Gavin's voice.

But no, another driver was jabbing his finger in the direction of the light, his face a dark scowl. Not heeding his warning, she quickly zigzagged her way through the other cars before they had gotten into gear.

She cut across the park and past the outdoor tourist market to the small, incut road used as a taxi station. The station was empty.

Forced to wait or walk up the darkened street alone, Callie wrapped her arms around herself and tried not to pace. She gritted her teeth and fought the chill that had settled between her shoulder blades, managing by sheer willpower to keep from glancing toward the ferry dock.

You're crazy, she told herself. *There's nothing to run from.*

"*Bon soir, Madame.*"

She nearly jumped from her skin at the friendly greeting. A tall, silver-haired gentleman in a suit stood beside her and she smiled faintly as she realized he, too, was waiting for a taxi.

"Bon soir," she answered.

"You're American," he said in a lovely French accent, and Callie only nodded. The last thing she wanted was to get embroiled in a conversation with a stranger. All she could think about was Tucker.

"You are alone," he said with obvious concern, and for once Callie grew impatient with the gallantry of the French.

"Not really alone," she quickly denied. "Just on my way home. I've been...shopping."

He glanced at her plastic bag, and it was then that Callie remembered what she looked like. Though she'd brushed the dust off her arms and legs, the grime on her white dress was distinguishable even under the fuzzy illumination from the street lamps.

And her hair. My God! It would be a miracle if she ever got the tangles out. With a sinking realization she wondered what her face looked like. Was it, too, covered with dirt? Gavin hadn't said as much and she was certain he would have at least mentioned that fact to her at some point. Even so, she began to feel extremely self-conscious.

Just then, a taxi slipped into the narrow roadway, and she sighed with relief.

"I live up the hill," she said to the driver, her knees bending so she could see through the window. She pointed in the direction she meant. "Can I show you the way?"

The driver nodded his understanding and the silver-haired gentleman lifted a hand and said, *"Au revoir, jolie femme."*

Callie smiled. *"Merci. Au revoir,"* she said as she climbed inside, then the taxi was speeding away from the curb and the city of Fort-de-France.

Goodbye, pretty woman. She was ashamed that she'd been so wrapped up in her own problems, she could scarcely be polite to a well-meaning stranger. She swallowed hard. Her nerves were raw. She couldn't seem to act sensibly.

Gavin's fault, Callie thought uncharitably. Now that she was away from his powerful influence she realized how truly awful he'd been to her. No wonder he'd wanted to fall all over himself apologizing. She should have let him. She should have forced him to get down and grovel for her forgiveness.

Not that it was going to matter anyway, she told herself as she looked out the taxi window. She wouldn't be seeing him again.

"And good riddance," Callie murmured to herself.

"Eh?" The taxi driver cocked his head.

"Nothing. Turn right . . . there."

The taxi swung into the narrow cobblestone street that fronted her building. Callie paid the fare and with a surreptitious glance in both directions, she crossed the street and let herself inside.

No small boy greeted her as she mounted the stairs, and though she knew she should be relieved that Tucker was safe at home, her heart was curiously heavy as she unlocked her apartment door and closed it gently behind her.

Gavin's taxi dropped him at the end of Callie's street. He wasn't certain which building she'd gone into, but he knew it was one of three. He walked toward the apartment buildings, his shoes scuffing on the uneven cobblestones. It was dark and quiet along the street, the sultry evening air heavy with the smell of frying fish and the omnipresent tang of brine lifting off the bay.

Gavin barely noticed. He was in a sullen rage that was almost entirely self-directed. *Almost* because a portion of his anger was meant for Callie Cantrell . . . or should he say, Teresa Thomas?

A muscle jerked beside his jaw. Whoever the hell she was, she had something to hide, and he intended to find out what that something was.

A light from a third-floor window switched on, spilling a trail of illumination over a wrought iron balcony and into the street. Gavin's eyes were irresistibly drawn and he inhaled a sharp breath when he heard a door slide open and Callie herself stepped onto the balcony.

He melted into the shadows. She hadn't seen him once as he'd followed her from Pointe du Bout; he was sure of that. He wasn't about to give himself away now. Not yet. Not until he'd had some time to think.

His chest tightened. He was aware that at that moment his interest in her was little short of voyeurism, but he didn't care. Somehow she'd gotten under his skin and he couldn't take his eyes off her. A hot awareness licked through him that he recognized as the early stages of arousal and he wondered about his own sanity. Was she Teresa? If so, Gavin had a new understanding as to why his brother had been so enamored with her.

He swore beneath his breath, trying to come to terms with this added complication to his quest. The woman on the balcony was involved, at least at some level; he could feel it. It was important that he ignore her obvious attractions and think about who she might be.

If he could turn back the clock he would seriously rethink his decision to help Victoria. He might even refuse her flat. Gavin grimaced, recalling his meeting with his grandmother. It wouldn't have been easy . . .

Victoria had sat straight in her chair at the head of the long, carved mahogany table in the Rutledge dining room, her white hair and cobwebbed, papery skin belied by her sharp blue eyes. Gavin had been amused and a little irritated by her invitation to come to the house; an invitation that in retrospect had been little more than a command performance.

"I'm being blackmailed," she'd said in her incisive way.

It had totally bowled him over. Blackmailed? He couldn't conceive of Victoria doing anything in her pristine life to warrant blackmail.

A smile had tightened the corners of her mouth as she'd witnessed his reaction. "Emotionally blackmailed," she corrected herself. "I see you're surprised, Gavin. Somehow I thought nothing could surprise you."

"What gave you that idea?"

He'd purposely slouched against the wall at the far end of the room, his jeans, boots, and two day's growth of beard making the gulf between him and his grandmother appear even wider. Gavin hadn't cared. He owed the Rutledges nothing and they owed him nothing. In fact, before the interview had even got under way he was itching to leave their forty-room white elephant home and get back to the windswept plains of Wyoming.

"You strike me as the kind of man who has a very realistic view of life," she'd continued. "I thought another scandal in the Rutledge family wouldn't surprise you in the least."

He hadn't missed her reference to "another" scandal. "Who's blackmailing you?" he'd asked evenly.

"Teresa. Stephen's wife."

Gavin raised his brows. He'd known little about Stephen's wife except that she was very beautiful—and that only because Stephen had called him out of the blue one day and sung her praises. He'd wanted Gavin to come to the wedding but Gavin had declined. Mixing with other Rutledges was something he'd avoided as much as possible. Until Victoria's letter Gavin hadn't even been to the family home since he was a child.

"She says she has a son. Stephen's son." Victoria's tone had been harsh. "She teases me with promises of seeing the boy if I send her money."

"And do you? Send her money?"

"Yes." She met his gaze deliberately. "I'm not proud of it, but if Stephen does have an heir I don't want to alienate Teresa entirely."

"Where do I fit in?"

She sighed, a little of her starchiness disappearing. "Ahh, Gavin, that's the one thing I've always admired about you. Even as a boy you knew when to get to the point."

It was easier to be the object of her censure than her admiration, Gavin recognized. He didn't want to like his grandmother too much. He'd suffered enough rejection in the past.

"And here I thought you wanted to see me because you'd missed me," he drawled sardonically.

"Don't be flippant. I need you to find Teresa and see if she's telling the truth. If there is a child, I want to know it. She sent me a picture."

Victoria had then spread two photographs on the table in front of her. Reluctantly, because he felt her pulling him into family affairs against his will, Gavin had walked to her end of the room. One picture was of Stephen with Teresa, and seeing his brother had brought a strange tightening to Gavin's throat. He'd loved Stephen; the only Rutledge he could really say that about.

Even Gavin's mother hadn't cared about him—nor he her—in the same way. She'd been too eager to find another wealthy man with the right genealogy, one who, unlike Gavin's real father, would be interested in marrying her. Stephen, on the other hand, had always treated Gavin with the kind of understood love that existed between brothers. Gavin's clearest memories of his childhood were the relatively few and precious times he and Stephen had been together.

The other picture had been of a small boy. Gavin's ambivalence about helping Victoria find Teresa had suddenly disappeared. If Teresa were responsible, however inadvertently, for Stephen's death, and if she were really holding her own son up to Victoria for blackmail... Gavin had suddenly wanted to kill her!

"Where do I start?" he'd asked in a rough whisper.

"She last wrote from Martinique. When can you go?"

He'd met Victoria's gaze directly. He might not have understood or agreed with his grandmother on most issues, but he wasn't going to let that get in the way of finding his brother's son.

"If I could, I'd leave yesterday," he'd heard himself say.

"Don't do anything rash," had been his grandmother's quick warning. "If you have to bargain with her, okay. But don't antagonize her any further!"

Now Gavin stared at Callie's lovely figure silhouetted against the light from her apartment. He felt the blinding anger of injustice. Why couldn't he hate her like he had when she'd been only a faceless image? Why did it seem so difficult to fit this woman into the picture he'd had of Teresa—the one where she was a greedy, heartless bitch?

He toyed with the idea of confronting her again, then changed his mind. He had precious little to go on; most of what he felt was gut instinct.

Sucking air between his teeth, he watched the mesmerizing woman on the balcony until she stepped back inside her apartment. A moment later he heard the glass door slide shut, then the final click of the lock.

There was another way, he realized, reluctant to move from the shadows. He could catch the early morning flight to Barbados, locate the jewelry store in Bridgetown, and find out if she were telling him the truth.

It was late evening before Gavin walked back down the cobblestone street and made his way along the roadway to the lights and sounds of Fort-de-France proper.

Callie awoke with the sensation of a mild hangover. She grimaced and turned her face into the pillow, her eyes flying open a swift heartbeat later as memory intruded. Tucker. The Bakoua Beach Hotel. Gavin Rutledge.

She threw back the covers and, shivering a little, hurried to the loud, clanking air conditioner sticking out of her bedroom window. She switched off the machine and almost instantly the sticky, sub-tropical heat pervaded the room. The bathroom was hot and Callie turned the shower to cool and washed her hair thoroughly. She had been too tired the evening before to do more than rinse the dirt off her body.

Stepping from the shower, she wrapped a towel around her head and another around her torso and walked back into her bedroom. It was 6:30 a.m. Early, but still a highly likely time for Tucker to be out and about.

Callie pulled on a sky-blue terry cloth beach dress then brushed her hair and waited for it to dry. She kept checking the clock, anxious for Tucker to put in an appearance. He didn't *have* to come, she kept reminding herself, but she'd told him she would bring him some pastries. He would surely find out if she had, no matter how late she'd been getting home.

She checked the white sack which held the creme-filled goodies and gave a rueful snort. Several of the pastries had been crushed flat. She salvaged what she could, arranged them on a plate, then made some iced tea and settled down to wait.

By nine o'clock she decided he wasn't going to show. By ten o'clock she was pacing the apartment.

She'd tied her hair back with a ribbon, transferred the pastries back to the sack, and was locking her door before the clock struck eleven. *I just want to know that he's all right,* she justified to herself. *That's all. Once I do, then I'll concentrate on packing and getting back to San Francisco.*

It wasn't far to Tucker's home but Callie took her time. Her fears were groundless, she told herself with more conviction. As she approached the run-down neighborhood, which was his home, her feet lagged. She knew how foolish she was being. There was no way something dire and dreadful had happened to the little boy, and there was no way Gavin Rutledge would have known where to find him. Tucker was safe with his mother, Callie told herself firmly, but a niggling doubt kept tickling inside her head.

A mangy looking mutt gave a half-hearted wag of his tail as she passed by an open doorway and three solemn-eyed children came outside to stare. Callie smiled but they didn't respond. Feeling like the outsider she was, Callie turned the corner to Tucker's street.

A breeze swept up from the bay, soothing her perspiring forehead and dissipating some of the shimmering heat. Beside the steps to Tucker's tenement stood a huge, gnarled and broken jade tree. Callie could smell damp earth and an odor she realized later was coming from an overloaded garbage bin further down the alley.

She stopped at the bottom step, clutching the sack of pastries with tight fingers. "Oh, Tucker," she whispered, heavyhearted. There was such a difference between his neighborhood and her own.

She'd been to his home once before but had forgotton—or maybe purposely blocked—what the surroundings were like. Not that Tucker's apartment was unclean. The woman who'd identified herself as Tucker's mother, Aimee, had only let Callie inside the living room, but the wooden floor had been swept clean, the furniture old and a bit dusty but cared for.

Callie climbed the stairs, opened the outer door and walked down the narrow hallway that led to the back apartments. Aged wallpaper was peeling away from the corners, and the overhead light gave off only the weakest illumination. Dirt had collected on the glass shade, adding to the dinginess, and Callie wondered when, if ever, the landlord had last cleaned the outer areas of the building.

She knocked on Tucker's door, wishing her heartbeat would assume a normal rate again. There was no earthly reason to work herself into such a state! Tucker had lived without her for over five years, for Pete's sake, and after this week she would be just a memory to him; it wasn't as if his whole life was at stake, or that she could do anything about it even if it were!

The door cracked an inch, a chain lock showing through the opening. Aimee Thomas peered out.

"*Allo?* Ah, Miss Cantrell," she said, recognizing Callie, but making no motion to open the door farther.

"Hello," Callie answered. "I was wondering if Tucker was home. I bought him some pastries from the bakery and I wanted to give them to him."

She tried hard not to appear as if she were trying to peek beyond the petite woman barring the doorway, but she couldn't help a glance over Aimee's head. From the limited vision provided by the cracked doorway Callie could only tell there was no one in the living room.

"Tucker is not here," Aimee said flatly.

"Will he . . . be back soon?"

Aimee shrugged and Callie inwardly sighed. What would it take to get beyond this woman's defenses? And where was Tucker?

"Could I leave the pastries?" she asked. "I told him I would bring them to him."

Reluctantly Aimee took the chain off the door and stood back, allowing Callie entrance. Pulling the white bakery sack from her plastic carryall, Callie held it out to Aimee. The woman accepted it with ill grace, her mouth tightening at the corners.

"Tell him I stopped by, won't you?" Callie said, and Aimee nodded.

On the way back to her apartment Callie was at first angry, then depressed. Her feelings for Tucker were very complicated, far more so than they should be. She knew Dr. Knox, the psychologist whom she had visited for a brief time after Jonathan and Joshua's deaths, would consider her attachment to Tucker unhealthy. But Callie knew she wasn't trying to replace Joshua with Tucker; her son and Tucker were nothing alike. It was just that Tucker needed the same thing that Joshua had—uncomplicated love and affection—and Callie was oh, so willing to give it.

Still, time was her enemy. The end of the week was fast approaching and the idea of leaving the little boy behind was growing harder by the minute.

"Tucker, where are you?" she murmured to herself as she trudged up the stairs to her apartment.

At twilight Callie gave up hope of seeing the little boy that day. He rarely stopped by in the evenings. She wasn't certain if it was because he had better things to do or if Aimee somehow prevented him from coming over. Not that the woman would care if he was out after dark, Callie thought uncharitably. But she was reasonably certain Aimee was doing everything in her power to disrupt Tucker's growing friendship and interest in Callie.

Leaning her head back she sighed and closed her eyes. She felt hot and sticky and frustrated. She'd paced the apartment for hours, afraid to go out in case she missed Tucker. Now she longed to take a walk by the water, but she wasn't willing to trek down the hill after dark. She debated on calling a taxi but couldn't seem to work up the enthusiasm. Instead she grabbed one of the rickety high-backed stools from around her dropleaf table—stools the management euphemistically referred to as dining room chairs—and hauled it onto the balcony.

The breeze fanned her flushed cheeks and the street was quiet enough for her to hear the drone of the cicadas. Using lessons she'd learned from dealing with the pain of losing her loved ones, Callie tried to unwind and relax her tightened muscles. She rationalized that her fears were excessive, an aftereffect from Gavin Rutledge's harsh treatment. There was absolutely no reason on earth to be so tensed up.

"Callie! Callie!"

Tucker's delighted cry sent Callie to her feet. She leaned eagerly over the wrought iron railing. "Tucker! Where have you been? I've been waiting for you all day!"

"Fishing! *Avec Michel!*"

"Well, come on up. I want to hear all about it!"

It was as if a terrible weight had been lifted off her shoulders. Fishing with Michael. Of course! Why hadn't she thought of that? Michael was one of the older boys who seemed to spend every waking minute at the water's edge, hoping some good-hearted fisherman would take him on board for a day. Tucker idolized Michael, dogging after him whenever he could. It was a testament to Callie's fears that she hadn't even considered the obvious.

Tucker bounded up the stairs, hurtling into the room with the unabashed enthusiasm of the very young. A stream of French poured around Callie's ears and she struggled unsuccessfully to get him to slow down. A day with Michael was not only exciting, but death on Tucker's knowledge of English.

"Whoa, Captain Bill," Callie interrupted, stopping his lips with her finger. "Start over at the beginning. In English. All I heard was *grand* and *poisson*. Did you catch a big fish?"

"Big, big *poisson*!" Tucker reiterated, holding out his arms.

"What was it?" At his blank look, she said, "What kind of fish?"

But that question was outside his command of English, or maybe even of French. He just shook his head and smiled, shrugging disarmingly.

"Who did you go with?" she asked. "What fisherman? What boat?"

"Oh, Francois fished us."

"Francois took you fishing? I don't think I know him."

"Michel is his friend."

Tucker's trust in complete strangers bothered Callie and she fought hard not to give him a lecture on being careful. It wasn't up to her to try and change Tucker's patterns. When she left at the end of the week he was beyond her care. She was a fool to dream otherwise. But her heart bled all the same.

"I wondered what you could be doing," Callie said with a trembling smile. "I stopped by your place today and gave your mother the pastries."

"You were not home yesterday!" Tucker said, his expression changing. "I waited forever!"

"I'm sorry." Callie heaved a sigh. "Something happened and I couldn't get back."

"What?" Tucker's gray eyes were wide and solemn.

"Nothing that concerns you," Callie lied. "Come here." She grabbed another stool and brought it out to the balcony. "Sit down for a minute. I want to talk."

Tucker did as he was bidden, perching himself on the bare wooden seat, his legs dangling in the air. For a moment Callie felt insecure and she glanced both ways down the road, worried someone might see her with him—that someone being Gavin Rutledge.

"You know when we became friends, you and I?" Callie pointed to him and then to herself. "We met on the pier. You remember? And then we found out we lived near each other."

The boy waited patiently for her to say something he didn't already know. Callie drew a deep breath and said, "Well, I knew right away that you were someone special—someone special to me. We both felt that way. We still do."

"You are going," he said with sudden certainty, his eyes huge. With that peculiar sense children have he'd understood she was about to say something terrible.

Callie tried to speak several times before the words finally came out. "Well, you know I have to leave sometime. But that's not what I want to talk about."

He dropped his gaze to the toes of his battered sandals. Callie's throat closed in on itself. She made an effort to clear it, hating herself, hating the world for unfairly treating herself and Tucker.

"I wanted—to talk about—your mother," she said unevenly. "That's all."

"I hate her."

"Oh, Tucker, you don't mean that."

"I hate her. I hate her. I hate her!" He slid off the stool and stalked stiff-legged back into Callie's living room. Seeing that he was heading for the door, Callie dashed after him, scared that she'd done something terrible.

She grabbed his small arm as he was reaching for the handle and Tucker struggled to get loose, furiously prying at her fingers, angry sounds issuing from his throat.

"Listen to me," Callie urged. "Tucker, listen—"

"Get away from me. I want to go! *I want to go!*"

"No, Tucker, please."

He fought like a tiger as Callie tried to hold on to him. She'd never seen him react so violently.

"I don't want to leave you, Tucker! Believe me, I would do anything to be with you!"

He jerked back with all his strength, tearing away from her hands. Desperate to make him understand, she grabbed him by his shoulders. "I love you, Tucker. I love you so much. I can't stand to think of losing you. It's killing me."

"Let me go!"

"Oh, Tucker..." Callie pressed her hands to her mouth and stepped away. She couldn't stop the tears. She turned away so he wouldn't see her cry.

She heard the door slam behind him and began to sob. She'd done it. She'd fallen in love with him, and she'd hurt him because of it. It was her fault—all her fault. Misery blinded her and she threw herself down on her bed, clenching her hands in the blankets, huge sobs issuing from somewhere deep and empty inside herself.

She cried all night and when dawn painted fiery streaks across the horizon she finally was worn out enough to sleep.

Chapter Five

Yes, William. I'll be there at the end of the week. No, I'm not going to change my plans. I'll be there." Callie listened into the receiver for several more moments and said testily, "Look, what do you want, an affidavit? *I'll be there.* Goodbye."

She hung up, angry. Then her anger melted as quickly as it had surfaced. It wasn't William Lister's fault that she was feeling so awful. She'd brought this upon herself.

Callie walked away from the public phone, tired and thirsty. She'd had to wait an hour before she could get the call placed, only to find that William was at lunch. She'd wasted another hour desultorily shopping, then had gone through the whole frustrating process of calling the states all over again. By the time William had answered, Callie's attitude had deteriorated to rock-bottom, and when all he'd been able to talk to her about were the ever-avaricious Cantrells, she'd wanted to kill him.

She didn't care about the Cantrell money! Couldn't William understand that? She was all for throwing the entire fortune back into their greedy faces!

Feeling completely out of sorts, Callie weaved her way through the tiny tables of an open-doored cafe, brushing strands of hair away from her eyes. An overhead fan did its best to cut through the heat but it did little more than add some decoration. Inside she felt as if she was burning up.

What was Tucker doing now? she wondered anxiously. Had he cut himself out of her life? Was Gavin Rutledge on his trail?

With a sigh, she sank into one of the cafe chairs. She should be glad, she supposed, that Gavin wouldn't be able to catch her with Tucker. Now there was no link between herself and the boy. Except that she still had the bracelet. She hadn't had a chance to give it back to Tucker.

A waiter with a white apron around his waist came to her table, pen and pad in hand. "Mademoiselle?"

"Oh, I don't know. Do you speak English? Anything." Callie waved an uncaring hand, then innate graciousness came to her rescue. "How about a cola? Do you have Coke?"

"Oui, Mademoiselle."

"A Coke would be great. Thanks. *Merci.*"

Alone, Callie thought about the bracelet. She needed to give it back to Tucker and she was bound and determined that she was going to see him at least one more time before she left. She wouldn't be able to go unless she did. Thinking about the lone little boy, she knew she might not be able to, anyway.

Grinding her teeth in frustration, Callie silently railed at herself for the mess she'd made of everything. Maybe William had read more into her voice than she'd been aware of, she thought with a faint smile. After all, she wasn't certain she *could* be back in San Francisco by the end of the week; everything depended on Tucker.

The Coke came and Callie accepted it gratefully, drinking it down in several long swallows. She left some change on the table and went back outside into the heat, shading her eyes as she began the long trek to her apartment.

Poor old William, she thought, making a rueful face. She'd been so glad to hear his voice—until he'd started talking legalese about the division of Jonathan's inheritance, that is. He'd warned her about the responsibility the fortune entailed, and the advisability of protecting herself against a possible unfavorable court decision. She'd suddenly become infuriated. How could he talk about money when she'd broken a little boy's heart? How could he expect her to care about Jonathan's sister and brother when Tucker's cry of *Let me go!* still echoed painfully in her ears?

"Don't talk to me about the Cantrells!" she'd blurted out. "Please, William. I just can't stand to hear about them now."

The pause that had followed was characteristic of the older man. "Are you all right, Callie?" he'd asked with fatherly concern.

As dear as he was to her, it had been all Callie could do not to bite his head off.

"I'm fine," she'd said shortly. "Just sick of the heat and everything."

"Then why aren't you back here?"

"Because...oh, I don't know. I'm just involved with a few things that need sorting out."

"Callie." William's voice had grown stern. "I'm sure I don't have to tell you that the problems here are getting bigger. Everyone's clamoring to know where you are. It's all I can do to keep Derek and Catherine from storming my office. They think you've run off with the money."

Callie had closed her eyes and tried to control her anger. Derek and Catherine, Jonathan's brother and sister, had been a thorn in her side since the first day she'd met them. They'd been as jealous of her as they had their older brother, and when Jonathan had died, though they'd feigned deep sadness and loss, the only emotion their eyes had reflected was relief.

That relief had quickly changed to disbelief and fury when they'd found out Callie had ended up with the fortune.

"Derek and Catherine are going to have to wait," Callie had told William firmly. "I've got other things on my mind right now. I'll face them soon enough."

"Will you be able to, Callie?" he'd asked, worried.

"Oh, yes."

She hadn't been able to explain why she felt so sure of herself when just a month earlier she'd been consumed by nervous indecision. Then, she'd needed to escape the pressure. But after meeting Tucker, realizing how much she cared about him and how difficult it was to let go, she'd realized confronting Jonathan's relatives would be a piece of cake.

She'd wanted to talk to William about Tucker, and about Gavin Rutledge, but though she tried several times to bring the subject up, she'd never found the right words. William was an old-time bachelor who'd understood Callie's loss of her husband and son, but she had known instinctively that he would never understand her emotional involvement with a ragamuffin little boy and the man claiming to be his uncle.

"I'll be there at the end of the week," she'd told him, but now she wondered if she'd be able to fulfill that promise.

Oh, Tucker. How can I every leave you?

Callie unlocked her apartment door, pushed it open, dropped her carryall on an empty stool, and sank onto the lumpy couch. She was hot and tired and depressed. There was nothing left to do but face Tucker at his apartment—and that meant facing him in front of Aimee.

She would rather face the dubious Gavin Rutledge again.

Feeling the oppressive heat, she got up, switched on her clattering air conditioner, and made straight for the chilled pitcher of lemonade. She would tackle Aimee Thomas in a little while. For now she just wanted to shake off the blues.

Gavin couldn't decide how he felt. One moment he was furious, the next his stomach would sink to his knees. All he knew for certain was that he'd been duped.

He flexed his right hand several times, finally balling it into an angry fist. The tendons strained with the effort. He counted to fifty before he released it and the small exercise in self-control had the desired effect. He wasn't going to go storming over to Callie's place after all; he was going to approach her quietly and calmly, and then blast her wretched story apart with cool, calculated logic.

He walked through Martinique's small airport, shifting his overnight bag from his left hand to his right.

Hailing a taxi, he reflected that he was going to have to do some serious physical self-improvement not to scare her into silence just by his appearance alone. The stubble on his jaw had turned into a black, scraggly beard, and his clothes were sticking to his skin.

"Bakoua Beach," he told the driver. *"Tout de suite."*

"Oui, Monsieur."

He leaned back and closed his eyes. He hadn't really been surprised that there was no jewelry store in Bridgetown named Weatherby's—or any facsimile thereof. Callie had manufactured it just as she'd probably manufactured a lot of other details; her name, for instance?

His eyes narrowed. It was galling to remember how much he'd needed to believe her.

Nevertheless, there was a tight constriction in his chest, an anxious feeling he couldn't shake no matter how hard he tried. He didn't *want* her involved. He didn't want her to be Teresa. But if she were, no amount of useless hoping was going to change the truth.

"Damn it all," he said under his breath. "Damn, damn, damn it all."

The bracelet was a complete puzzle, Callie decided, turning it over and over in her hands. She was half inclined to take it to a jeweler, to find out its worth.

She slipped it on her wrist and held it up to the weak overhead light. But what good would that prove? She'd known it was valuable even before Gavin Rutledge had said the stones were part of his family's heirlooms. The real question was how Tucker had come to possess it.

Afternoon shadows were creeping through the window as Callie checked her appearance in her tiny bureau mirror. The effects of her crying binge weren't visible anymore, she decided critically. It was time to find

Tucker and make him understand how hard their separation was going to be on her, too. She already had a hundred half-baked ideas about having him come and vacation with her, and sometimes when she really wanted to forsake reality, she even dared to dream of adopting him.

She refused to let the truth of the situation even be considered: that there was no way in the world Tucker's mother would let him anywhere near Callie once she was gone.

Pushing the bracelet up her arm, Callie grabbed her carryall and headed for the door. She was reaching for the knob when several hard raps sounded from the other side, freezing her hand in midair. Tucker? Not likely. He never knocked; he yelled.

Her heart constricted. It was Gavin Rutledge. She knew it! He'd found her. He'd found out all about her and Tucker.

"Mrs. Cantrell?" Gavin's familiar voice sounded through the door panels, cool and wary.

She thought about hiding. Maybe he hadn't heard her. Maybe he didn't know she was home.

In disbelief she watched the knob turn and the door inch open. Then he was there, staring at her, his expression unreadable except for the white line of tension that tightened his lips. Callie's heart plummeted. He knew, she thought despairingly. He knew about her and Tucker.

Callie cracked a thin smile. "Well, hello..." she said, as he opened the door fully, his hands pressed against the panels.

"Going somewhere?" he asked.

She followed his gaze, focusing blankly on her white plastic carryall. It hung from her hand in mute testimony. "Yes...to the store...I'm out—I need some groceries."

"May I come in for a minute?"

She recovered by degrees, feeling each painful beat of her heart. "It looks like you're already in," she observed as Gavin came forward. "Have a chair."

As she closed the door she saw him looking over the room, examining each and every item with deceptive lack of interest. Callie wasn't fooled. He was as alert as a watchdog. She set down her carryall and leaned back against the door, her trembling hands hidden behind her.

The transformation in him took her by surprise. Two days earlier he had looked rough and dangerous. Today he had a sharp, chiseled appearance; the dark stubble gone, his manner less driven. He seemed more civilized and she had to remind herself how easily that veneer could be chipped away. He'd nearly frightened her out of her wits in the alleyway.

"How did you find me?" she asked, a friendly smile on her face.

"I followed you."

The muscles around Callie's jaw froze. "When?"

"After you left me at Bakoua."

"You followed me—from the hotel?"

Gavin nodded. "You said you were going to take a taxi home." He regarded her wordlessly for a moment, then added, "But you didn't."

It was all she could do not to rush into explanations. She wanted to apologize, to make some excuse. The urge was so strong that she had to physically swallow back the words.

"I took the ferry," she said quietly.

Gavin stalked toward her with such swift strides that she couldn't help inhaling a startled breath. He thrust his face to within inches of hers. "There wasn't a Weatherby's in Bridgetown, or anywhere else on the whole damn island," he growled, fury turning his eyes to chips of blue ice. "Lady, I don't know who you are or what you're doing, but you've got yourself a shadow until I find out. You got it?"

"I can explain—"

"Don't explain." His command cut off her words with the speed of a guillotine.

Callie regarded him helplessly. "What do you want?"

"I want you to show me. No more words. I'm tired of words. I want action, and I want it now. Show me where you got this bracelet!"

He yanked her arm from behind her. Callie looked unseeingly at the bracelet. She'd never made a man so angry. Her fights with Jonathan had been few and far between and they'd never been this intense. Even dealing with Derek and Catherine, though draining, had never resulted in the kind of volcanic emotions she was seeing now. And it had happened so fast! One moment he was cool and composed, the next he was in for the kill.

For the space of two unsteady breaths, Callie could only stare. His mouth was a thin line of purpose. His eyes made it clear she'd taken one step too many over the boundary. His body was as tense and watchful as any predatory cat's and Callie knew she had to tell him the truth.

"It was given to me," she said, clearing her throat at the odd sound of her voice. "Right here. Tucker gave it to me."

"Tucker?"

"Stephen Tucker Thomas."

A heartbeat passed. "My God." Gavin's jaw slackened in disbelief.

"I couldn't tell you about him," Callie whispered urgently. "I didn't trust you. Maybe he is your brother's son. I don't know."

"You don't know?" Gavin's palms crashed against the panels on either side of her head. Callie shrank backward, afraid. "Who the hell are you? Teresa?"

"No, I—"

"Don't talk. Don't lie." Contempt grooved the lines that ran from his nose to his mouth still deeper.

Callie's head ached with strain. "I'm not lying," she managed to choke out.

"Where is he?"

She hesitated. It was one thing to admit the truth, quite another to send Gavin after him.

"Where is he?" Gavin repeated softly, his eyes narrowing to glacial slits.

There wasn't a lot Callie could do. He was primed to react to her slightest movement. She thought hard for several seconds, but her mind was overloaded, her senses far too aware of his heat and smell. It was a heady mixture, heightening the tension crackling between them.

"I can't tell you."

He was so close she could see the texture of each pore, the flecks of deeper blue radiating from each iris.

"You'll tell me," he said positively.

"No." Callie swallowed. "I won't."

Her heart was pumping so fast she could hardly think for the pounding in her ears. She wasn't used to defying anyone so blatantly; she was afraid of what he would do.

"You lying, lying bitch!" he snarled furiously. "If you think I'm going to let you continue blackmailing my grandmother, you're out of your mind! I'll break you first!"

"You can threaten me until eternity," she said in a shaking voice, "but I won't change my mind. Not until I know for certain who you are. Tucker means too much to me. I'd rather die than hurt that little boy again."

"Again?"

His tone said it all. Callie stared into his steely eyes and felt a glorious surge of anger. "Tucker's a friend of mine," she said through her teeth. "He's hurting because I told him I was leaving at the end of the week. It's killing me to know how he feels—and it's *my* fault! But I'll be damned if I'll help you find him and hurt him, too!"

Her chest was rising and falling with emotion, her breasts nearly touching the front of his shirt with each movement. She refused to drop her eyes. She'd be damned if she gave in first! *You can go straight to hell!* her measured glare told him, and she saw the glitter of challenge in his own gaze.

Strands of fiery red and gold hair were caught beneath his palm. She waited for him to move, to release her, but she made no move herself. If it was a battle of wills, he'd find out what she was made of. She would never, never sacrifice Tucker for her own sake.

"You're an enigma," Gavin ground out at long last.

"So, Mr. Rutledge, are you."

"You're going to get burned," he warned softly.

Callie laughed shortly. "I can take care of myself."

"Why won't you tell me where he is, Callie? Afraid I'll learn too much about you?"

"I'm only afraid for Tucker."

Gavin shook his head in frustration. "God help me, I almost believe you!"

Hope filled her heart. If Tucker really were a Rutledge she would give anything to connect him with his family.

But she had to be sure. She had to trust this furious man in front of her first. Couldn't he understand that?

"I love Tucker," she said unevenly. "He means more to me than he probably should."

"What's your connection to him?"

"I told you, I'm a friend."

"How long have you known him?"

"About a month, I guess."

"What the hell does he look like?" Gavin suddenly exploded. "God! Is he Stephen's son or not?"

Callie's eyes were wide and eloquent as she shook her head. She understood his frustration but she had no answers for him. In many ways, she was further in the dark than he was.

"I honestly don't know. I wish I could tell you what you want to hear, but I can't."

"Tell me where he is."

Callie twisted her hands together. "He's just a little boy. I won't let you hurt him."

"I won't hurt him! Good God, lady. I want to find out who he is. I want to know if he's a Rutledge. What does it take to convince you my intentions are strictly honorable?"

"A lot more than what I've seen," she said, lifting her chin.

Gavin swore beneath his breath, as much at himself as at Callie. The corners of his mouth quirked briefly and his expression softened.

"Ahh, Callie," he said on a sigh, meditatively stroking the gold and red strands caught between his fingers. "I don't know who you are but I can't hate you. I want to, but can't."

She felt his shift in mood and it sent a frisson of apprehension down her back. She'd found him dangerous

before, but she realized he could be a lot more dangerous in other ways. "Gavin..."

"What?"

She hadn't meant to, but her involuntary plea had focused his attention back on her face. His gaze caught hers
then slid, with agonizing slowness, to her mouth.

Callie inhaled. "I wanted to tell you about Tucker but
I needed to find out some things first."

"What things?"

"Like if his mother was really named Teresa."

Gavin's gaze lifted. His eyes regarded her with deceptive laziness but she saw a flame of desire burning,
building, in their cerulean depths. "Do you really believe," he asked slowly, "there could be two children on
this island with the name Stephen Thomas, in possession of that bracelet?"

He glanced toward her arm. Her hand was in the folds
of her white skirt but the bracelet's beauty stood out,
glowing richly against her lightly tanned skin. Gavin
touched the triangular stones and Callie felt a thrill up her
arm.

He stared at his darker fingers against her skin, then to
Callie's alarm and shock, those fingers closed around her
arm, inching steadily upward, raising goose bumps on
her flesh.

"Don't..." she said.

"Let me," he whispered.

Her lips quivered unconsciously. Though she'd half
ached for this kind of male response from him she was in
a mild panic now that it had happened.

His head bent down, and his mouth fit possessively
over hers. She felt his tongue circling her lips, seeking
entry, and with a wild flutter of her heart she realized this

kiss was going to be a thousand times more devastating than the last.

She tried to protest but no sound issued forth, only the faint rustle of her clothes against his as he moved closer, the hard angles of his body meshing with her softer curves. Her lips parted of their own accord and his tongue explored the moist recesses of her mouth, eager and thrusting. Callie's own tongue tentatively responded, and for her effort she felt his arms tightening around her.

Her own arms were slack at her sides. Now she lifted them, her hands slowly sliding around his back, feeling the contours of muscle and bone beneath the thin fabric of his shirt. One of his hands cupped her head, tipping up her chin, allowing him freer access. There was a feverish need to his kisses that made her heart thump heavily, her hands tightened the material of his shirt into her fists. The moan she heard was her own, and when she felt him tremble she fought her mouth free, only to turn her lips against the pulse beating erratically beside his jaw.

"Callie..." he groaned, his body pressing her against the panels of the door. It was a pleasure to feel his muscular thighs pushing heavily against her trembling legs. Her hands at his nape urged him closer, her own needs as driven as his. She ached inside. Throbbed. Desired in a way that was frightening in its searing intensity.

His palms were molding her breasts through her clothes, then they were urgently pushing down her elastic bodice. Callie was dazed at the pace of their lovemaking. She stood helpless as he watched the material fall away, as mesmerized as he to see her rosy, heat-tinged skin change to milky whiteness.

"Oh, Callie..." he said unsteadily, as the fabric scraped lightly over her sensitized nipples. When she was bared to the waist his hand cupped one breast, touching it in a way that made her knees sag.

His mouth closed over one swollen nipple and she gasped, feeling a belated return of conscience. No man had touched her but Jonathan. She'd never wanted another man. She'd never even looked at another man.

What was happening to her? Callie wondered, frozen. It wasn't like her to be so swept away. And Gavin Rutledge was a stranger! Moreover, he was a stranger she couldn't trust.

But she was powerless to change the tide of desire now. Her wants ruled her mind, and the touch of his hands, the taste of him in her mouth, and the feel of his tongue upon her were all she needed.

His mouth recaptured hers in a fierce kiss that she met with equal fervor. His tongue teased and taunted and Callie's senses were inflamed. Her arms wound possessively around him, her body rubbed against his in an invitation as old as time itself.

Distantly, she heard the sound of footsteps on the stairs. A part of herself tried to respond but Gavin's hands were sliding down her waist and hips, journeying to the gentle swell of her buttocks. She could feel him pulling the material of her dress upward, could feel the cool flutter of air around her thighs.

The knock on the door behind sounded as loud as thunder. It froze them both.

"Callie?" Tucker's innocent voice called.

Wordlessly, Gavin's eyes met hers, their fever slowly fading as he realized who it could be. Callie hesitated for only a heartbeat then she pushed herself away from him, hastily straightening her clothes. Her horror over what had happened was overridden by her relief in knowing Tucker had come to her. She grabbed the door handle,

glanced back once, uncertainly, toward Gavin's closed
face. Then she twisted the knob.

Tucker, seeing only Callie, took a tentative half step
forward. Callie bent to her knees and held out her arms
and the little boy's dam of resistance broke. He threw
himself toward her, wrapping his thin arms as tightly
around her as her arms were wound around him. Callie
cuddled him close, crooning soft love words against his
tousled dark hair. Over the top of his head she met Gavin's eyes, her own eyes issuing a fiercely maternal, silent
warning: *I'll never, ever let you hurt him!*

Chapter Six

D on't go. Don't go," Tucker pleaded, his face pressed against her neck. "I want you here! I want you with me."

Callie rested her cheek against the crown of his head, overcome by emotions she couldn't express. She ignored Gavin but felt his presence keenly. She knew Tucker was unaware that someone else was in the room.

"Oh, Tucker, I'm so glad to see you," she said tremulously. "I was afraid you weren't going to talk to me again. I felt awful."

"Don't go," he reiterated.

Up to this point Gavin hadn't moved but now the floor squeaked as he shifted his weight. Tucker heard and looked up, his tear-drenched eyes moving blankly from Gavin back to Callie.

"This is Gavin," Callie explained, straightening, holding Tucker's hand tightly within her own. "He's a— friend of mine."

"Hello, Tucker." Gavin's voice was careful.

Tucker sidled closer to Callie, watching Gavin with those heartbreakingly solemn eyes she'd grown to love. He looked up accusingly at Callie and she read his mind.

"I'm not leaving with him. He's not from my home. It's a coincidence—a surprise—that he's here."

He was silent. It was plain to Callie he didn't believe her.

"I promise I won't leave until I have to," she said, bending down once again. "Honest."

"How much?" he mumbled, turning his shoulders so he effectively ostracized Gavin.

"A few more days. Three or four."

It hurt Callie more than she could stand to see Tucker so upset and disillusioned. She had no one to blame but herself. She'd been as anxious for his companionship as he'd been for hers, but being the adult, she should have seen this soul-wrenching outcome far more clearly.

She glanced toward Gavin and thought she saw compassion and something akin to pain on his lean features. But a second later he said, "I'm going outside for a while." She heard the sliding door to the balcony open then click shut behind him, a gust of sweltering air ruffling Tucker's hair in its wake.

Swallowing, she kissed his smooth forehead and said, "Come in the kitchen and I'll get you a drink."

With a last, studied glance toward the man on the balcony, Tucker clasped Callie's hand and followed after her.

It was one of life's great ironies that he couldn't be indifferent to the family who'd been so cruel and callous to him, Gavin reflected as he leaned on the balcony's railing. If he had a whit of sense he would clear out and leave the child with Callie. She loved Tucker. That was obvious. And it really didn't matter who she was and what she was doing in Martinique because Tucker loved her, too.

That was the bottom line.

A trickle of sweat slid down his temple. He ignored it, just as he ignored the dazzling pink and scarlet sunset ribboning across the horizon. All he could concentrate on was that little boy—and the woman with him.

Tucker was Stephen's son. One look and Gavin had known the truth. That solemn expression, those gray eyes. Tucker looked more like the Rutledges than he did himself.

He wondered if Callie's insistence that she was leaving was for his benefit—at the poor child's expense. It sure as hell was effective. He'd wanted to turn on his heel and leave them alone, stop complicating their lives. He'd wanted that misery, so deep in the boy's eyes, to vanish.

Whoever Callie Cantrell was, she held Tucker's heart in her hands. And who was *he* to intervene?

Gavin drew a deep breath. The choice wasn't simple. But he had to stop Teresa from bleeding Victoria dry. There was no other alternative. Yet it went against his deepest convictions to separate Tucker from Callie, or Teresa, or whoever the hell she was! He *knew* how the boy was going to feel when the whole thing came down. He knew, better than most, what it meant to be betrayed by one's own family. Tucker would never truly forgive Callie for using him. He would never trust adults again.

Gavin ran a weary hand over his face. He had no other choice. He was going to have to start proceedings against the woman and take her son from her.

* * *

Callie handed Tucker a glass of lemonade. "Now don't gulp it down. I don't have any more lemons to make more. I'll have to go to the store and buy some so sip it."

"Sip it?"

"Drink slowly." Callie racked her brain for the appropriate word in French, but Tucker innocently supplied it.

"Bois lentement."

"Sounds good. Whatever. Just enjoy it, okay?"

He nodded and managed a brief smile.

Callie glanced for the hundredth time toward the sliding glass door. She could see Gavin's tense shoulders and the tight grip of his hands around the railing. She was nearly frantic, wondering what he was thinking. She couldn't help but recall the passionate scene Tucker had unknowingly interrupted and she shuddered inside. She was crazy to react to Gavin the way she had! What in the world had possessed her?

And what about Tucker? What was going to happen now?

"Tucker," Callie said softly, trying to keep her voice casual. "Your name's Stephen Tucker Thomas, isn't it?"

"Uh-huh."

"What is your mother's name?"

Sensing the tension Callie was unwittingly giving off, Tucker gave her a searching look. *"Maman?"*

"Yes, what's her name?"

"You know. Aimee."

Quizzical humor lightened his eyes, as if he thought she was playing a game with him. Callie smiled uncertainly.

"You're right. I know her name is Aimee. But is she..." Callie grappled for the way to broach this subject, hating herself for what she was about to do. She cleared her throat. "Is she your real mother, sweet-heart? Or is she just taking care of you?"

Tucker seemed to be having a hard time comprehending what she was asking. She didn't blame him. She was having a hard time herself.

"Is your real mother's name Teresa?" Callie asked gently.

Something flashed across his eyes. Fear, perhaps? He set his glass down on the counter with a clink. "I want to go home now."

"Oh, Tucker I don't want to upset you," Callie said, distressed. "I love you. I just don't want to have to leave you. If I just knew what was going on maybe I could—" She cut herself off before she started making empty promises. She had to face the fact she might never see him again. "Are you living with your mother?" she asked. "Please tell me."

The muscles in his face worked; he was close to tears. Callie, knowing she shouldn't, swept him close to her again, holding him with all her might. "I don't know what I'm going to do without you," she said brokenly. "I can't think about leaving you."

His small arms squeezed her neck, then she felt him fingering her red-gold hair. Callie kissed his forehead. "Does Teresa have red hair, too?"

His tousled head moved against her. Was that a nod? Or was she just hoping so hard that he wasn't Aimee's son that she was reaching for an answer he couldn't give?

"Who is he?" Tucker asked, twisting his neck and pointing a finger in Gavin's direction.

She looked past his outstretched finger to Gavin's broad back.

"I don't really know," she admitted.

"I don't like him."

"Oh, Tucker, you don't even know him."

"I don't want to."

Callie wondered if Tucker was using Gavin as a scapegoat for the fact that she was leaving. Probably. It would certainly be easier to blame an outsider than to recognize it was really no one's fault.

Except her own, she reminded herself bitterly, for getting so involved in the first place.

"Do you love him?" Tucker asked, bringing Callie's thoughts back with a bang.

"Good heavens, no!"

"Why you say it that way?" he asked, his eyes serious.

"I hardly know him, that's why." She was knocked off balance by his directness. "I just met him several days ago. He's looking for someone, and he thought I could tell him where this person was."

"What person?"

Callie regarded him blankly.

"What person he's looking for?" Tucker asked patiently.

She hesitated in answering just a moment too long, wondering how smart it was to be truthful with Tucker about Gavin's search for him and Teresa. But the boy felt her indecision and he backed away.

Though he couldn't understand all the reasons, she saw him jump to the right conclusion: Gavin was looking for him.

"He's not a bad man," she heard herself saying, but Tucker had had enough. He took several more steps backward, eyeing her with distrust, then he spun on his heel and headed for the door.

Desperate, Callie glanced over her shoulder. Gavin was slowly turning around. She opened her mouth to beg

Tucker to wait but it was too late, he was already turning the knob.

"Be careful," she said, her maternal habits surfacing even while she felt close to panic. Her fists clenched. She had to let him go. He was someone else's child.

The door shut behind him with a careless bang and Callie heard the balcony door slide open at the same moment. She turned quickly, only to meet the censure in Gavin's dark blue eyes.

"Where did you send him?" he demanded.

"I didn't send him anywhere. He's going home."

Tucker's footsteps resounded on the stairs, growing steadily fainter. Gavin wheeled back to the balcony, straining over the railing as Callie heard Tucker running full tilt down the cobblestone street in the direction of his tenement.

Gavin watched the retreating boy for a long time. Callie held her breath. She half expected him to tear out after Tucker, but he stood like a statue, every muscle tense. Eventually he walked back inside the apartment, shut the balcony door, then stalked to the air conditioner, switching it off with an arrogant flip of his wrist.

The quiet was deafening.

"He's Stephen's son," Gavin said. "I'd bet my life on it."

Callie's knees felt weak. She sank onto one of the nicked stools. "I don't know if that's good or bad."

"I'll find him, you know, whether you tell me where he lives or not. I'll find him."

"I'm sure you will," Callie said tiredly.

"What the hell is going on? Who *are* you? You can't fit in unless you're Teresa Thomas."

So they were back to that. She wasn't surprised. His trust in her had been infinitesimal at best and at worst,

well...if the situation were reversed she would undoubtedly come to the same conclusion.

"I don't fit in," she told him. "Tucker picked me,
probably because of the color of my hair and we just...I
don't know...we *clicked*. We needed each other."

"Then where's Teresa?" Gavin's grim face wasn't en-
couraging.

"I've never seen her. The woman Tucker lives with is
not the woman in that picture you showed me."

"She could have changed her hair—her appearance—
anything. She could have—"

"This woman's French, for God's sake! Her accent's
real."

"Even changed her name," he finished pointedly.

Callie glared at him. "I am not Teresa Thomas."

"So you've told me over and over, but lady, I can't
believe you. I don't know what to believe!"

His exasperation did Callie's battered self-confidence
a lot of good. "Aimee claims to be Tucker's mother. He
even calls her *Maman*. But she's French. Is Teresa
French?"

"No. She's American."

"Then Aimee is not Teresa. She's a Martinique native. I don't know how she got hold of Tucker, or what
their situation is, but Tucker doesn't like her."

Gavin's eyes narrowed. "He likes you."

"I'm not Teresa, either. Don't look at me like that. I'm
telling you the truth."

Gavin seemed to want to argue, but he clamped his lips
into a thin line and slowly sat down on the lumpy couch.
Callie let out a sigh of relief and ran her hand over her
throat. The heat was oppressive.

"May I turn the air conditioner back on?" she asked
with a hint of rebellion.

He nodded curtly, then slid his hands around the back of his neck. She saw she wasn't the only one tired of going over the same ground again and again. Then he suddenly said, "Let's get out of here," as if the room had suddenly become too close. "Let's go into Fort-de-France. I'll buy you dinner and try to make up for—all of this."

He didn't have to say what "all of this" was. The list was long and still growing. But with a wince of conscience Callie knew the passionate lovemaking had been as much her fault as his.

She shook her head, knowing it would be best to keep completely away from him. "I'm surprised you're not charging after Tucker. He *is* the reason you're here, isn't he?"

"He's not going anywhere without you. I could read that much on his face."

"I have no control over him," she said.

"I don't think you give yourself enough credit. Come out with me, Callie. I promise to return you unharmed."

Callie looked away. Why, oh, why did he make it sound so enticing? She should be shot for even considering spending time with him. When ever had she become so reckless? It was on the tip of her tongue to refuse again when she thought about Tucker. Being with Gavin was an excellent way to divert him from the boy. And that's what she wanted, wasn't it?

At least that's what she told herself when she answered, "All right. Just give me a minute. I need to buy some more lemons for lemonade anyway...."

They sat at an outdoor table under a red-and-blue umbrella, a light at the corner of the restaurant, street lamps outside the wrought iron fence, and a flickering candle in the center of the table their only illumination. As Callie surreptitiously studied the shadowed planes of Gavin's face she wondered if her memories of Martinique would consist mainly of tense meals with him—and the remembrance of Tucker's solemn gray eyes.

"I need something stronger than iced tea," she remarked, and was rewarded with a flash of white as Gavin smiled.

The courtyard was wedged between two rustic buildings, one open to the street except for the low, wrought iron railing done in the ubiquitous grillwork style so common to Martinique. Callie faced the street and she could see a parade of shoppers and tourists as they passed under the streetlamps, their arms overloaded with parcels, the women mincing carefully between the outrageously parked automobiles and uneven curbs.

Gavin ordered wine for her and a beer for himself. He told the waiter it would be a while before they were interested in the dinner menu and Callie realized tiredly that he wanted to question her some more. When the drinks arrived Gavin poured his into his glass, letting some foam dribble over the side as he filled it to the brim. He looked up to catch her staring at him.

"Tell me how you met Tucker," he said.

"I did tell you."

"No, I mean every little detail. I want to know where exactly you met him and when. Please. It could be very important."

"Why are you even bothering with me? You've seen Tucker. You've got a good idea where he lives. I would think you'd be itching to close in on him."

"Itching?" Gavin took a long draft of his beer, then pulled back his lips in a grimace. "You really have me cast as the villain, don't you?"

"Yes." Callie was truthful. "Tucker's all I care about. I can't afford to trust you."

"We're even, there. I can't trust you either, and I'm finding it difficult to leave you."

"Afraid I'll run out on you again?"

He smiled again and deliberately said, "No."

There was a lurking sensuality in the depths of his eyes and Callie knew he was recalling the scene in her apartment. Her throat felt hot. She swallowed, picked up her wineglass and narrowed her eyes toward the open street. She couldn't deal with her feelings for Gavin right now. They had no place.

"Well, maybe you should be. I think being with you is dangerous to my health."

Gavin laughed. "That cuts two ways, lady. I haven't had a moment's peace since I saw you."

"Since you *accosted* me," she corrected him.

"Callie..."

The way he spoke her name brought a shiver to her flesh. Reluctantly, she turned back to him, waiting.

His eyes caught hers and held. It was suddenly difficult to breathe. Callie felt suspended and afraid, her eyes wide. But then the spell broke. Gavin shook his head and said, "Tell me about Tucker."

Callie sighed. "I met him on the pier," she said. "It was a hot day—well, they all are—but this one was really hot. My feet were burning in my thongs. Tucker just leaped off a returning fishing boat, right in front of me. He stopped and stared."

"I can imagine," Gavin said dryly. "I did a little staring myself."

Callie looked down at her wineglass. "Anyway, I asked him what his name was and eventually he told me it was Tucker. Then he wanted to know mine. We talked for a while and that was it."

"There must have been a good deal more to it than that."

"Not really. The next day I thought about him and I went to the bakery and bought some goodies. I went down to the pier again and there he was, almost waiting for me. He walked me home and I found out he lived just down the street. He started stopping by and I—encouraged it." Callie's face clouded. She'd been selfish, she realized now. She should have known falling in love with a Martinique street urchin would be trouble.

"What about the bracelet?"

Callie lifted her palm. "He just wanted me to wear it. I told him I couldn't. I knew it was an expensive piece."

"Didn't you wonder how he'd come by it?" Gavin asked.

"Of course! But I had a feeling I wouldn't want to know. So I tried to give it back but it obviously meant a lot to him to have me wear it. I promised I'd wear it for a while, but that was it—he'd have to take it back."

Gavin finished his beer, then twisted the glass mug around and around in his hands. "Was he with anyone when you met him? Was there anything unusual?"

"No." Callie was positive. "It was only when I met Aimee, the woman he calls *Maman*, that I thought there was something strange about the whole setup."

"What do you mean? You noticed something?"

Callie shook her head. "They were poor, yet Tucker had this fabulous bracelet. And Aimee was very secretive and made it clear that she didn't want me around. It didn't matter how nice I was...I just wasn't wanted."

Callie made an exasperated sound. "There was nothing that unusual, I guess, but it felt strange. And then Tucker was such a dear and I knew she didn't like me seeing him..."

Her voice trailed off. She didn't realize it, but her feelings were clear on her face: anguish, and love, and a kind of bittersweet hopelessness. Gavin saw everything, and his own confused feelings mounted.

"I have to believe you," he said, as if the idea were so foreign to him that it defied understanding. "I have to."

Callie didn't answer. What could she say? To her the truth was so plain. It worried her that he had to try so hard to believe her, yet what did she expect?

"I saw you on the pier," Gavin said reflectively. "You looked just like Teresa in that picture, shading your eyes and squinting into the sun. Then you waved to that man on the sailboat."

"That man on the sailboat...?" It was news to her that Gavin had seen her at the pier. "That man waved to me first."

"You didn't know him?"

"No. Why? Should I?"

Gavin frowned. "I was told he knew a woman with fiery gold-red hair, possibly Teresa. I thought maybe he'd brought her to Martinique aboard his boat, and of course, I thought you were Teresa."

Callie felt as if she'd been hit with something out of the blue. No wonder Gavin had been so certain she was this other woman! She could recall that incident with the sailor as if it had just happened. He'd waved to her—as if he'd known her—and she'd felt as if she must have known him, too. It made a peculiar kind of sense that he might have mistaken her for Teresa.

"I don't like this," she murmured, rubbing her bare arms against a sudden chill.

"I don't like it, either. That particular sailboat's been out to sea ever since. It hasn't worried me since I figured I'd already found my link to the boy." His smile was self-deprecatory. "And I guess I have."

"So where do we go from here?" Callie asked.

"We?" A slow smile crossed Gavin's lips.

"You know I'm involved, Gavin. Very involved."

"How involved?"

The look he sent her smoked with remembrance. Callie's heart pounded unevenly and she didn't move as his fingers crept across the table, enfolding her hand within his own.

"I meant—with Tucker."

"And what about me?"

"I don't think I want to know you any better," she admitted candidly.

Gavin laughed and Callie tried to rescue her fingers. But there was no hope for her. His touch was light but strong, and the only way she could get free would be by creating a scene. Inexplicably, she felt her cheeks warm, and desperately, sensing the situation was growing out of control, she said, "You really are the most arrogant man."

He lifted his brows. "Name calling? I guess I probably deserve it."

"You do deserve it."

A light danced in his eyes, but a moment later his face grew serious. "I know you're involved with Tucker. You didn't have to tell me. I saw it."

His thumb lightly rubbed over her knuckles. She tried very hard to forget that he was holding her hand, but every nerve seemed attuned to that one, small part of her body.

"I can't get involved with you," she told him a little breathlessly.

"Why not?"

"I can think of a dozen reasons."

"Name seven."

"Stop it, Gavin."

"Why?" His blue eyes regarded her with celestial innocence.

"Because I don't have time for this! I'm not crazy enough to have a wild romantic affair with a man who only a few days ago wanted to strangle me."

"The way you responded to me earlier says otherwise."

Callie could not believe his nerve. "That was then," she said deliberately. "This is now. I've had time to think things through."

"Uh-uh. You can't think your feelings away. No one can."

The fact that he was right infuriated Callie. She had a million arguments to blast him with but she knew—just as he did—that the bottom line was that she was attracted to him. Still, she resented him for being aware of the fact.

"I'm going to be leaving in less than a week," she said. "I don't want to do something I'll regret."

"Would you regret it?"

Her lips parted in disbelief. What kind of woman did he think she was? There was no way she could have a quick, heated affair then go back to her life in San Francisco without regrets.

She saw the passion lurking in his eyes, waiting to ignite and all her indignation withered in her throat. Her heart thumped. A deep hidden woman within her reached out and embraced the idea.

Unsteadily, she said, "I don't even want a memory, Gavin. I don't want something to pull out when I'm lonely, something wonderful and illusionary. I don't want to spend the rest of my life comparing other moments to 'that passionate time in Martinique.' Do you know what I'm saying?"

Gavin's face was taut. "I hear you saying you want me."

"That's not it at all!"

"Isn't it?"

Callie looked away. Yes, that's what she was saying all right. She could hear it in her own voice. She could *feel* it deep inside herself. "In the long run I would be sorry. I can't afford to be sorry. Don't expect things out of me I just can't give, Gavin. You don't know me that well."

Gavin half smiled. "You're not listening to your instincts."

"Yes, I am. Every instinct I have is telling me to stay away from you."

"Not every instinct." Gavin sighed as he witnessed Callie's tense expression. "You've been honest with me, so far. At least you've been honest about how you feel about Tucker. I can almost believe in you. But today I held a soft, trembling, eager woman. She just didn't disappear. That I can't believe."

Callie slipped her napkin from under her silverware, searching beyond Gavin for the waiter. If only the service weren't so damned slow! "I don't want to talk about this anymore," she said, folding her napkin in her lap.

"You don't want to face your feelings."

"I'm facing my feelings!" Callie whispered harshly. She signaled the dark-suited waiter setting the table next to them. "Could we have some service now, *s'il vous plait*?"

The waiter nodded and went to the podium near the door of the restaurant to get some menus.

Gavin let go of her hand. "If I said I'd follow you to San Francisco, that I think there's more between us than a wild, passionate affair what would you say?"

"I'd say you have a terrific line."

"You're afraid, Callie."

"You're damn right I am!" Callie's hand was trembling as she lifted her wineglass, then seeing the betraying tremor she set it back down. "What do you expect from me? All I know about you is what you've told me. No, don't give me any more reasons for believing in you," she added tautly when it appeared he was going to interrupt her. "I can't listen to them. Not for myself. I've got so many problems in my life already it's—" Callie stopped herself, taking a deep calming breath. "There's no room for this kind of insanity," she finished flatly.

The waiter returned with the menus. Callie accepted hers with a faint smile of thanks than buried her nose inside. But a pair of lazy blue eyes were superimposed on the printed pages and she wished her heart would stop beating so painfully.

Why was this happening to her? She didn't want to know any more about him, yet there was something dangerously seductive about him that was irresistible.

"I don't want to talk anymore," she said again, refusing to look up.

His laugh was full of promises and Callie had to grit her teeth together to keep from adding fuel to the fire.

"Okay, you're off the hook until after dinner," he said. "Then we'll go find Tucker..."

* * *

The table had been cleared except for Callie's half-full glass of wine. She pushed it aside and realized she needed something to clear her head. The events of the day were taking their toll, and she felt unprepared to do more battle.

Gavin ordered espresso, asking, with a lift of his dark brows, if Callie wanted a cup. She nodded and the waiter sped away to do their bidding.

The silence deepened. It had been difficult for her to keep the conversation flowing during dinner; Gavin had made it difficult. She'd wanted to make certain they kept to safe topics, but he'd disappeared into his own little world. Her remarks, without a response from him, had begun to sound shallow and inane. As a result, conversation had trickled off and finally ceased to exist altogether. They were now what they'd been all along: two strangers whose paths had accidentally crossed. Without Tucker, there was nothing left to talk about.

"We don't trust each other," Gavin suddenly said, his face shadowed as he lounged back in his chair. "And that's the problem."

"One of them."

The tiny cups of espresso were placed in front of them as the waiter discreetly left the bill. Gavin fingered the edge of the paper.

"What would it take to get you to trust me?" he asked.

She lifted one shoulder. "What would it take to get you to trust me?"

"Finding Teresa."

"Well, I'm afraid I can't do that. That's a trick you're going to have to pull out of the hat all by—" Callie cut herself off and demanded, "You never called William, did you?"

"I haven't had time. I went to Barbados, remember?" he said, stressing the last word.

Blushing slightly, she asked, "Wouldn't it help to call him? You'd find out I was telling the truth."

"Would I?"

"Unless you've closed your mind to the truth already," Callie snapped. "Call him!"

"And leave you here all alone? I don't trust you that much," he said blandly.

There was no point in butting heads with him; he was even more stubborn than she was. Working on a different tack, she said a trifle testily, "The way I see things, we're working toward the same end—at least as far as Tucker's concerned," she amended quickly. "You're looking out for his welfare as well as your grandmother's, right?"

Gavin nodded.

"All I want is what's best for Tucker, and somehow you're a part of that. I want you to call William. Right now. I want you to know who I am once and for all so we can do what's best for the boy.

"You'll be convinced," Callie assured him. "Ask him any questions you want. I'll even come with you."

"How come I get the feeling this is another stall to keep me away from Tucker?"

Callie sipped her espresso. "Because you're a suspicious man."

His mouth slanted appealingly. "*Touché, mon amie.* Lead me to the telephone."

Jubilant—for no good reason other than that a decision had been made—Callie eagerly pushed back her chair. "There's one down the street and around the corner. I used it earlier to call William. He'll probably worry for days over why I've phoned him twice in just a few hours.''

"He's like that?'' Gavin stood up also, collecting the bill.

Callie laughed, the sound so clear and unexpected it arrested Gavin. Several other people turned and smiled. Unaware, Callie's smile was full of warmth. She felt good all of a sudden, as if she'd finally started on the right path. "Just wait until you talk to him,'' she encouraged. "The man's a natural born worrier but a tiger when it comes to dealing with the Cantrells. He looks out for me.''

"How old is this Mr. Lister?'' Gavin asked casually.

Her eyes twinkled. "Old enough to be my father. Why?''

"Just curious,'' Gavin murmured, but his gaze was lazily sensual as he followed Callie out of the restaurant.

It was easier to place a call in the evening rather than the middle of the day, she found out, as the phone rang through to William's office. With the time change, it was late afternoon in California, and she hoped she could still catch him at work.

As the line rang on and on she shifted from one foot to the other, earning her an amused glance from Gavin as he stood a few feet away from the open-air phone booth.

She was just about to give up when the connection clicked. "William Lister,'' William said in his most professional, and slightly irritated, voice.

"Oh, William, thank God you're still there!'' Callie said. "I was afraid I wouldn't reach you.''

"Callie! Is anything wrong?''

"No. Nothing's wrong.'' She twisted to catch another glimpse of Gavin. "I just needed to talk to you again.''

"Well, I'm glad you called back," William said agitatedly. "I just found out Derek and Catherine have hired Caldwell Mathison to represent them. That's bringing out the heavy artillery, Callie. Mathison's a man to be reckoned with."

Talking to William about the Cantrells was like being forced to take a bitter medicine: it left a bad taste in her mouth. And the trouble was that medicine was her reality, her life. Martinique was the illusion. Martinique and Gavin and Tucker. The realization made Callie feel depressed.

"I don't care what Derek and Catherine do," she said firmly. "Let them have the money. Divide it equally. They can circle each other for a bigger share and snarl over what they've got. I just don't give a damn, anymore."

"Jonathan meant you to have that money or he would have made other provisions," William reminded her.

"He left it to Joshua. He never counted on Joshua dying with him."

Callie wondered how much of this Gavin was picking up, then decided it didn't matter, anyway. She was impatient to get to the purpose of her call, but William was hard to turn off once he got started.

"That's probably true," the attorney agreed. "But Jonathan was farsighted enough to at least consider the 'what ifs.' He knew you would end up with the inheritance if Joshua didn't. It's what he wanted."

Her forehead was damp. Strands of hair were curling at her temples. "I'm tired, William," she said. "Tired of fighting."

There was more to her complaint than just the Cantrells. Gavin must have understood what she meant because to her surprise he came up behind her, dropping his hands lightly, supportively, on her shoulders. She could feel his breath stirring her hair, and an intense longing suddenly sprang out of nowhere, tightening her chest.

"Let me fight the battle for you," William said grimly into her ear. "Don't give up yet."

"There are other things—happening, William. More important things. I can't really explain but, believe me, the Cantrell money isn't important right now."

"What's wrong?" the attorney demanded, alarmed, finally acknowledging the strain in her voice.

"Oh..." Callie pushed her hair away from her face. She felt Gavin's fingers, long and sensual, against her shoulders. Risking a direct look into his eyes, she felt a wave of heat travel up her body. His intensity frightened and thrilled her, and it was difficult to keep her mind on track.

"William, would you talk to a friend of mine?" she said urgently. "He's here on Martinique with me and seems to think I'm...well, never mind. Just answer any and all questions he asks, okay? It's really important."

"Who is he? For God's sake, Callie, I can't give him information about the Cantrells!"

"You don't have to. Please," she begged on a sigh. "This has nothing to do with the inheritance. Here, I'll let you talk to him."

She twisted around until she was face to face with Gavin, her nose bare inches from his. She didn't move right away, confused by how much she wanted him. Then, like some sacred ritual she slowly held out the receiver, trying to negate in her own mind the importance of having him believe in her.

Gavin seemed reluctant to accept it. Very slowly he placed the receiver to his ear, his eyes still locked to hers. "My name's Gavin Rutledge," he said in his low, rough way, a way that sent Callie's senses tumbling. "I only have one question: does Callie have to get back right away?"

She didn't understand what that meant. What was he asking? William's answer was lengthy but she couldn't hear the words. She just waited, suspended in a kind of dread mixed with hope, like a defendant watching the jury file back into the courtroom after a long trial.

Gavin hung up soon afterward. While Callie searched his face for some kind of clue, he led her back onto the crowded sidewalk.

"Okay." He let go of her and shoved his hands in his pockets, unconsciously stretching his shirt across his chest and drawing her eyes to the gap at his throat. Dark hair showed against firm skin, and she saw muscles flex as he eased the tension in his shoulders.

"You're Callie Cantrell," he said. "Just like you said."

A smile crept across her lips. "I won't say I told you so."

"I need your help."

She wanted to milk the moment for all it was worth but she couldn't. He was referring to Tucker.

"How?" she said simply.

"By showing me where Tucker lives. I have to face this Aimee person and find out the truth. Gut instinct tells me the boy's Stephen's son, but I need proof for Victoria before I can start legal proceedings against Teresa."

"Gavin, you're forgetting something," she said softly.

"What?"

"You trust me . . . but I still don't trust you."

"In that case, I'll do it alone."

She'd been testing him, seeing how far she could push him. Now the limits were clear. She tilted up her chin. "Not on your life."

Gavin had been looking past her, up the road, his brows drawn in furious concentration. Now he glanced back, a sensual smile curling his lips. "Then you'll have to take me on faith," he said, lifting a hand to graze the slope of her cheekbone.

She licked her lips. "Anything for Tucker."

"Don't say 'anything,' Callie, unless you mean it."

His hand caressed her jaw, capturing it, making it a prisoner as his mouth descended, his lips rubbing lightly over hers.

"Don't read too much between the lines," she murmured a trifle breathlessly.

"Let me know when I reach 'too much.'"

The kiss was soft and warm and promised far more than it gave. She knew she should push him away but she couldn't. She yearned, throbbed, for more. She was helpless to lie about her feelings when the touch and taste and smell of him was so near.

Her mouth was trembling when he finally pulled back to look at her. She felt something more had happened than one simple kiss. Something frightening and dangerous. Something irresistible.

Love is just a kiss away.

Callie swallowed. Where had she heard that before? She didn't like the idea, rejected it outright. She would never, ever fall in love with him.

"There's just one more thing," Gavin said, his eyes drifting lazily over her face.

"I'm afraid to ask."

He laughed, wrapping his arm around her as they walked away from Fort-de-France. "Don't be so quick to give up your inheritance, Mrs. Callie Cantrell. You never know when it might come in handy...."

Chapter Seven

"This is it?" Gavin asked, his voice edged with horror.

The tenement building where Tucker lived looked even more decrepit by night. The smells were thick in the still air, the scent of sour milk emanating from a white puddle beside the stairway.

"It's not as bad as it looks," Callie said, feeling compelled to defend Tucker though she, too, was sometimes overwhelmed by the boy's situation.

"My God." Gavin stepped off the curb on the opposite side of the street, staring across at the tenement. "She sure as hell isn't spending the money on him," he snarled furiously, kicking at a soggy piece of cardboard.

"His apartment is clean. Aimee seems to be a pretty good housekeeper."

Gavin whirled around. "That's really comforting—a pretty good housekeeper. Where the hell's his mother?"

Callie didn't answer. Inside, her stomach was churning. What if they were wrong? What if Tucker wasn't Teresa's son? Now that she'd accepted the idea she really wanted it to be true—for her sake and Gavin's. And for Tucker's sake most of all.

"What's she doing with Victoria's money?" Gavin demanded savagely. "How many furs has she bought? How many diamonds?" His eyes narrowed into angry slits. "God, it makes me crazy."

"What if Aimee has adopted Tucker?" Callie asked, carefully broaching her worst fears.

"The Rutledges will fight for him with their last dime; at least Victoria will. Tucker's a legitimate heir," he said with a faint smile.

"And what about you?" She folded her arms beneath her breasts and shivered.

"I'll fight, too."

His tone suggested a determination Callie might have found frightening another time. Now she applauded it. "Are you going to approach Aimee tonight?"

"No time like the present," Gavin muttered grimly, as he took hold of her arm and led her toward the stairway.

If Callie had found Aimee's reception to her cool, the woman's reaction to Gavin was positively glacial. The door was only opened as far as the chain allowed and Aimee made no further effort to let them inside.

"Mrs. Thomas?" Gavin's tone was carefully constrained. "Could we talk to you for a moment? I believe you know Callie already."

Aimee just regarded him with cold dark eyes, and Callie wished she'd warned Gavin a little more about the woman's unapproachability. But then from what she'd seen, Gavin rarely let an obstacle block his way for long.

"That is your last name, isn't it?" he asked. "Thomas?"

"Oui." Aimee flashed a withering look at Callie. "What do you want?"

"I want you to take the chain off the door and talk to me about Tucker. Think you could do that?"

Gavin's steel determination slipped through his affable veneer. Aimee's eyes moved from him to Callie, then back again. For a moment she seemed undecided, then her jaw tightened and Callie half expected her to slam the door in their faces.

"Don't do it," Gavin warned softly. "I'll break it down if you do. And I hope to God you decide to call the police, too. *Comprenez?*"

A stream of French poured out of Aimee's mouth, half-angry, half-fearful. Callie only caught the occasional word but she understood *mon enfant* as "my child."

"Occupez-vous de ce qui vous regarde!" Aimee sputtered at the end and would have shut the door entirely if Gavin hadn't shoved his foot inside.

"It *is* my business," Gavin bit out tersely. "I'm Tucker's uncle. His father's brother."

"Mon Dieu! You are *fou!* He is my son."

Callie put a trembling hand on Gavin's arm. "Gavin..."

"If I'm crazy," he grated through his teeth, "why don't you explain this?" He twisted up Callie's arm, and even in the dingy light the bracelet glinted its worth.

Aimee's bottom lip quivered in shock. She looked as if she wanted to reach out and snatch the bracelet off Callie's arm. But then she pulled herself together, straightening her shoulders. "I have no more to say to you!'' she told Gavin, nostrils flaring in outrage. ''Now go away!''

''*Maman?*''

Tucker's voice came on the heels of the sound of a creaking door. From her vantage point Callie saw his dark head peek around the corner at the far end of the room.

In rapid-fire French Aimee told him to get back in bed, and he obediently ducked out of sight.

Seeing him brought a catch to Callie's throat. *Oh, Tucker. I hope we're doing the right thing.*

There was no break in the tension between Gavin and Aimee. Neither was willing to give in. Aimee glared hatefully at Gavin and he met her gaze evenly. Callie's nerves were stretched to breaking. Even her battles with the Cantrells were far more civilized than this!

Seizing the moment, she ripped the bracelet from her arm and pushed it through the narrow opening. ''I meant to give it back,'' she said. ''I know it's Tucker's. He wanted me to wear it.''

Aimee's hand lifted automatically, her eyes on the bracelet. Then she dropped her arm, stating firmly, ''It is not mine or my son's.''

''But he gave it to me,'' Callie objected, dumbfounded.

The dark-haired woman shook her head.

It was clear Gavin was going to have to use force if he wanted to gain entry and Callie was afraid he would do just that. He stared Aimee down with such cool calculation that eventually she had to look away, resentment tightening her jaw, her fingers curled whitely around the door's edge.

''The bracelet's hers then,'' Gavin said, inclining his head toward Callie.

Aimee hesitated, her eyes on the lovely piece of jewelry. It dangled between Callie's fingers and, seeing Aimee's interest, Callie held it out to the woman, tempting her.

At the last moment Aimee's sense of survival overcame her greed. "It is not mine or my son's. Take it and go."

Callie's heart sank. She looked at Gavin for support.

"It's a Rutledge bracelet," he said. When Aimee continued to stare at him he made a quick decision. "We're leaving," he said, shocking Callie.

"Do not come back," Aimee warned, but there was relief in her voice. "You are not welcome to see my son again."

To Callie her words were a crushing blow—more crushing than the effect the deed could actually have. Common sense said that Tucker would find a way to see her if he wanted to; Aimee couldn't stop him. But hearing Aimee's self-satisfied declaration blew Callie's hopes to dust. She wanted to cry.

Gavin was not so intimidated.

"You'd better hope Teresa comes back soon and takes Tucker away because if she doesn't, I'll bring the police down on your head for kidnapping."

"Je ne comprends pas," Aimee whispered dazedly.

"I know that child is my brother's son. My brother's name was Stephen Thomas, too. My guess is your name isn't Thomas at all; Teresa left the boy with you while she's off doing God knows what. Now I'm giving you thirty minutes. When I get back we're going to talk."

With that Gavin grabbed Callie's arm again and steered her away. The sound of Aimee's door slamming shut behind them resounded like the last report of a gun.

"Do you think leaving her was wise?" Callie worried aloud, pacing the floor of her apartment. She was heartsick. Everything had gone all wrong.

Gavin was leaning against the wall, propped by his shoulders. His features were set in stone. "She might need time to get her priorities straight."

"How do you know?" She twisted her hands together. "You weren't exactly subtle, for God's sake. What if we're wrong?"

"We're not wrong, and I don't feel *subtle*! Didn't you see that tenement building? The whole damn thing makes my blood boil."

A tender smile found its way to Callie's lips. She was growing used to Gavin Rutledge's ways. His fury didn't frighten her as it had in the beginning and she was glad one of them could express their feelings so accurately.

"So what are you going to do now?"

Gavin checked his watch, pushing up his sleeves to the middle of his forearms. "I'm going over there. I'm going to break down the door if I have to, but that woman's gonna let me inside."

"I'm coming with you."

"No."

"Gavin, I have to. I can't stay here."

He pushed himself from the wall, walking to the center of the room, clasping her by her upper arms. "I know how you feel about Tucker," he said. "And I appreciate it, more than I can say. But you're a weak link, beautiful lady. Let me handle this alone."

She didn't know whether to be pleased or insulted. "What do you mean by a weak link?"

"You're too emotionally involved to be tough enough."

"And you're not?"

"Oh, I'm emotionally involved all right." His teeth gleamed in a humorless smile. "But I don't have any problem being tough."

"Gavin . . . don't . . ." Callie bit her lip.

"Shhh." He drew her to him. "I'm not going to get into any trouble I can't handle."

"You wouldn't . . . hurt her, would you?"

A trace of amusement entered his eyes. "I promise not to kill her until after she tells me the truth."

"That's not funny, Gavin."

For an answer he merely shook his head, tipping up her chin with one finger, his mouth finding hers with unerring accuracy, his tongue setting her senses aflame.

"You're going to have to learn to trust me a little," he murmured when he released her a moment later. "I'm exactly who I say I am. And Aimee's going to find out just what that means."

If Callie had been asked just how long she expected Gavin to be gone she would have come up with an answer of between two and three hours. It had been late when they'd approached Aimee at the tenement, later still when she and Gavin had gone back to her apartment. But it was hours past midnight and though Callie, in an effort to hear better, had left open the sliding glass door and turned off the air conditioner there was not a breath, not a sound not even the scrape of a sole against stone, to indicate Gavin was anywhere near coming back.

Her mind played tricks on her. What had he found out? Had Aimee still been there when he'd gotten back? Had he taken off with Tucker on his own?

All she could think about was how many mistakes she'd made herself. She hoped relying on Gavin hadn't been one of them.

A faint lifting of darkness warned her that morning was rapidly approaching. Still fully dressed, she rose stiffly from the couch and walked to her balcony. She stepped outside, feeling the humidity settle around her like a cloak.

Callie stood like a statue as the sky grew lighter, the horizon turning to cloud-puffed streaks of orange and gold. The cobblestone street was damp with dew, shining dully in the pale morning sun, and children were already calling to one another. She watched as the sun drew morning shadows over the whitewashed buildings, and she returned indoors only when the blinding full force of daylight began to hurt her eyes.

She'd forgotten the lemons the day before so she was forced to settle for coffee. She made it by rote, all the time waiting, waiting, waiting.

By ten she knew she'd been had. Gavin Rutledge had left. He'd gotten what he wanted from her: Tucker's whereabouts. It was time for him to move on.

Callie dashed the remains of her coffee into the sink, her apathy disappearing, fury ticking away inside her like a live bomb. It was Tucker who mattered. If Gavin hurt that boy in any way...

She sluiced cold water over her face, then with a sound of impatience, stripped off her clothes and showered away the accumulation of dust, sweat, and—she hoped— lingering nostalgia where Gavin was concerned. She'd put on a pair of white slacks and cotton sweater and was in the process of wiggling her toes into her thongs when she heard running steps against the cobblestones.

"Tucker!" Callie's heart flip-flopped.

She heard his familiar thunderous approach on the stairs, and she ran for the door, yanking it open. Her knees shook and she felt weak.

By the time he rounded the last corner Callie was in control, standing in the foyer, a wide grin on her face. Tucker didn't hesitate. He threw himself into her arms and she swept him off his feet, squeezing him, feeling traitorous tears burn behind her eyes.

"My boy, my boy," she whispered, hating herself for promising too much, helpless to do otherwise.

"Mommy," he answered, burying his face into her hair.

The shock went through Callie like an electrical jolt. So the truth was just as they'd suspected. "Oh, I wish I were your mommy," she told him. "I have the same color of hair, don't I?"

This time Tucker's nod was clear. "Yes," he said, and the pent-up tears drizzled down Callie's cheeks.

She took him inside, kicking the door shut behind them, unwilling to release Tucker from her arms. And he was unwilling to go. He clung to her neck like a burr.

It took a tremendous effort of willpower for her not to bombard him with questions but she knew, from experience with her own son, that she couldn't push the issue yet. But thoughts of Gavin were burning in her brain. What had happened? Why was Tucker here?

She eased down to the couch, brushing off her tears with the back of her hand, swallowing against her hot throat. Eventually Tucker crawled off her lap and sat beside her, his small form curled beneath the safe protection of her arm.

"I'm sorry we were fighting with *Maman*," she said at last. "I didn't want to."

Tucker burrowed closer. "She mad about the bracelet," he whispered.

Callie gave him a long look. "Did she say that to you?"

He shook his head. "She tells that man she need it."

"*Gavin?*"

Tucker nodded, his gray eyes wide and sober.

"Is he still there? Talking to Aimee—to your *Maman*?"

Tucker lifted his shoulders, his cheek still pressed tightly against her.

Callie felt jubilation. She'd been wrong. Gavin hadn't left. He was still on the island, determinedly searching out the truth. In her relief she gave Tucker an extra hug, smiling down into his serious eyes.

"He's trying to work things out for all of us, sweetheart. He doesn't mean to make Aimee upset."

For an answer the little boy managed a faint smile and Callie prayed her predictions where Gavin was concerned would work out for the best.

Gavin rubbed his thumb and forefinger over his eyes, feeling sticky and hot and weary. He walked aimlessly through the crooked streets until he finally sat on one of the dirty tenement's front steps, certain that he looked as tattered and unkempt as the children he saw laughing and chasing after a skinny, well-seasoned alley cat.

He needed time to think. He wanted to go back to Callie with a set plan. He'd learned what he needed to know; now he just had to decide what was best to do.

He watched the children for a long time, his mind filled with thoughts of Tucker. Then, sighing, he stood up, dusting his hands on his thighs.

"Callie Cantrell, I need your help," he muttered beneath his breath. It was time to find out how willing she was to give it.

* * *

Callie stared into Tucker's innocent, boyish face and wondered what was going on behind those beautiful long-lashed eyes. She had the terrible sensation you get when you realize a child might be smarter than you are.

"What do you mean you're going to live with me?" she asked.

"I heared him. He said I could stay with you."

"Tucker, love, as much as that might be what I want, even maybe what you want—"

"He said it!" His gray eyes flashed obstinately.

"Gavin told you that you were going to live with me?"

"He told *Maman*."

Hope was thudding within her breast. Callie had to be very careful not to listen to its pounding. It would be oh, so easy to be seduced by what she wanted most of all.

"Exactly what did he say? Word for word, if you can remember. Please, Tucker. Repeat what he said to Aimee."

His serious effort etched a line between his brows and Callie's breath caught at his resemblance to Gavin. The Rutledges didn't look a great deal alike, but there were certainly definite characteristics that seemed to pass from generation to generation.

"He said, 'The boy stays with Callie until I find Teresa. We'll decide about the bracelet later.'"

Callie licked her lips. "And what did *Maman* say?"

"She say she need it. She *said*—" Tucker corrected himself "—'You have no authority!' and he said, 'I'm the boy's uncle. And I can prove it!'"

Her lips parted. Gavin could prove it? Tucker's mimicry of Gavin's tone was uncanny. If Callie hadn't been so strung out herself she would have smiled. "So the upshot was that you're here," she reflected. "I wonder where Gavin is."

"Maybe he is in hot water," Tucker said seriously, and Callie couldn't help laughing.

"Maybe we all are," she said, affectionately touching the tip of his nose, "and if you learn verbs the same way you learn sayings you'll be a master of the English language in no time."

"A master?"

"An expert. Someone who knows everything."

"Can I go with you?"

Callie blinked at his sudden change of topic. "Go with me?"

"When you go. I want to go, too."

The reality of the situation struck her and her shoulders slumped. He wanted to go away with her. She didn't know what to say. How does one explain legal rights to a five-year-old? she wondered.

She heard footsteps in the hall just before the knock on her door. Tucker stood up when she did, clasping her hand. Callie had to fight the desire to ask him to hide in her room. Once again she had to remind herself that Tucker was someone else's child. Maybe not Aimee's, but someone else's, nevertheless.

"Gavin," she said with relief when she saw him standing in the hallway. Impulse won over protocol and she embraced him with open arms, surprising them both.

"Callie..." His hesitation embarrassed her, but then his strong arms squeezed her tightly for several heartbeats until he saw Tucker standing awkwardly to one side.

"What happened?" she asked, once they were all inside.

"It's a long story." Gavin bent down and smiled at Tucker. "Thanks for coming over to Callie's."

The boy said nothing, just looked at Callie for support.

"He said he's supposed to stay with me," she offered uncertainly.

"He is. Do you mind?"

She gave a snort of disbelief. "Be serious, Gavin. I'd love to have him here. But what about . . . ?"

"Tucker." Gavin crooked his finger in his direction. "Come over here and talk a minute. Then I need to talk to Callie alone. *Comprenez?*" At the boy's hesitant nod, he continued, "Michael—Michel—is waiting for you at the pier. I've hired a boat to do some afternoon fishing. Both you and Michel are invited to go if you want to."

Tucker's glance toward Callie glowed with disbelief. He couldn't believe his luck!

"But, Tucker, changes are coming for you at home. Do you understand?"

"Oui." Tucker's tone was as grave as Gavin's.

"Aimee won't be taking care of you much longer. You'll be with me—and Callie," he added, his sharp look in her direction a question in itself. "We're looking for your real mother, and Callie and I need to talk about that."

"I don't want her," Tucker said with cruel honesty. "I want Callie."

"I understand," Gavin said, ignoring Callie's unconscious intake of breath. "But Callie and I need to talk this over. We want to help."

"What is a uncle?"

Gavin looked at Callie, obviously stumped by the child's directness. Putting an arm on Tucker's shoulders, Callie said gently, "A relative, sweetheart. In this case, Gavin might be your father's brother."

Tucker examined Gavin critically. "My father is dead."

"I know." Gavin's voice was gentle. "My brother is dead, too."

The boy's gaze dropped to the floor, then he frowned. "Can I go fish now?"

"Right now. I'll take you there."

Tucker had been walking toward Gavin, the man's honesty slowly winning his trust. Now he twisted his neck to see Callie. "You don't go away while I'm on the boat."

"Oh, Tucker, *never*!" Callie was horrified that he would think she could do such a thing.

Gavin's jaw was rigid. "We'll both be waiting at the pier when you get back."

Tucker placed his small hand in Gavin's larger one and the decision was made.

The wind off Fort-de-France bay blew Callie's slacks flat against her thighs as she followed Gavin to the end of the ferry dock, her hand clasped tightly in his. They both waved after Tucker's fishing boat and Callie blew a kiss. Tucker and Michel waved their arms enthusiastically.

"Okay, let's have it," she said, her gaze still following the boat. She had to step aside as people swarmed to get on the ferry. Gavin guided her out of the fray toward a more quiet area where she leaned on one of the outdoor canopy's posts.

He squinted against the glare off the water. "Aimee's last name is Rouseau, not Thomas. Tucker is Teresa and Stephen's son. She finally told me."

The salt air filled Callie's lungs. She inhaled deeply, trying to clear her senses. "She told you that?" she asked incredulously, and at Gavin's nod, added, "What kind of coercion did you have to use?"

"Threats, promises and bribery. I stopped short at physical abuse."

"I don't think I really want to know."

Gavin laughed. "Actually, I just wore her down. She's one tough lady."

Aimee's thin-lipped image formed in Callie's mind. There was nothing remotely soft about the woman. "Tell me about it."

"But I think she really cares about Tucker's welfare," Gavin said reflectively. "Teresa gave Aimee the bracelet as collateral, proof that she would come back for the boy. I'm sure Aimee was paid for her trouble, too, but even so, I got the feeling she's grown used to having Tucker around."

Snorting her disapproval, Callie gave Gavin a quick, hard glare. She hadn't forgotten the way Aimee had treated her, nor could she forget Tucker's reluctance to be with the woman. "I don't trust her," she said flatly.

Gavin leaned his elbows on the rail, the wind ruffling his black hair. Tucker's boat was a dark speck on the horizon. "Don't think I'm so ready to accept her innocence either, Callie. She and her husband have a lot of explaining to do. But I wanted you to know that Tucker's been well cared for. At least as well as Aimee can care for anyone," he amended dryly.

"How did Tucker get hold of the bracelet?"

"He took it." The corners of Gavin's eyes creased with humor. "Aimee never even knew it was missing until she saw it on your arm. Tucker's craftier than anyone gave him credit for."

"It runs in the family."

Gavin slid her a sidelong look. "We Rutledges do what's necessary to survive."

The ferry horn blasted twice, shattering the silence. It was so loud the air seemed to vibrate around them. Startled, Callie straightened at the same moment Gavin did. His shoulder brushed her breast. For an electric instant her eyes met his, then slowly, almost reluctantly, he pulled her into his arms, close against his broad chest. She could feel the heavy beating of his heart.

"I need your help...again," he said, his sensual mouth twisting a little.

"What can I do?"

"Stay with Tucker. Know where he is every minute of the day. Don't let him out of your sight."

She licked her lips. "But I—"

"Don't leave Martinique. Your friend, Mr. Lister, wants you back, but even he admitted it wasn't necessary right this moment. One more week. That's all I ask. For Tucker."

She shifted, but only succeeded in rubbing against him, her body thrillingly aware of the differences between them. "You don't play fair, Mr. Rutledge."

Gavin's eyes were intensely blue. "I play to win. You know Tucker needs you."

If she could have summoned a single solitary reason to deny him she would have. But she couldn't. Tucker was everything to her, and Gavin Rutledge knew it. "You're certain you can wrap this up in another week?"

"I can try. I've got some ideas."

His hands slid to her waist. She looked down, seeing his dark skin against the waistband of her white slacks. Memories danced behind her eyes and she saw his tanned flesh against her pale breasts. She cleared her throat. "What ideas?"

"Aimee's husband, Jean-Paul. She was very careful to tell me he wasn't due back for many weeks. I think she's lying. I think he took Teresa off the island on his sailboat and I mean to catch him the next time he sails to Martinique. He may know Teresa's whereabouts."

"And if Aimee's not lying?"

"Then I'll think of something else."

Her eyes were focused on the tanned column of his throat and with an effort she dragged them away, staring blindly toward the horizon. Tucker's boat had disappeared around the peninsula on the other side of the bay.

Gavin's gaze stayed firmly on her face; she could feel it. But when he spoke, it was about Tucker. "He's all right for the afternoon."

"Are you worried?" Callie felt a pinprick of fear. "What do you think might happen to him?"

"Anything." Gavin was grim. "Until I find Teresa, Tucker isn't safe."

A cold emptiness filled her stomach and she sucked her breath through her teeth. She would rather die than let anything happen to Tucker.

"So where do you think Teresa is?" she asked, her worried blue eyes meeting Gavin's once more.

"I don't know, yet, but I may when Jean-Paul returns. He went to sea again the same day I found you. In fact, I think he's the sailor who waved at you."

He was moving too fast for her. "Why?"

"I'd been watching that boat, Callie; the captain was my only contact to Teresa. And he fits Jean-Paul Rouseau's description to a tee."

She tried to visualize the captain of the sailboat and remembered how he'd blown her a kiss. "But I thought the captain—the man I waved to—was French . . ."

"He probably is. Aimee had to have some way to explain Tucker's command of English, so she said her last name was Thomas and spun you a story about her husband being an American fisherman. Where else would he have learned it?"

The pieces did fit. It seemed so simple in retrospect. Overwhelmed, Callie shivered and Gavin's palms tightened on her hips, almost automatically.

"He must have thought, like I did, that you were Teresa," he mused, frowning. "He probably assumed you'd come back for the boy."

She was far too conscious of Gavin's virility; it seemed to set her nerves, where he touched her, on fire. "I'm not good with this kind of thing," she murmured, dipping her head.

"What kind of thing?"

His voice was low and attractive and so very close to her ear. She tried not to notice, but her heart quivered. She was sunk, she thought wretchedly. There was no hope for her. A treacherous throbbing had centered itself inside her, and she tried carefully to remove herself from his grasp.

"Pressure. I fold under it. I did after Jonathan and Joshua died. I even had to see a doctor."

Now he would know the worst of her, the weakest part. As Callie tried to shift away, she tightened her shoulders, expecting his rebuff.

She was not prepared for the deep rumble of laughter in his chest. "Are you crazy?" His voice was richly amused. "You're a tigress. You battled me in the alley— my shin still hurts, lady! You deceived me. You sent me to Barbados. You fought for Tucker with every wile you had. Don't ever tell me you fold under pressure, because it just isn't true."

As he spoke his jaw rubbed against her hair and Callie felt a shimmer of desire. Surprised, she turned in his hands, and in doing so unconsciously fitted her hips perfectly to his.

Gavin sucked in his breath, his hand tangling in her hair. "Callie..." he murmured unsteadily.

Her eyes flew to his, widening. "I didn't mean to—"

"What?"

She couldn't answer. Emitting an unhappy sound, Callie looked past his right ear, anywhere but at his ruggedly handsome face.

Peripherally, she saw his lips pull into a self-deprecatory line. "Neither did I," he admitted huskily, then abruptly let her go. Running a palm around his neck he slowly let out his breath.

Bemused, Callie wrapped a hand around the post, glancing this way and that. She wasn't thinking straight. Parts of her were still warm where Gavin's body had touched.

She slid him a look from beneath her lashes. He was staring out to sea, his jaw working, his hands thrust in the pockets of his jeans.

"When the ferry comes back, let's take it," he said unevenly.

"Where to?"

"Hell, I don't care!" he said explosively. Then with an odd laugh, he muttered, "My God, you make it hard to think straight."

She'd been under the impression that he wanted to have an affair with her; he'd even gone so far as to hint it might last after she returned to San Francisco. But now he appeared to be having second thoughts, and though Callie knew she should be glad, she couldn't put their earlier lovemaking out of her mind.

"Here comes the ferry," she said.

Gavin twisted his neck to see. The boat was halfway across the bay from Pointe du Bout to Fort-de-France. He looked her way, his chin set and determined. "We've got some time to kill and I need to think."

"Do you want to be alone?"

"No."

She took some measure of hope from his tone. He still wanted her; he just didn't want to want her.

And you're out of your mind to even care!

As the ferry docked and began to empty Gavin shoved himself away from the rail, turning to wait for Callie. His blue eyes looked into hers and for a moment, while the sounds of the crowd faded, Callie saw the mirror of her own desires. She swallowed and walked across the boarding ramp ahead of him, feeling the power of his gaze boring into her sweat-dampened back.

The sea spray was wet against Gavin's face and neck as he shifted position on the ferry's bow. Callie was beside him, her bare arm within touching distance. From the corner of his eye he could see her sun-lightened hair, the smooth, supple contours of her skin. He hurt inside, from a familiar numbing ache that was more frustration than actual pain, and he tried very hard to thrust her slim, sensual image from his mind.

It was an impossible task, he already knew, and it was all he could do to keep from hauling her into his arms again, molding her lithe figure to his. God, when he remembered the burn of passion he'd felt when he held her it drove him wild. But he'd made a decision in the past few hours and he intended to stand by it: Callie Cantrell was a woman to leave alone.

He gritted his teeth together and half closed his eyes, pretending to be lost in thought. He needed time to get himself under control. Being assured of Tucker's safety had been a mixed blessing: now there was too much time to think about Callie.

With an inward groan he remembered having dinner with her, discussing their relationship, testing the idea of an affair with her. She'd resisted, but he'd known she was interested. Everything he'd done to this point had pushed that idea, and now . . . now he was going to be the one to back away.

And it was going to kill him.

Through narrowed eyes he looked at her, then wished he hadn't. It only made him feel worse. But he knew she deserved better than a passionate affair on a Caribbean island with a man she barely knew; and unfortunately that was all he could offer her. There was nothing else he could give, and there was no other way. Especially now— now that his own feelings were involved and he'd learned the depths of her.

Like the last nail in his coffin, he recalled how she'd responded to his lovemaking. His pants began to feel terribly tight and his head throbbed with the force of fighting his emotions. God! Would this ferry ride never end?

She turned toward him and smiled. "I don't know how you did it, but you've managed to give me some hope."

Her eyes sparkled, smokey blue between gold-tipped lashes. The sultry scent of her wafted to him as she raised an arm to push her hair back, still smiling.

With an effort, Gavin turned away from her. "Don't expect too much yet."

"Oh, I don't. But just knowing you're looking out for Tucker's welfare is a big help."

He didn't disillusion her. Tucker's problems were a long way from over, as were his own. Callie's growing trust in him only added to his burden of guilt, especially when he remembered how much he'd wanted her and had planned to have her—no matter what her feelings were. Life had taught him to take what was offered, no questions asked, and he'd planned to do that with Callie since she'd so conveniently put herself in his way.

But each time he'd seen her with Tucker he'd admired her a little more—and liked himself a little less. He was in awe of her uncomplicated love for the boy. It made him ashamed of his own inability to love that deeply.

When she'd thrown her arms around him at her apartment he'd been bowled over. No one had ever greeted him with such uninhibited affection.

And now that Tucker was safely aboard the fishing boat and Callie installed as the boy's temporary guardian angel, Gavin had the time to think about her, his feelings for her, and what the future would be without her.

He felt a noose slowly tightening around his neck.

"Gavin..."

Pulling himself back from his thoughts was difficult. With reluctance, he turned to face her again, seeing her concerned eyes upon him. "You're not hiding something from me, are you?" she asked anxiously.

"No."

"Then why are you so grim?"

The ferry crested a wave and Callie was suddenly thrown forward. He grabbed for her and her hands gripped his upper arms. He heard the rustle of fabric brushing fabric, the low, urgent throb of the engine, then felt her hips slide unknowingly across his pelvis. He fought back a groan of agony.

"I'm sorry," Callie said, stepping back.

"Don't apologize."

She flicked him a look that asked a thousand questions he couldn't answer, then her eyes slid away. Her hands fumbled for her sunglasses.

"Are you okay?" he asked in a strange voice.

"Yes."

There was a breathless quality to her tone that made Gavin's ache deepen. Inside he knew, regretting it, that his control was already weak, and slipping.

"I'm not trying to be grim," he told her huskily. "We'll take care of Tucker."

Callie's smile was a brilliant reward. "Thank you," she said.

With relief, he watched the familiar sight of the Pointe du Bout marina approach, and as he followed Callie to the exit he desperately tried not to watch the way her long limbs moved and her hips swayed. The curve of her buttocks made his throat go dry. Using more willpower than he'd thought himself capable of, he dragged his eyes away from her and concentrated with stiff-jawed determination on the beauty of the marina.

There were a lot of questions still to ask but Callie was loath to voice them. With the wind rippling her hair, and Gavin's hand touching her arm to guide her through the marina's shops, she couldn't think of a reason to break the spell. Tucker was safe and that was all that mattered.

She peered through her sunglasses at Gavin's lean face. Something was going on inside his head, she concluded, and for some reason it made her want to latch on to him, hold him. His detachment scared her and she wondered if, after all, his words of need had been empty ones. Maybe he didn't want her help anymore. He had Tucker and he had his link to Teresa, Aimee Rouseau. Who was Callie Cantrell, anyway, but just extra baggage?

"Talk to me, Gavin," she said. "Say something. I know you said you need to think but it's driving me crazy. Can't I help in some way?"

"No."

They were standing on the wharf in front of a small clothing store, its windows bedecked with skimpy bikinis. Callie bit into her lower lip and persevered. "What else did Aimee say?"

"I don't want to talk about Aimee."

"You don't want to talk about anything."

"That's right," he snapped, then pinched the bridge of his nose and grimaced. "Do you want one of those?" he asked.

He was gesturing to the bikinis. Callie lifted her brows. "I wouldn't be caught dead in one."

"Why not?"

He looked at her for the first time in what seemed like hours.

"Because they're not me," she said.

"I'd love to see you in one."

She laughed. "Don't hold your breath."

A smile actually teased the corner of his mouth. "Be fair, Callie. It's cold in Wyoming. I'd like to see you once, like that, before I go back."

"Wyoming? You told me the Rutledges were from Denver."

"They are. I'm not."

"What do you do in Wyoming?"

"I'm a wildcatter."

With a bang that other world—the real world—intruded on her, and for a disoriented instant Callie didn't know how to react. "A wildcatter?" she repeated blankly. "I didn't know you were a wildcatter."

"You didn't ask."

"You're a complete stranger to me," she murmured, the revelation unpleasant and scary.

He shook his handsome head. "No I'm not."

"Oh, yes you are! My God...." She choked on her own disbelief. It was incredible—insane!—that she'd begun to care so much about a man she didn't even really know.

Scowling, he muttered, "Don't worry so much, Callie. I'm just who I say I am. You're trying to find more problems than there are."

"It's just that you expect so much from me on faith, and oh, God—" she laughed shakily "—it's so easy for me to believe."

"Well, don't stop now." Gavin exhaled in frustration. "Do you honestly think you don't know what kind of man I am? Hell, woman, you've seen more of me than most of my family has!"

"Why are you so angry?" she asked, blinking in surprise.

"I'm not angry."

Callie stared at him with total lack of understanding. "Then why are you closing me out?" she asked in a small voice.

"I'm not, Callie, I—" He swore, glanced toward the gate that led to his hotel, and said, "I need a drink, that's all. You want one? We can go to Bakoua."

Callie sipped her second glass of wine and ran her fingers around the base of the wineglass, trying not to be alarmed. Gavin wasn't the same man he'd been when he'd arrived at her apartment that morning. Then he'd been eager and primed to take care of Tucker but now...she had no clue to the workings of his mind.

He was drinking his third glass of straight scotch; that alone was enough to worry her. But there was no notice-able effects, Callie concluded, studying him surrepti-tiously.

Unwilling to wait any longer, she reached across the table and touched his hand. "It's Tucker, isn't it?" she guessed. "You've left something out because you're afraid to tell me. What is it, Gavin? I have a right to know."

"There's nothing wrong," he said in exasperation. "Look, I know I've been terrible company. It's the calm before the storm, I expect. Why don't we go back to Fort-de-France and wait for the fishing boat?"

"Gavin..."

"Callie, don't."

His tone was so final she stopped short. What had happened to the tenderness she'd glimpsed in him? Where had that Gavin Rutledge gone?

"I don't know what's wrong with you, but I mean to find out," she said, rising. She pointed a finger at his chest and added, "If I have to, I'll hire a boat of my own to find Tucker's and make sure he's all right."

"Callie..." Gavin rose, too, but she was all through with platitudes. She swept her purse from the table and left, stalking down the tiered stairway to the beach.

He caught her on the bottom step, his grip so tight it hurt. "Damn it, Callie," he growled.

"Do something, Gavin. For God's sake, do some-thing! I can't stand not knowing."

"You're jumping off the deep end."

"Am I?" Callie swallowed hard. "How come I don't think so?"

"Just let it be. Tucker will be back before you know it and—"

"You're scaring me," she whispered. "You're keeping something from me. What is it, Gavin? Please..."

He made an angry sound, grinding his teeth together. Callie's hands crept to her throat as she envisioned all sorts of terrible endings. Then Gavin abruptly came to a decision; she saw it flicker in his eyes. His hands gripped her shoulders and he lowered his head and kissed her, hungrily, until she was breathless, in full view of everyone on the beach.

Her eyes widened, her fists pressed against his chest.

"It has nothing to do with Tucker," he grated. "Can't you see?"

In dawning recognition Callie finally understood, and she was embarrassed by her dull wits. Her lips trembled, trying to form words, and Gavin yanked her away from the hundreds of staring eyes.

"You don't want an affair," he said harshly, pulling her up another stairway, one farther away from the crowd. "You said so, and I believe you. But that's all there is with me."

"Let go of my arm. I can move under my own power."

"I don't want to let go of you. I don't want to let go of you at all."

Callie's pulse was drumming light and fast. "Then why have you been fighting it?"

"Because, damn it, woman, you deserve better!"

He couldn't have said anything that made less sense. Callie gaped at him in disbelief. "I'm a big girl, Gavin. I make my own decisions. And since when did you have this...?"

"Sudden turn of respectability?" he finished when she'd trailed off. "Since I got to know you better."

"I think I'm insulted."

"For God's sake," he expelled in frustration. Then, overcome by amusement, he hung his head and silently laughed. "Don't worry, Mrs. Cantrell. My respectability won't last—you can count on that."

They were on the second landing of the beachfront cabanas. Callie looked down the vine-trailed walkways at the rows of dark wood doors. She licked her lips. "What if I don't want it to last?"

Gavin groaned, "Oh, Callie...don't..."

"Which one's your room, Gavin?"

He regarded her wordlessly for an endless moment then turned down the covered walkway, Callie following behind him. A few minutes later they were in front of his door, and he twisted the key in the lock, then opened the door.

She didn't know what to do. Bravery, especially in the sexual battlefield, was a new experience for Callie. As the door closed behind them she knew a flash of panic, then Gavin was standing in front of her, watching her.

"You chose the venue but you can still back out," he said in a low voice.

"I don't think so."

"It's up to you."

There was a trembling somewhere near her knees but she was powerless to stop it. "I'm not an impulsive woman," she whispered. "But I'd hate to grow old thinking about lost opportunities."

He took a step nearer, his gaze intent. "Isn't that an abrupt change of attitude?"

"Yes..."

He cupped her face and Callie's racing pulse nearly leaped out of control. She was frightened; she didn't kid herself on that. But she was alive, too, with a powerful need that shook the very foundations of her existence.

The first kiss was tender. Callie's lips quivered beneath his and he soothed them with a gentleness in direct contrast to his taut body.

"I can't think about tomorrow," he said. "It doesn't exist yet. I live for today and today only."

"I don't know how to be that way," she said tremulously.

"I'll show you."

He fit her to him, drew her arms down, found her hands, placed them on him. Callie's heart pounded, ringing in her ears. She gasped for air and found only the salty taste and texture of Gavin's skin as he rubbed his jaw across her mouth.

Buttons were coming free. A triangle of skin was exposed at her throat and she bent backward as he lowered his head to taste her. Her legs were flooded with warmth and she sank against the wall.

"Maybe...I...can't do this," she moaned, wide-eyed.

"Why can't you?"

"I don't know. I'm afraid..."

His tongue was wet and slick as it found sensitive places by her jaw she hadn't known existed. His knees propped her trembling form against the wall, supporting her. She felt his rough maleness, the forces that drove him, and she could only submit as his mouth plundered hers again and again.

Shock melted away, burning to fire. She moved her hands, and Gavin's quick intake of breath was enough to give her courage. She began to explore him as he was exploring her and his uneven, ragged breaths were an eloquent reward.

She placed her hands on his firm buttocks, drawing him closer, and Gavin complied with a movement that thrilled her deep inside. She held him as he held her, as if they were trying to slide within each other's skins, all the time moving to a hot, quick tempo that was totally out of Callie's experience.

Her splintered thoughts fixed on Jonathan. It hadn't been like this with him. It hadn't been anything like this!

"I can't afford another mistake," she said, but her voice shook with longing and Gavin wasn't listening anyway.

She moved instinctively as his hands dipped lower, his mouth leaving a trail of wetness down one bared breast. "Don't," she tried to say, but no words came. She was slipping, slipping, down the cool plaster wall and into his waiting grasp.

He carried her to the bed, wordlessly resting her on the soft coverlet. In hazy bemusement she watched as he undressed her, her only motion an uncontrollable tremor that shook just beneath her skin. Then his mouth returned with a vengeance and she rose up to meet him, her hands tangling in the silky richness of his hair, her breasts scoured by the sweet abrasion of his beard.

His knee was between her legs, his hands supporting her buttocks. He'd warned her, she realized dazedly. She'd had her chance to leave. But fires were stoked in a dark, feminine part of her and she raged to feel more. With feverish hands she helped him from his clothes, then pulled his mouth back to hers with a vengeance. His weight covered her and her limbs slid restlessly against his flesh until he was suddenly poised above her.

"Callie . . ." he murmured, wrenchingly.

For an answer she wound herself around him, her legs tangling in his own, her breasts crushed beneath his pounding heart. She wasn't going to let him hate himself for this; she wanted him as much as he wanted her.

Against her yielding abdomen she felt his hardness, and with infinite tenderness she fitted herself to him. With a groan he took what she offered, making her his with one, deep plunge that tore a gasp from her throat.

He swept back damp tendrils of hair from her forehead, his eyes searching hers.

She smiled tremulously. "Love me," she whispered, aching for him.

"Ah, Callie..." he sighed in uncertainty, but there was no turning back. Pressure built with each movement. There was a breathless feeling in the back of her throat that made her want to cry out, but she said nothing. The moan that wrenched itself free was his, but then in answer, the small whimpers of need were her own.

"Please, please..." she murmured, her hands digging into his tautly muscled back. Searing passion suddenly erupted within her, startling her, shattering her, running through her like a river of fire. Callie had never been so quickly transformed, and as she reveled in the sensations Gavin reached his own climax, shuddering. With a groan of satisfaction he spilled himself inside her, his mouth bent to the supple curve of her neck. She heard his labored breathing as his straining body slumped on top of her and she kissed his damp forehead, treasuring the moment.

With the crystal clarity of true wisdom she finally realized and accepted the truth: she'd fallen in love with him.

And now she had no idea what to do about it.

Chapter Eight

So how did you convince Aimee that you're Tucker's uncle?''

Callie lay against Gavin's broad chest, her fingernails gently moving through his dark, curling hair. She twisted to look up at him, then tugged on the sheet as one rose-tipped breast slipped out of confinement.

With brazen male arrogance Gavin's finger circled the dusky peak, her nipple turning button-hard beneath his touch. He smiled and Callie pressed her face into his neck, hating herself for loving him so much.

"The picture," he said, lying back again and cradling her to him. She could feel his warm limbs under hers. "My identification. I told her a few things about the Rutledges that apparently jibed with what Teresa had told her, and let's face it . . ." Gavin smiled. "My sheer obstinacy over the matter was almost proof enough."

"Tucker said you did have proof that he's Stephen's son," Callie murmured. She rubbed her face against his lower jaw, tasting him with her tongue while her hand resumed its foray through the forest of chest hair. Her courage was a sobering revelation to her. Sex with Jonathan, though wonderful, had never been so addictive, so wonderfully dangerous. Or did that just come from loving a dangerous man? she wondered.

"That's what I told Aimee." Gavin regarded her with lazy, sensual eyes. "God, Callie, what are you doing to me?"

"Touching you."

"That, I know," he murmured, his own hand sliding down the curve of her back. Then he emitted a mock groan of ecstasy that made her laugh.

"We were talking about Aimee," she reminded him.

"Were we?"

"Sort of." Callie sighed and closed her eyes. Good Lord, she was a mess! Without a thought for her safety she'd taken a step over the edge of a cliff, blithely expecting life to give her a soft landing. The hell of it was she didn't care.

"I convinced Aimee I could prove the stones in that bracelet are Rutledge heirlooms," Gavin said.

"Can you?"

"I doubt it. Maybe. But it sounded good and Aimee was so rattled by then that she was ready to believe me."

He was so inordinately pleased with himself she felt compelled to bring him down a notch or two. "She's probably planning dark dastardly deeds even as we . . ."

"As we what?"

Callie heard the smile in his voice and she slid him a look. His blue eyes danced and his teeth flashed in a wicked grin.

"As we reconnoiter new territory, and—" his wolf whistle nearly ruined her straight-faced delivery "—devise new stratagems to overcome and subjugate our oppressors."

"Would you listen to her," he said, lifting his brows.

"I was an English teacher before I married Jonathan," Callie answered, coquettishly tilting her chin. "I learned myself a few things along the way."

"Really. Will you learn them to me, too?" he asked, pulling her atop him.

"You seem to be a very able pupil already."

"Ready, willing, and..." he agreed. "English teacher, huh? Now who's been holding back? Here I thought you'd been wallowing in the lap of luxury all these years."

"Only since my marriage. Before that I was struggling to make ends meet."

His stroking hands were doing wild things to her senses. "It's hard to give up wealth once you've had it," he murmured, kissing her lightly. "I wouldn't do it, if I were you."

"You mean the Cantrell fortune?"

"Callie, you're holding all the cards, don't blow the game now."

"But I don't want the money."

"What do you want?"

She looked into his ruggedly handsome face. *You,* she thought, *and Tucker.* But she didn't say it. She couldn't.

"I want...a taste of happiness," she said shyly. "That's all."

The seriousness in his face made her wish she hadn't said anything. "We have to talk about what's happening here, you know."

"Please, not now..." she whispered.

"Don't make me hate myself later, Callie."

She already knew he wasn't going to offer undying love and marriage; he'd said as much already. She didn't have to hear it again.

"Why don't you tell me what you want," she suggested softly. "And we'll work from there."

He seemed about to argue with her more, but then he sighed, a faint smile lifting one corner of his mouth. He rubbed his bottom lip against her mouth and hunger began to simmer like a blue light between his lashes. "What was it you said awhile ago? 'Love me'?"

She blushed. "It was something like that," she murmured.

"It was exactly that. Say it again."

"No." Callie laughed and tried to turn away.

His finger brought her chin back, her eyes in direct line with his. "Say it again."

"Love me."

"Nah...that needs work. Where's the passion?"

"Gavin..."

"Come on, say it again."

Callie was embarrassed and totally beyond doing as he suggested. But she could feel the changes happening between them and she wasn't immune.

"You asked me what I wanted," he reminded her, a dangerous, passionate flame flickering in his eyes. The humor around his mouth had all but disappeared, and as he stared at her Callie's heart lurched in spite of herself. With a groan of surrender she dipped downward and kissed him, open-mouthed, her hair falling around them like a silken curtain.

"Close enough," he murmured roughly, rising up to wrap himself around her.

* * *

The pier was crowded as they waited for the fishing boat to return. Shoppers and sightseers strolled along the sidewalk, adding to the city's evening hustle and bustle, making it necessary for Callie to squeeze closer to Gavin. Not that she minded. She could get very used to having those strong arms around her, she thought ruefully. Maybe too used to it. Like Tucker, Gavin was only temporary. She had to face the fact that she was setting herself up for another colossal letdown.

She swallowed. "Shouldn't he be here by now?"

The street lamps' glow reflected and quivered in the dark water. Gavin's eyes followed the illumination out to sea. "Soon, I imagine. Don't worry. He's with Michel and I made certain the captain understood how important it was that I know when they return."

"You don't think we missed them already, do you?"

Gavin shook his head, pulling Callie back against him as a laughing group of young men and women swaggered by in front of them. His arms were draped loosely over hers, clasped at her abdomen. "We're not going to miss that boat," he said with hard-jawed determination.

"Why do I feel I'm missing something again?" Callie asked, hearing more in his tone than should be there.

"Teresa left him that way," Gavin explained flatly. "Something Aimee said made me realize Teresa took off while he was out on one of the fishing boats. Tucker came back to find out she was gone."

"That's terrible!" She felt sick, remembering Tucker's last question to her. "He thought I might do the same."

"He has no reason to trust adults."

"I hate this!" Callie pressed her palms to her forehead. "I really hate this."

"So do I."

"What are we going to do next?" she asked. "I mean, when Tucker gets back."

"We're going to take him to your apartment."

"And then?"

His arms squeezed tighter, his hips pressed firmly against her buttocks. "Do you have to ask?"

Callie smiled, ducking her head. "There's only one bedroom. I'm afraid Tucker gets to sleep with me."

"Good God. Something's got to be done about that."

She agreed with his sentiments, knowing her time with him was running out. But she couldn't abandon Tucker. "Are you sure Aimee expects him to stay all night?" she worried aloud. "Isn't she afraid we'll spirit him away?"

"She's more afraid of an investigation. She has no legal right to the child, and Teresa left her nothing in writing. I could cause her a lot of problems . . . problems she doesn't want to have to deal with. Aimee knows I'm Tucker's uncle. She knows you love the boy. It's simpler all the way around if she tries to cooperate now."

"I guess if I were her, I wouldn't trust *me*." Callie's eyes were on a returning boat, but she soon realized it wasn't Tucker's. "I'd like to spirit him away," she admitted softly. "I wish he were mine."

Gavin didn't answer for a long time. Eventually he said, "Who knows what'll happen when I find Teresa. It may be simpler to wrest him away from her than we think."

Her heart leaped. "You're trying for custody?" she questioned, afraid to believe his dreams were so close to hers.

"Teresa Thomas likes money, so much so that's she's using Tucker to extort it. It don't think it's such a giant leap to believe she might sell him to me."

"Gavin!"

"Call it what you will." She felt him shrug. "The boy's an albatross around her neck except for the money she can wring out of him. She might be glad to accept a settlement on the condition that I get the legal right to raise him."

It was beyond Callie's comprehension. "No mother would do that," she murmured, knowing deep in her heart she was being naive.

"Teresa would." Gavin's confidence hammered at Callie's ideals. "I'm almost certain of it. There's the boat."

The fishing boat moved slowly into the bay and anchored. One of its small rubber launches was lowered to the water. In the darkness Callie couldn't make out which boy was Tucker, but she saw two figures climb inside, followed by the burly captain. Then the familiar buzz of the motor grew louder as the launch sped through the water, making for the end of the nearest pier.

"Come on." Gavin clasped Callie's hand and they walked across the wooden slats, their steps creaking on the worn planks.

Tucker scrambled from the launch, saw them and waved. *"Ici! Le grand poisson!"* he shouted.

He stood only in bathing trunks, the fabric still wet. It was obvious he'd taken a dip in the water somewhere. The captain, after slapping a huge fish on the pier, explained with gestures and broken English that Tucker and Michel had taken time out from fishing for swimming.

Gavin looked closely at the subject of Tucker's enthusiasm, a medium-sized kingfish. "It is a big fish," he agreed. "Did you catch it yourself?"

"Avec Michel," Tucker admitted, glancing at the older boy, whose dark hair was also tangled and sandy.

"What happened to English?" Callie asked affectionately.

"A day with those two would probably drive it from anyone's head," Gavin remarked as Michel and the captain got into a lively discussion over the apparent ownership rights of the kingfish.

Then Tucker, in lightening French that was way beyond Callie's grasp, began a long discourse that ended with a question. His gray eyes looked eagerly into hers and she turned to Gavin, whose own command of the language was infinitely stronger, for help.

Gavin was laughing. "Fat chance, Tucker. We've got problems in that area already."

"What did he say?" Callie asked.

"Fat chance?" Tucker repeated, lost.

"He wants Michel to spend the night with us, too," Gavin said.

"Us?"

Gavin's sexy eyes slid over her. "Did you really expect me to go back to my hotel? I can probably live with the couch."

She didn't know what to say. She wanted him so much it was crazy, and terrible, and wonderful.

Tucker, all shyness gone, tugged on Gavin's arm. "Fat chance?" he demanded again. *"Qu'est-ce que c'est ca?"*

Callie smiled. The boy's idiomatic English was growing by leaps and bounds.

"Gros . . . hasard," Gavin ventured, trying to translate directly. "And if you can figure out what it means, let me know. I've never understood."

Tucker looked at Gavin as if he'd lost his mind, and Callie, torn between laughing and chastising Gavin for confusing the poor boy, said, "It makes no sense. It just means we can't have Michel tonight. Maybe another time."

"No. You are leaving," Tucker said with simple logic.

"I'm going to be staying for a while longer than I'd intended," she assured him with a loving smile. She looked up at Gavin and saw he was relieved by her decision. Her heart swelled. "Gavin's staying, too."

"Come on." Gavin held out a hand to him. "Let's go eat. The captain can sell the kingfish to the cannery." In French, he said the same to the captain and the man grunted in satisfaction.

But Michel was affronted. He argued long and hard, furious when the captain made a dismissive movement with his hand and hauled the fish over one burly shoulder.

"Tell Michel he can come to dinner with us, too," Callie said, and Tucker, who had reluctantly clasped Gavin's hand, suddenly beelined toward her, throwing himself around her in gratitude.

She hitched him up to her hip. "Now you've done it, sweetheart. I'm a mess!"

"No problem. We'll eat at your place. I'll buy some cheese, bread and wine," Gavin said, gesturing to the still-angry Michel.

"And fish," Tucker proclaimed autocratically.

"We'll buy some fish, too," Gavin agreed.

Plans were set into motion before Callie could offer a word of protest—not that she would have, even had she wanted to. She purchased the bread while Gavin selected the fish and allowed Michel and Tucker to pick out a thick wedge of cheese. Then Callie brought some tropical fruit—pineapple, mangos, and papaya—and the troop of them walked through the sultry night to her apartment.

There wasn't room at her tiny table for all of them, so once the fish was cooked, they sat cross-legged on the floor, except for Gavin who stretched out on his side. Michel, who at first said very little, quickly became quite animated, talking exclusively to Gavin when he realized how little French Callie actually understood, his indignation over losing the catch still darkening his young face.

"Where did you learn your French?" Callie asked Gavin as she tasted the succulent fish.

"Ahh...you think a wildcatter from Wyoming shouldn't speak French. Snob," he accused with a grin.

"I'd say it's unusual. And I'm not a snob."

"I haven't been a wildcatter all my life, Callie. I worked for several years on a French freighter."

She stared at him. "When?"

"I'm thirty-eight. I've done a lot of things."

She took another bite of the butter-poached fish, struck silent by how different her life was from Gavin's. She was a fool to even hope there might be something lasting between them, something more than Gavin had yet realized.

"How do you like the Dolphin?" he asked.

"Dolphin?" Callie nearly choked. "This is *Dolphin*?"

"It's a fish, love. Not the mammal. It's just called Dolphin because it jumps out of the water and does some of the same aerial leaps a dolphin can."

"You're sure?" Callie suspiciously lifted part of the meat with her fork, turning it over.

"Positive. You are *not* eating one of man's friends. It's just a fish."

"A good fish," Tucker said.

Callie smiled at the little boy. Next to Michel, whose adolescent limbs were long and muscular, Tucker seemed so much younger, though he would have been filled with indignation had he known it.

Michel stood up, wiping his hands on his shorts. *"Merci,"* he murmured.

"Michel needs to go," Tucker said as if he were a world authority. "His Papa needs him back."

"Goodbye, Michel," Callie said. "You're welcome."

He smiled uncertainly, then turned to Gavin, speaking rapidly in French. With a wave he hurried out of the apartment, pounding down the stairs with even more noise than Tucker did.

"What did he say?" Callie asked, retrieving the boy's plate.

"That he would like to go fishing again tomorrow and he hoped I would like him to, too."

"The little con man." She laughed. "He thinks he's found a sucker."

"Can we go fishing?" Tucker piped in eagerly.

Gavin looked at him, tenderness easing some of the harsh angles of his face. "We'll see."

"Do I really sleep here?"

"For tonight, at least," Callie answered, unable to give false hope. "Come on. Let's wash up and get you into bed."

Tucker scooted closer to Gavin, stretching out on the floor in endearing mimicry. "You are staying here, too?"

"On the couch."

"Tomorrow, we go fish."

Gavin was amused. "You want that in writing?"

"What?"

"Come on, Tucker," Callie said. "You two can debate in the morning, but for now, it's bedtime."

Going through the motions of getting him ready for bed was a bittersweet experience for Callie. Joshua's image kept floating before her eyes. She helped Tucker climb into the bath, toweled him off, slipped one of her T-shirts over his head, and loaned him her toothbrush— all the while drifting through memories that had once been too painful to touch. They were still painful, but she had since learned to live with them.

"Tell me a story," Tucker begged, the sheet pulled to his chin.

"Okay." Callie climbed on the mattress and put her arm around him. "Let's see. Do you know *The Tortoise and the Hare*?"

Tucker shook his head.

She began telling the story, poignantly aware that it had been Joshua's favorite. Before long Tucker had slipped into deep sleep, his lashes sweeping down the soft curve of his cheek, his chest rising and falling evenly.

Callie untangled herself from him and watched as he burrowed into the pillow, and suddenly there were tears, falling down her cheeks, dripping off the tip of her nose. She couldn't stop them. She wiped at them but they fell, faster and faster, until a huge sob filled her throat, choking her. Blinded, she slid off the bed and stumbled into the bathroom.

She was shaking over the sink, crying in silence, holding back the wrenching sobs for fear that Gavin would hear. Why now? she wondered, wiping away pouring tears with the back of one trembling hand. Why now?

There was a soft tap on the door but she couldn't answer.

"Callie?" Gavin called softly.

She closed her eyes and misery swelled in her lungs. Then Gavin was in the room, his hands on her shoulders, pulling her to his chest. She crushed her face into the fabric of his shirt and squeezed her eyes shut. A low, tearing sound came from her own throat.

"Oh, love, love," he whispered.

She sagged against him. She had no more strength. He helped her to the living room, sat on the couch with her, gathered her to his chest. Callie tried to pull herself together but the release, once begun, was refusing to turn its tide. All the pent-up anguish over losing her own child couldn't be contained; there was nothing to do but let it out.

Finally, exhausted, she fell asleep on Gavin's chest. She held on to him as tightly as Tucker held on to her. And Gavin understood.

Callie held her breath, stroked cleanly through the clear water, and then buckled up, diving down into the pool. She skimmed along the bottom, her toes touching the plastic coating, then she shot upward, her lungs suddenly bursting for air.

Gavin laughed as she tossed hair out of her eyes. "You look wonderful in wet," he drawled.

She skewered him with a glare. "Why don't you try it?"

He was sitting at the edge of the pool, his feet in the water. All the while she'd been swimming he'd watched her, but he hadn't attempted to join in.

"It's your hotel," she pointed out. "You should use the facilities."

Gavin sighed loudly, then lay back on the cement, his eyes closed to the sun. "I am."

Swimming to his side, she lifted herself out of the pool, dripping water down his torso.

"Hah!" he yelled, stomach muscles contracting.

"Get in." Callie wrung out her hair and the water streamed over his chest.

She howled with laughter when he grabbed her ankle. With a muscular twist he was suddenly sitting up, then he swung her around before she could get her balance and pushed her back into the pool.

"You son-of-a—" was all she managed before the water closed over her head. When she surfaced, his deep laughter was filling the air and several sunbathers had been diverted from the serious business of achieving the perfect tan to actually lift their heads and stare.

"Take pity on me," Gavin said to the murderous glint in her eyes. "I can't swim."

She snorted. "I don't believe you."

"No. I never learned how."

"You're kidding."

His dark head shook from side to side. "Can you teach me?"

"Gavin, if you really can't swim, you need an expert to teach you how." Callie swam back to his side and pulled herself up beside him.

"But I want you to," he said, and before she could stop him he'd slid off the edge—and promptly dropped right to the bottom of the pool.

She was frozen. *This couldn't be happening.* Collecting her wits an instant later, she dived after him and, her hands in his hair, yanked, pulled, and dragged him to the surface.

He was laughing when he came up and she was furious.

"You damn fool! You could've drowned."

"Nah . . ." He turned around to face her, treading water. Then before she could blister him with her thoughts he was off, slicing cleanly through the water like the expert swimmer he was.

"You lied to me!" she shouted.

"Tit for tat, love. You lied to me a few times, too." He swam back to her, pinning her indignant body against the side of the pool. "Besides, I liked feeling your wet arms and legs around me," he whispered in her ear.

"You're . . ."

"What?"

She couldn't stay mad at him, no matter how she tried. It was just wonderful that he'd honored her plea not to talk about the future—their future—and enjoy this time-out-of-time together in Martinique. With a sigh she laid her arms on his broad shoulders and said, "I'm sorry about last night. I don't know what came over me."

"Don't be sorry. Crying's good for you."

"Do you ever cry?"

"Not anymore. But then, I don't have anything to cry over."

She wasn't certain she liked the sound of that, but she let it be. "Thanks for taking me swimming. And thanks for paying for another fishing day for Tucker and Michel."

"It's what he wanted to do and he might as well do it while he still can." Gavin leaned forward, then hesitated, as if he were making an awful mistake. He made a frustrated sound before kissing her on the bridge of her nose then floating backward.

They swam for several hours, but the time seemed endless. Inside, Callie knew this was just the calm before the storm and so she savored each moment. Decisions were on hold. For now Gavin was hers and she was his, and Stephen Tucker Thomas was safe.

Later that morning the pool began to fill up with hotel residents, and Callie climbed out, throwing a thin beach robe over her swimsuit. She was nearly dry by the time Gavin hauled himself out, and she couldn't help the feeling of feminine pride as she watched him towel off, his muscles fluid and effortless beneath his tanned skin.

"I'm going to have to check with Aimee again," he said, after he'd pulled a pair of disreputable shorts over his swimsuit and a shirt over his head.

"I know."

"She didn't seem to know anything about Teresa's whereabouts but I don't know... maybe if I press her, something will come out."

"She's had no contact with Teresa since she left?"

"That's what she says." The look on his face said he felt her word was doubtful. "Maybe she'll tell me more about Jean-Paul."

"What do you want me to do?"

"If I'm not back by the time Tucker and Michel return, go to the pier without me. I'll meet you later at your place."

"Be careful."

Gavin took her arm, tucking it in the crook of his elbow. "Careful is my middle name."

Callie stood first on one foot and then the other, watching the boats. She was impatient for Tucker to get back, impatient for Gavin to show up, too. Rubbing her upper arms briskly, she walked down the sidewalk along the bay. It was dusk, and though the weather was warm, she felt chilled with the coming of nightfall.

Her skirt swirled around her legs but her skin felt clammy. She paced, watching the passersby with more than casual interest, seeing Gavin in every man who remotely resembled him.

She was early; she knew it. Yet she couldn't help checking her watch again and again. She thought about strolling through the open-air market just across the road. But even it was too far from the pier. She had to be here when Tucker returned.

Pacing aimlessly, Callie was lost in thought, her eyes skimming over each new arriving boat, then disregarding it when she realized it wasn't the fishing boat Tucker and Michel had taken. Stopping, she clenched and unclenched her hands around the railing that ran along the sidewalk, feeling anxious and uncomfortable.

It was her lack of interest in the other boats that kept her from seeing the blue-and-white sailboat anchored just west of the ferry dock. She didn't give it a second look. Fishing boats were her targets.

Only after an argument broke out on board between two men, the sound carrying clearly across the water, did Callie even turn in the sailboat's direction.

It was the boat of the man who'd waved to her.

Aimee's husband. Jean-Paul Rouseau.

Callie helplessly looked around herself, hoping against hope that Gavin would miraculously appear. She bit her lip. She didn't want to leave the pier but she didn't want to lose sight of Aimee's husband either.

There was no sign of Tucker's fishing boat.

"Damn."

A red rubber launch was lowered from the aft deck of the sailboat and Callie saw two figures climb down a rope ladder. The engine roared to life and grew louder as the launch approached the pier.

Callie faded back from the railing, blending with the crowd. She was thankful for the growing darkness, glad her hair wouldn't be an unwanted beacon.

The two men drew up to the pier, clambered out of the launch and stood together, hands on hips, still arguing. One was shaking his finger at the other.

Callie moved slowly in their direction, her hand trailing on the rail, her heart thudding. As she approached, the men's voices grew to a shout and she was afraid they might come to blows. But then they suddenly threw their arms around each other, clapping one another on the back. Laughing heartily, they weaved in the direction of the nearest bistro. It didn't take an expert to see they were drunk.

Pausing halfway between the pier and the bistro, Callie was torn with indecision. She couldn't leave Tucker abandoned, especially knowing that's how his mother had left him. But she was afraid to lose sight of Jean-Paul. If he was Aimee's husband, if he had taken Teresa from the island, then he knew where she must be now!

She searched the bay for any sign of Tucker's fishing boat, but none of the approaching vessels was familiar. Her palms were sweating. She wiped them on her dress.

Gavin, where are you?

She took several steps toward the bistro, hesitated, then took a few more. A scan of the horizon showed no familiar fishing boat and she concentrated on the lively-sounding bistro.

She was perhaps a dozen yards from the door when it suddenly swung outward, spilling yellow light and loud voices onto the quay. The two men from the sailboat swaggered out and Callie froze to the spot.

They saw her and one of them leered, lurching forward. *"Allo,"* he said drunkenly. *"Comment vous appelez-vous?"*

Thankful for the shadows, Callie said, "I don't speak French. I'm waiting for someone."

She recognized Jean-Paul, the man who'd waved at her; his grizzled beard and hulking shape were unmistakable. He was standing back, eyeing her, while his friend drew closer.

The friend was thinner but still a big man. It was all Callie could do to stand her ground as he came right up to her, reeking of beer. "I speak English, too," he told her with a happy slur. "Right, Jean-Paul?"

The die was cast. Gavin had been right. Callie felt her hands begin to sweat.

"You are familiar," Jean-Paul told her in a gruff voice.

"Am I?" Callie's voice was forcefully light. It was a major test of willpower to keep from twisting her neck, looking again for Tucker's boat.

"What are you doing here?"

"I'm waiting for someone," she repeated.

"At the bistro?"

"No... I'm waiting for a... fishing boat."

The door opened again. Callie jumped as the screen banged shut, and in that moment, a flash of illumination highlighted her hair.

"I saw you on the pier," Jean-Paul said with dawning recognition, his fingers digging into his beard.

Callie swallowed. "Oh? Maybe. I'm here a lot."

"I thought you were someone else."

All she had to do was ask. With those few words he'd unknowingly committed himself and Callie only had to bring up Teresa's name to learn the truth.

The friend swayed on his feet, tripped, and swore good-naturedly. He threw his arm around Callie and she stiffened. She lifted one shoulder and said plainly in body language that she found his nearness offensive. He was too drunk or uncaring to notice.

Jean-Paul's bushy eyebrows were drawn together, as if he were thinking hard, trying to remember. But he, too, had had a lot to drink; it showed in the way he balanced his big body on his feet.

Callie craned her neck to watch an approaching boat. It wasn't Tucker's. *Where was he?*

She would have walked away had Jean-Paul been anyone else. The fact that she was still there was undoubtedly giving them the wrong impression. Taking the bull by the horns, she said, "You thought I was Teresa Thomas, didn't you?"

There was no immediate reaction, but as Callie watched, Aimee's husband finally made the connection. His eyes lit with surprise, then suspicion. He thrust his thick neck forward and demanded, "Who are you?"

"A friend of Tucker's."

She hadn't given much regard to her own safety; the situation had arisen and she'd seized it. But now she felt afraid. Just because Gavin had frightened Aimee into helping didn't mean her husband would react the same way.

The friend backed away, but Jean-Paul continued to glare at her, narrow-eyed. This was the man who'd taken care of Tucker? Callie wondered fearfully. His very size was threatening.

"Pretty ladies should know better than coming down to the wharf alone," he said, taking a step nearer, standing so close that Callie couldn't help the trembling step she took backward. This wasn't going as she'd planned at all.

"You know what happens to pretty ladies?" he went on harshly. "They are sorry they did not stay home."

"You'd better have a damn good reason for scaring this pretty lady, friend," drawled a deep, dangerous voice just behind Callie's head. "Otherwise you're gonna wish you'd stayed home, too."

Gavin strode up to Jean-Paul and grabbed a hunk of the man's shirt. "Now, back up," he growled, "unless you want a fist in your face. This pretty lady is mine."

Chapter Nine

Callie had never witnessed an actual fight, but she was certain she was going to see one now. She wanted to intervene but she couldn't move. She could only watch in mute terror as Gavin's grip on Jean-Paul's shirt tightened and his body shifted in readiness.

Jean-Paul hesitated, his eyes traveling over Gavin with careful consideration. Though Aimee's husband was bulkier, bigger, and looked strong as an ox, he wasn't a fool. Gavin wasn't quite as tall or as huge, but he possessed a deadly kind of determination. His lean form was built of solid muscle; his weight was poised on the balls of his feet. Showing more common sense than Callie would have credited him with, Jean-Paul made a faint conciliatory movement.

"I don't fight with you," he said, wiping the back of his hand slowly across his grizzled beard. "Take your woman away."

Your woman. Callie glanced at Gavin to catch his re-action, but his blue eyes were fastened on Jean-Paul's face. He wasn't nearly as willing to back down.

With a feeling of facing the inevitable, she said tiredly, "He's Aimee's husband. The man who waved to me from the sailboat."

Gavin's hand was still white-knuckled within the stained folds of Jean-Paul's shirt. "Is that so?"

"I am Jean-Paul Rouseau," he stated flatly. "My wife is Aimee, but I do not know you."

"I know your wife. And I know about the boy, too." Gavin jerked on the man's shirt and Callie held her breath. "I'm his uncle. You got that, friend? *His uncle!* I want some answers from you *now.* We can talk peace-ably or we can...work this out another way. It's your choice."

"Take your hands away," Jean-Paul warned.

The muscles in Gavin's back tightened. "That's your answer?"

"You misunderstand. I want no fight. I believe your woman has made a mistake, that's all." He spread his hands.

Callie would have risen to her own defense but Gavin was one step ahead of her. He gave Jean-Paul a shove and said coldly, "I've been with Aimee all afternoon. There's no mistake. Tucker's Teresa's son and you and your wife have been taking care of him. But that's going to change. I'm bringing the authorities and immigration down on you tomorrow."

Gavin's words doused the flare of anger in the bigger man's eyes. "You have no right," he growled. "I have done nothing wrong. You have empty threats, *mon-sieur.*"

"What kind of living do you make, Jean-Paul? You sail—for what? Tourism, or something else...? You want a custom's inspection on your neck?"

Jean-Paul angrily drew up his chest and Callie quailed inside, wishing Gavin weren't so bloody determined to pick a fight.

"You are accusing me of smuggling?" the Fisherman roared.

"Yes." Gavin's voice was chilling.

"I am no smuggler! I am a charter sailboat captain!" He swore lividly in French and Callie turned her head, reaching blindly for Gavin, certain the first blow was about to hit. But Jean-Paul was more intent upon setting the record straight than physically fighting. He pushed his face into Gavin's. "I take care of a small boy. What is wrong with that? His mother pays me. I am good to the boy. I am no smuggler!"

"How much does she pay you?"

"Eh." He lifted his broad shoulders. "Enough."

"Where did she go?"

"I take her to St. Lucia."

"St. Lucia?"

"Hey..." Jean-Paul narrowed his eyes, his beer-fogged brain sluggish but still functioning. "You think I am smuggler? Bah! You want information."

For the first time since he'd approached Jean-Paul, Gavin's tight body relaxed a little. "I want Teresa Thomas," he said grimly.

"You should have asked! I would tell you. It is no secret. I have taken her to St. Lucia, the island south of here. She will be back."

Callie didn't know what to make of the man's sudden friendliness. She was anxious for this scene to end, anxious to get back to Tucker.

"When?" Gavin asked him.

"I do not know. I am no smuggler."

Gavin's jaw tilted, his mouth knife-blade thin. "What you are, *Monsieur* Rouseau, is an opportunist, like your wife. I learned that much today and more. When I leave this island, I'm taking Tucker with me; I don't care how."

Jean-Paul cursed, flung a look toward his friend and gestured toward the bistro, snapping orders in angry French. The man threw up a hand and walked away. "You will be kidnapping," he bit out. "He is not your son."

"And neither is he yours," Gavin said in a deadly tone. "I'll take the matter of kidnapping up with Teresa, when I find her. Somehow, I think we'll be able to work out a deal."

"The boy has no passport."

"That's not what Aimee said."

Callie's head was swimming. She hadn't considered how difficult it would be to get Tucker back inside U.S. borders.

Jean-Paul cursed his wife, shaking his fist at the fates. Then his eyes glittered and he rubbed his jaw. "It is possible that I could find one..." he said.

"Name your price. I'll pay it."

She could scarcely believe the manner the conversation had taken and she held her breath. As if suddenly remembering her, Gavin looked her way, his jaw still dangerously set. "Where's Tucker?" he asked.

"His boat hasn't come in yet."

He stared at her through the inky night. "What?" he demanded softly.

Fear filled her breast. "I've been waiting. He hasn't come back and it's late, isn't it? Oh, God, what's happened?"

"Get to the pier." His voice was the crack of a whip. "I'll finish here."

Jean-Paul responded to the urgency. "The boy," he said in concern, and Callie understood then, that Gavin had been right. The Rouseaus did care about Tucker and had been kind to him, even though Teresa's money had been their main objective.

Her feet were winged as she sped back to the pier. She hadn't seen Tucker's boat but she'd been distracted part of the time and her vision of the pier had been limited. Now she ran, jumping on one foot to rip off a thong, then the other, to remove the thong's mate. Her throat was dry as cotton. *Oh, Tucker. Please be there!*

He was there. Standing forlornly on the pier, his shoulder held up as a shield against the comforting words Michel was trying to offer. Seeing Callie, Michel eagerly came toward her, relief covering his young face. Tucker glanced her way and it was then she saw the tears. Her heart broke.

"I let you down," she whispered, eyes burning. She went to him, arms outstretched, but he turned his head. He hadn't wanted Michel to see his tears and he didn't want Callie to.

"I wouldn't ever leave without telling you," she said, standing beside him, lovingly touching his tangled hair. She dropped her arm when he flinched away, her heart twisting wretchedly.

Michel looked on gravely, and Callie searched her mind for the right words to tell him he could leave. *"Allez-vous, s'il vous plaît,"* she said, and Michel understood enough to flash her a commiserating smile, then with a last look toward his little friend, he headed home.

"No fish today?" Callie asked, seeing the empty pier.

"No."

"Gavin's with Jean-Paul."

Tucker feigned disinterest, swiping surreptitiously at his cheeks.

"I'm sorry, sweetheart," she whispered. "I should have been here." She wanted to launch into all the reasons why she was late but she didn't think he was ready to listen. The bottom line was she should have been on the pier, no matter what. She shouldn't have let him think she'd abandoned him the same way his mother had.

"Ahh, Tucker." Callie sighed, hurting. "I don't blame you for being upset. But please believe me: I would never, ever leave without saying goodbye."

He hunched his shoulders and she realized he was trying to get a grip on himself—tough duty for one so young. Tightening her jaw against her own need to cry, Callie waited for Gavin. She hoped the situation with Jean-Paul hadn't worsened.

Heavy footsteps sounded on the pier and Callie saw Gavin, hair tossed by the furious pace he'd set, hurrying toward her. Obviously the argument hadn't escalated into an out-and-out fight. Relieved, she wanted to throw herself into his arms, but she didn't move. She couldn't depend on him that much.

His brows lifted in a silent question when he saw Tucker's stiff-backed stance.

"He was waiting for me," was all Callie had to say.

Gavin crouched down. "Feel like taking the ferry across the bay?" he asked. "My hotel's right across there." Gavin pointed to the lights of Pointe du Bout. "I'd like to take you and Callie over there, if you feel like it."

"You—stay there?" It was difficult for Tucker to throw off his anger, but curiosity was a strong force.

"Since I've been in Martinique. But I really live in the United States. Do you know of the United States?"

"I comed from there first."

"I know."

Callie wondered why Gavin wanted to take Tucker to his hotel at this late hour, but she couldn't ask with the boy still so upset. The way he was ignoring her hurt. Especially since the ostracism apparently didn't extend to Gavin.

"It might be simpler to go back to my apartment," she murmured, but Gavin's look told her not to argue.

What had happened? Callie was dying to know. She ached a little as she watched Tucker slide his hand into Gavin's, and she followed a pace or two behind as they met the approaching ferry. Was this a sign of the future? she thought wearily. Even though she'd been warned, she'd been hopelessly kidding herself into believing she might be a part of their lives.

"Jean-Paul swears he has no idea where Teresa is now," Gavin whispered in her ear as they boarded, "but I don't believe he's telling the whole truth. Let's get Tucker to bed and then I may have to track the man down again."

"But . . . are we going to your hotel? Why?"

"Might be safer," he muttered, then he took Tucker up to the top deck to ensure he got the best view. Disturbed, Callie looked around herself, seeing ghostly enemies in every dark shadow.

"The message light's flashing," Gavin said, as he pulled the key out of the lock on his door.

Callie was looking at Tucker's bent head. How long was he going to punish her? As if in answer to her question he suddenly glanced up and his small hand reached for hers. In relief she squeezed it, and he squeezed back.

"The message light?" she repeated, as she and Tucker walked inside.

"Yeah... Callie, think you could take Tucker up for a late snack, or... how about a swim?"

"A swim!" Tucker shouted, delighted.

"Okay, sure, but just a minute, Tucker. Okay?"

"I go ahead," he said and was out the door before she could stop him. Callie quickly followed, hesitating just outside the door, holding it open with her palm. "What's happening?" she asked Gavin. "Who is it?"

"It has to be Victoria. She's the only one who knows I'm here." He grimaced. "I'd just rather not have Tucker overhear my conversation with her, knowing how it's bound to go."

"Are you really thinking of taking Tucker back to the U.S. without Teresa's consent?" Callie asked worriedly. "Is that legal? I don't want you to get in trouble."

"Because Teresa would set the authorities on me?" Gavin laughed coldly. "She wouldn't slay the golden goose. She'd be too afraid Victoria would cut her off."

"You're supposedly not in favor with the family," Callie reminded him.

"Stop worrying. It'll all work out."

There was simply no warning Gavin about risks; he just took them and said, damn the consequences. While a part of her admired his daring, another part fretted endlessly. With a last anxious glance at the man she loved, Callie followed after Tucker.

Perching on the edge of a lounge chair, she watched Tucker as he swam. He boasted to her about his prowess, magnanimously urging her to spend the time with Gavin; he was, after all, no baby. But she couldn't get used to his independence and allow him to swim unattended; her maternal instincts wouldn't let her. She stayed and watched as the boy swam in the Bakoua's lovely, night-lit pool, her mind tortured by a million questions.

She felt as if circumstances were growing beyond her control. And Gavin... what did he think about her? She had no clue. That he cared was self-evident, but it was no guarantee for the future, and at this point Callie was desperate for just that guarantee.

She was in the act of standing, to call Tucker from the pool, when Gavin suddenly materialized beside her. "Oh, there you are," she said, reaching for a towel, "I was just about to—"

Her words died in her throat as his hand dropped on her shoulder. She looked at him, puzzled. In the shadowed darkness she saw a strange expression on his face. "What is it?" she asked fearfully.

"The phone call was from Victoria, just as I thought."

She folded the towel over her arm. "And?"

"She's been trying to get hold of me. Teresa's in Denver, Callie. She arrived on the Rutledge doorstep last night."

Callie laid her sweater on top of the other clothes in her suitcase. She tested the lid and found, as she'd suspected, it wasn't going to close. How had she ever packed everything in before?

Discouraged, she sank down onto the couch. Her eyes ached from several nights without sleep, and her shoulder muscles were weary and sore. If she could live the past few days over again she would live them just the same... and end up hating herself as she did now.

She'd begged Gavin to take her to Denver with him, and his reaction had been lukewarm.

"Callie," he'd said, his mouth slanting unhappily, "I don't think it's the best idea. You don't know the Rutledges. This could be really sticky."

"But what about Tucker? He'll be alone with people he hardly knows!"

With more than a trace of sarcasm, he'd answered, "Teresa will be there."

"Are you telling me you don't want me to go?" Callie had drawn herself up straight. "Don't lie to me Gavin. Please, please don't lie to me. I couldn't stand it."

His hesitation had scared her but then he'd said in a low, uneven tone, "I want you to go. For me." But before Callie could feel jubilation, he'd added, "I just don't think it would be a good idea . . . at least for now."

The conversation had ended, and he hadn't tried to talk her out of it again. He'd just left the situation up in the air, letting her make her own decision. While Gavin put things together with Victoria—even managing to get the older woman to convince Teresa to wire the Rouseaus and have them turn over Tucker's passport—Callie stayed at her apartment, drinking coffee and packing, vacillating between chasing after Gavin and Tucker come hell or high water, or cutting her ties and heading home to San Francisco.

Neither alternative was the answer. She wanted Gavin to relent and plead with her to come with him, but it wasn't going to happen.

The timer on her oven went off, breaking into her thoughts, and she checked the erratic coffeepot, pouring herself a cup. Wiping an arm across her forehead she ruefully surveyed the wreckage of her packing: dresses and pants thrown over chairs, shoes tossed haphazardly across the floor, her coat folded on the arm of the couch.

Her wardrobe wasn't right for November in Denver. She should go back home.

"Damn," she muttered, knowing it was impossible. Gavin Rutledge aside, she needed to be with Tucker.

Rationally, she could understand why Gavin didn't want her there. She knew with a woman's instinct that she could cause worse problems for Gavin and Tucker. Teresa might easily see her as more of a threat than she saw Gavin. Callie was too much of a "mother replacement." Lord, she even looked like the woman! Though Gavin hadn't voiced these same fears she knew he had to feel them. But what about Tucker . . . ?

Her need for action forced Callie out of the apartment, down the hill and into Fort-de-France. She would call William, she determined. He would help her decide what to do.

As she waited while the call was being placed, she wondered what Gavin and Tucker were doing. Tucker had had the chance to be with Callie, but he'd become more and more interested in being with his uncle—a situation that didn't really surprise her, but hurt nonetheless. As a result Callie had spent most of the past couple days alone while they packed and made plans to return to the States.

"William Lister and Associates," the receptionist for William's firm answered.

"I'd like to speak to Mr. Lister, please. It's Callie Cantrell."

She'd heard the swift intake of breath that meant she was about to get the brush off, but at the mention of her name, the receptionist warmed up and said, "Oh, I'm sure he'll want to talk to you, Mrs. Cantrell. Just a moment, please."

Callie counted the seconds, feeling oddly nervous. When William's familiar voice came on the line, it was all she could do to keep herself from cutting him off before she spoke. She didn't think she could stand to hear any more about Derek and Catherine right now, and it was practically a certainty William would bring them up.

"Callie! My God, I was about to fly down to Martinique myself and make certain you were all right. Who is this Gavin Rutledge? I've been worried sick!"

Her brows lifted. She'd never heard such an impassioned speech from the normally dry-toned attorney. "I'm fine. Really."

"Why did you have Rutledge talk to me? What's he doing there, Callie?"

"It's a long story, one I'd rather wait and tell you when I get back to San Francisco."

"Does that mean you're coming back right away?"

The lift in William's voice couldn't be disguised. She made a face and prevaricated, murmuring, "I'm thinking about it."

"Good. From what Rutledge said I was afraid you weren't coming home for a while."

"Well, I don't know..."

"Callie, what's going on? Who is this Gavin Rutledge? Where's he from and... how are you involved?"

His last question was given diffidently, as if she knew he might be stepping over bounds he shouldn't. She smiled, unable to be angry at his endearing, fatherly concern. "Gavin Rutledge came to Martinique to find his nephew, and as it happened, the boy lived right down the street from me. We, er, met during the process, and now he's going back to Denver."

"Denver?"

"That's where the Rutledge's are from, although Gavin lives in Wyoming. William," she hurried on, unwilling to reveal more about her relationship with Gavin than was absolutely necessary, "I may take a roundabout route back to San Francisco. What would you say to another week or ten-day delay?"

He sighed. "Where are you planning to go now?"

"Maybe—Denver."

"With Gavin Rutledge?" the attorney demanded. "Callie, I can't let you do it! What do you know about this man? This isn't like you at all."

"It's the boy I'm thinking of," Callie said, telling only part of the truth while she burned her last bridge.

"What boy?"

"Gavin's nephew, Stephen Tucker Thomas. William, he means a lot to me."

Cringing, because she knew what had to be going through his mind, she waited for a response. But it was long in coming. William never rushed headlong into anything. Eventually the attorney cleared his throat and suggested carefully, "Mightn't this have something to do with Joshua, Callie?"

"In a way," she admitted. "But Tucker's not a substitute, if that's what you're thinking. He's just a little boy I care a lot about who needs me right now."

"I'm going to be frank, Callie. If Derek and Catherine hear about this they'll think you're still suffering, mentally suffering, over the loss of your own son. They could use it against you."

Frustration suffused her. "Let them!"

"They'll go after you on mental incompetency," William said gravely. "Do you want that?"

The heat was sending a trickle of sweat down her back and Callie closed her eyes. There was no way to win. She didn't want the money, but no one believed she should give it back—even Gavin—though she was digging herself a deeper grave by holding on to it.

"I'm not crazy—yet," she said through her teeth, "but I sometimes wonder about the rest of the world. Do what you have to do, William. I don't care anymore. I'm going to Denver. I'll call you when I get there."

"Callie!"

"I'm sorry. There's really no other answer. Don't worry so much," she added gently before she hung up. "I know what I'm doing...."

The private drive that led to the Rutledge home was long and winding and bordered by giant spruce trees. Outside the taxi window and beyond this black-topped concession to civilization, the forested hills loomed wild and remote. It was beautiful and scary, and Callie couldn't help shivering a little, more from apprehension than the cool Denver temperatures. She hadn't expected the house to be so far from the city's center.

Tucker's arm was linked through hers but he, too, had his nose fairly pressed to the window. He gave her an unfathomable look, and she realized he was as overwhelmed as she was. The poor child probably couldn't remember life outside Martinique. Teresa had left him with the Rouseaus when he was still a baby and had, according to Aimee, only visited him a few times in the intervening years.

Snuggling Tucker closer to her, Callie slid a glance toward Gavin. He was as cold and distant as the approaching Tudor home. This remoteness wasn't new. Since she'd told him about her decision to come with him to Denver he'd been the same way. It hadn't taken a mind reader to see how he felt, but she kept reminding herself that he did care about her. He was, she supposed, trying to protect her in a way. He didn't want her to have to face his family.

But rejection, whatever the reason, was difficult to take, and Callie had to swallow against a lump in her throat. He'd warned her not to fall in love with him, but she'd done it anyway. The little hurts he heaped on her now were only because she cared so much; they were unintentional on his part.

Only the flash of longing she sometimes caught in his eyes kept her going. It gave her dogged hope. In his own way, she knew he cared, and Callie had swallowed her pride again and again, hiding her sensitive feelings during the long, tiring flight from Martinique and the tense taxi ride from the airport. She just hoped she was doing the right thing.

The taxi slid to a halt in front of the tiered bluestone steps. As Gavin paid the driver, Callie held tightly to Tucker's hand, wrapping his pitifully inadequate sweater around his shivering frame. She wished she'd had time to buy him a coat. Denver in November was a far cry from Martinique at any time of the year.

"So what do you think?" Gavin drawled as he led them to the front door.

Callie seized on this crumb of affection, smiling and looking upward, her eyes skimming the outlines of the Rutledge home. Its gabled eaves were sharp against the pewter sky. "I don't know."

Tucker moved even closer to her. "I don't like it."

"You get no argument from me, pal," Gavin muttered as he clanged the door knocker against the heavy panels.

The door was opened by a middle-aged woman with a pompous air. She looked down her aristocratic nose, and there was the faintest sign of recognition when her eyes fell on Gavin. "Ahh, Gavin, Victoria's been expecting you."

Gavin gave her a sardonic look and ushered Callie and Tucker inside, turning in the direction of a pair of double doors.

"Wait! I haven't had a chance to—"

"Don't worry. We'll show ourselves in."

"You can't! Victoria's just gotten up and she's not ready for visitors," the woman sputtered.

"Laurene, I don't have time for this, okay? Play nursemaid for someone else for a while. Victoria doesn't need you."

As Gavin held the double doors and Tucker cast a wide-eyed glance at the speechless Laurene, Callie forced herself not to stare. She ducked past Gavin and waited inside a magnificent, high-ceilinged parlor room. A fire burned in the grate, and as Tucker went to warm his hands Callie looked around for Victoria. The room was empty. Seeing her look, Gavin indicated another door at the far end and said, "Come on."

"Who was that?" Callie murmured, inclining her head to the way they'd just come.

"Just another blood-sucking Rutledge. Laurene is a second cousin, I believe. She's hoping she'll be left something when Victoria dies."

"You are cynical, aren't you?"

"Uh-huh. What you see is what you get."

He strode to the other end of the room and pushed his hand on the ornately carved swinging door. Callie followed behind, more slowly. She wished she knew why Gavin was trying so hard to push her away. Maybe it wasn't that he was trying to protect her, she fretted. Maybe he was having second thoughts after all.

"Do you think you should see your grandmother alone, first?" she suggested slowly. "Tucker and I could—"

Gavin's palm closed around her upper arm. "You chose the venue, my love. Don't back out now."

She couldn't continue the charade. "Why are you doing this?"

"Doing what?"

She was infuriated with him. This wasn't the same man who'd held her in his arms when she'd cried out her grief over losing her son. It couldn't be. "If you're trying to hurt me," she whispered unevenly, "you're doing a good job. I ache, Gavin."

Regret flashed deeply in his eyes and he looked away, frowning. It gave Callie hope and she silently begged him to relent.

"Tucker!" he called, clearing his throat against an unnatural huskiness. He ignored Callie, pushing open the door and holding it while she, her shoulders slumped in defeat, preceded him through.

Tucker was at her heels as she stepped into a huge, oblong dining room hung with glimmering crystal chandeliers. At least twenty chairs surrounded the mahogany table, and an enormous flower arrangement was centered under the largest chandelier. Where they'd fallen from the petals, drops of water stood in perfect circles on the gleaming patina, and as Callie walked forward she heard the door swing shut behind her and the soft, musical clink of crystal brushing crystal as the chandeliers' silvery teardrops swayed from the draft.

"Gavin."

The white-haired woman at the head of the table raised herself up, her hands gripped tightly around the chair's shining wooden arms. She pinned Callie with her bright blue gaze for just an instant, then her glance slid over Gavin to rest on Tucker.

Gavin stepped to one side. "Victoria, this is Callie Cantrell, and this is Stephen Tucker Thomas. He goes by Tucker."

There was another entrance to the dining room, and that door suddenly opened, admitting Laurene. Lines of outrage bracketed her nose and mouth. "I told them to wait but they wouldn't!"

Victoria waved her away as she sat back down. "Don't coddle me, Laurene. I want to talk to my great-grandson."

With a glare meant for Gavin alone, Laurene turned on her heel. Gavin's lips twitched, and Callie herself had to swallow a smile. Oh, the absurdity of pretension. Many times she'd wanted to sigh and toss up her hands at the way Derek and Catherine acted.

Tucker's chin was to his chest. He was eyeing Victoria with distrust.

"Well, come here, child," Victoria said with an impatient wave of one wrinkled hand. "Let me get a closer look."

Tucker was rooted to the spot.

"She doesn't bite," Gavin put in. "At least she's never bitten me—yet."

"Go on," Callie urged gently. "Meet your great-grandmother, then maybe we can have a tour of the house, hmm?"

"Laurene will show you around later," Victoria assured him, giving Callie a considering glance. "What kind of name is Tucker? I'll call you Stephen, like my grandson, your father."

"My name is Tucker," the boy said, but he took a reluctant step forward.

It was some time before the older woman could convince Tucker to come within touching range and when she did finally clasp his hands, Tucker, showing more constraint than usual, stood very still and silent. As a first meeting, it wasn't going too badly, Callie concluded, resisting the urge to cuddle the boy close and reassure him that everything would be all right.

Tucker's mother was noticeably absent and she wondered what that meant. Was Teresa somewhere in the house? When Callie had told Tucker they would see his mother, his reaction had been less than enthusiastic.

Laurene returned with a tray of cakes and a pot of tea, and Victoria, after managing to squeeze a hug out of Tucker, told her to give Callie and Tucker a tour. With a tight smile, Laurene beckoned them from the room and Tucker eagerly pounded toward the door. Callie threw a questioning look over her shoulder to Gavin.

Something in her face must have softened his heart because he said, "I'll catch up with you later," then touched her arm, briefly and reassuringly, before he walked the remaining distance to meet his grandmother.

"Where's our loving Teresa?" she heard him softly ask Victoria just as the door shut behind her.

"Who is that woman?" Victoria demanded autocratically, motioning Gavin to a chair.

"Callie?" Gavin stayed on his feet, propped against the nearest wall.

"What does she have to do with the boy?"

"She's a friend of Tucker's and she's a friend of mine. Now where's Teresa?"

Victoria reached for the pot of tea, pouring two cups with a steady hand. She held one up to Gavin and he reluctantly accepted it. "Teresa's staying at a hotel. I didn't want her at the house."

"Doesn't she know her son's here? Or doesn't she care?"

Victoria's lips thinned to a humorless smile. "She has different priorities right now. There's a man involved...and I don't think he wants a five-year-old child hanging around."

With a snort of disgust, Gavin restlessly paced toward the lead-paned diamond-shaped windows. "So you've talked to her about all this. What does she plan to do with Tucker?"

"Isn't it obvious?"

Gavin turned to his grandmother, watching as she smoothed a pink linen napkin across her lap. "She's going to give him up," he said, relieved, yet angry at the callous Teresa, too. "What did you offer her? Money?"

"That's right. My lawyer's already drawing up the papers. I get custody."

Gavin spun to look at her, his tea slopping over the side of the cup. "What?"

"Well, what did you expect?" Her white brows raised. "The boy needs his family."

"Yes, but *you* want custody?"

Victoria stared at her grandson. "I don't see why you're surprised. It's a logical answer."

"Maybe I want custody myself," he said casually.

Victoria Rutledge was a woman who lived by a strict code of ethics, and having her daughter come home pregnant had been outside the boundaries. She'd never been able to accept Gavin as her grandson. But there were times—oh, yes—there were times when she saw a lot of herself in him. This was one of those times.

Her lip curled in amusement. "*You?* Your life-style hardly condones it, Gavin. What in heaven's name would you do with a five-year-old?"

He coolly met his grandmother's challenging gaze. "I could ask you the same thing."

"He'd have a home here."

"Yes, I know. Everything that money can buy."

"What's wrong with that?"

Gavin walked around her chair, restless and tense. "This may come as a surprise to you, Victoria, but there's more to life."

"Oh, I know. Better than you think. You don't know me as well as you think, Gavin, and it doesn't matter anyway. Stephen stays with me. Teresa and I have it all worked out."

She jumped, startled, when Gavin's fist slammed into the table, then she pressed her lips together and glared at him. But Gavin's memory of his own childhood was too strong. He knew what it was like to be an unloved child, and he didn't trust his grandmother to have warmed over the years—legitimate heir or not.

"I'm going to fight you," he said next to her ear. "I'm not going to let you ruin that boy."

"You can't threaten me, Gavin. I'm too old."

"Oh, it isn't a threat." He leaned a hip against the edge of the table and solemnly crossed his arms over his chest. "I know how you are, Victoria, and I'd rather cut off my right arm than leave Tucker with you. I'll fight you and I won't play fair. You're not going to raise him in this mausoleum."

Her mouth drew into a scowl. The game of parry and thrust with her grandson was over. "I've never known you to boast about what you couldn't do. Don't start a bad habit now."

"The shame of it all is that you really believe you're doing the right thing," Gavin muttered, half to himself. "But some of the worst crimes were done for the right reasons. Tucker needs someone to love him," he said, straightening. "And you don't know how to love anybody."

Two high spots of color were flaming in Victoria's paper-fine cheeks. "You're a single man riding a worthless dream, Gavin," she said tautly. "You'll be penniless before you're forty, if you aren't already. Wildcatting—" she snorted in disgust "—is for fools. You should have accepted that position with our oil company. And since when are you an expert on love?"

His steely blue eyes met hers evenly. "I know when it doesn't exist."

"Don't be so sure. Where are you going?" she demanded as Gavin headed for the door.

"To find Teresa." His footsteps echoed his decision and he paused at the door, his smile cold. "Whatever you've offered her, I'm going to double it. I'm not penniless yet...."

Callie was startled when somewhere behind her a door slammed violently shut, shaking the very foundations of the house. Even the taciturn Laurene showed a moment of animation, a gleam coming into her eye.

"No, don't go into that room," she scolded Tucker. "Here. Play in here."

"In here" was a cold, empty room that looked as if it hadn't be used in a century. Tucker, used to exploring on his own, regarded Laurene with those penetrating, sober gray eyes. Fidgeting, Laurene looked back down the hall, as if she were anxious to know what was happening at the other end of the house.

Callie pulled out her most charming smile. "Why don't I stay with Tucker? I'm sure you're busy and have lots to do."

"I do have some things to attend to," the woman murmured, peering closely at Callie as if she wasn't at all certain if she could trust her.

"Then go. We'll be fine."

Laurene was still undecided when forceful footsteps rang through the hall and Gavin called out, "Callie!" in a voice cold with fury.

"I'll be back," Laurene said, and slipped away.

"We are here!" Tucker sang out, racing around Callie in his effort to find his uncle.

Callie followed more slowly. She'd been through the upper corridors of the home, had seen the perfectly decorated rooms that were hers and Tucker's, and had followed Laurene back to the first floor. Several other servants had looked at her curiously, then quickly glanced away as Laurene bore down on them. Altogether, Callie's impression was of a cold, empty home without a family heart and she was appalled that Tucker was even here. Had he been better off in Martinique? Her conscience twinged.

Gavin was toward the front of the house, and she and Tucker met him in the outer hallway. He scooped up the boy and placed him on one strong shoulder, but his face was carved in stone. What had happened? Callie wondered fearfully.

"I've got to go out for a while," he said, setting Tucker on his feet again. "Will you be okay here?"

"I want to go," Tucker pleaded.

Callie's desires were an echo of Tucker's but she held them in check. "Is something wrong?"

"Just the usual." He seemed to want to tell her something but Tucker was standing between them, tuned in to their every word.

Gavin turned to her and something must have shown on her face because his eyes softened. With a groan he pulled her into his arms and for a breathless instant Callie forgot everything in the pure joy of his touch. "What am I going to do with you?" he muttered.

"Take us both. Wherever you're going."

The moment passed and he released her. "Not this time."

"Why not?"

"Look—" he spread his hands against her growing resentment "—you've done a lot for me, and I—"

"Don't you dare tell me it's time to leave. Not now." Her eyes flashed fire.

Gavin raked his hands through his hair, pulling on the long strands at his nape. "I wanted to say I'm glad you're here," he expelled frustratedly. "And damn it all..." He suddenly remembered Tucker and whipped around, scooping the little boy up again. "I want you both," he said huskily, looking at Tucker.

She was so relieved she wanted to laugh, but Tucker said with a child's simplicity, "You can have us."

"I'm going to give it one helluva try," Gavin said, and this time he didn't hesitate as he placed a kiss on Callie's lips. "Just one more hurdle. A big one."

She knew then what he meant. Teresa. He was going to see Teresa, wherever she was. Palms sweating, Callie was afraid to consider what would happen if the outcome went the wrong way—for herself as well as Tucker.

She was about to wish him luck when a string of musical chimes sounded through the house, echoing and ending on a curiously somber note.

Gavin didn't wait for Laurene. Balancing Tucker, he pulled open the front door.

On the steps was a petite and unquestionably beautiful red-headed woman. Teresa Thomas.

She blinked several times at the sight that met her eyes. "Why, Tucker, darling, there you are!" she said, extending her arms to him. "Come here, pet. I've missed you so much. Come give Mommy a kiss."

Chapter Ten

Callie had never been the type to instantly size up another woman as the competition, but seeing Teresa Thomas did strange things to her. She wanted to find some flaw in her, make certain she wasn't good enough to raise Tucker. With the kind of critical eye she had seen used on herself once or twice—and had squirmed beneath—Callie looked Teresa over. Her hair was almost the same shade as Callie's own; her eyes a bluish green; her small frame endowed with lush curves. Other than a jaded weariness around her mouth the woman was beautiful, and Callie was engulfed by a strange desolation. Teresa Thomas was indeed formidable.

Gavin slowly placed Tucker on his feet, but the boy kept close to his side. Even Callie's sizing up of Teresa was nothing in comparison with the inspection her son was giving her.

Growing impatient with his sober-eyed silence, Teresa came forward and ruffled Tucker's hair, smiling with a kind of forced naturalness that Callie recognized as tension. "You've grown so-o-o big," she said brightly, but her attention drifted to Callie as she did her own quick assessment of the competition.

Tucker said nothing. He looked up to Gavin for support.

Instantly Teresa redirected her gaze. Her blue eyes widened fractionally. "You must be Gavin," she said, and this time her smile was easier.

"You must be Teresa."

Callie felt the hairs at the back of her neck rise. Anyone who knew Gavin well could hear the ominous tone of his voice. Teresa, however, was blithely unaware.

"Victoria told me you'd, er, found Tucker," she said, pulling off her gloves. They were trimmed in mink, Callie noted, as was the small wool hat on her crown.

"With the Rouseaus," Gavin agreed.

"They've taken excellent care of him," Teresa said a trifle defensively, not totally unaware of Gavin's censure. "They love Tucker. I had to do some heavy explaining to get them to let you bring him to me. How was the flight?"

This last question was meant for her son but Tucker was immovable. Callie was glad those gray eyes weren't watching *her* so judgmentally.

With an impatient twitch of her lips Teresa turned back to Gavin. "You're not quite what I expected," she said. "It was silly of Victoria to send you after Tucker. I was bringing him here myself."

"Were you?"

She flushed, looking piqued. "Well, of course I was. Tucker's Stephen's son. He's a Rutledge," she reminded him.

"He's a Thomas, too." Gavin's expression was a miracle of tolerance. "Tell me, does my mother know she's a grandmother?"

"Your mother and Stephen's father are in Europe," Teresa said crisply. "I thought I should wait until they got back to Denver to tell them about . . . Tucker."

Tucker pressed himself against Gavin's legs. Gavin placed a reassuring hand on his shoulder and said softly, "You waited too long to tell my brother. He never knew."

"Your *half* brother," she said with some malice. "Just what is it you want? Heavens, if I didn't know better I'd believe I was getting a lecture on behavior!"

"What makes you think you aren't?"

Lines of anger carved beside her nose. "Because I'm considering the source, Mr. *Rutledge*."

Callie had stood like a statue during this entire exchange, but Teresa's cruelty filled her with indignation. She didn't want Tucker to witness any more. "I'm going to go upstairs," she said, reaching a hand in the boy's direction. "Want to come along?"

"I haven't finished saying hello yet." Teresa's blue eyes raked over Callie. "Come here, Tucker."

Callie's lips parted in dismay. How could Teresa play emotional tug-of-war with her own son?

Gavin was quick to react. "You and I need to talk alone, Teresa," he said in cold fury. "Tucker, go with Callie. I'll be up in a few minutes. Teresa, you and I need to face Victoria together."

"That's not exactly—" Teresa began hotly.

"Just do it!"

Tucker's gray eyes were wide as he turned to Callie, and she instinctively held her arms to him. He ran to her and she clasped him to her breast, reluctantly letting him go a moment later when she heard Teresa's sharp intake of breath and realized what a challenge this scene must be to her. Then, grabbing for Tucker's hand, Callie blindly turned toward the stairs.

"Who the hell do you think you are?" Teresa hissed to Gavin as Callie mounted the stairs.

"I'm the answer to your prayers," Gavin said mockingly. "Victoria's in the dining room. I suggest you follow me and find out just what that means . . ."

"Callie . . ."

Gavin's voice through the panels of the door made her pulse leap. With a glance at the sleeping boy curled in the center of the bed, Callie hurried to the door.

She'd been beside herself with anxiety, straining her ears each time she heard the raised tenor of Gavin's voice. It unnerved her to realize how loud he must be shouting, and she'd read a bedtime story to Tucker in a louder voice than normal to drown out the noise. Tucker was too tired, or too apathetic, to listen anyway. He'd dozed off before Callie was halfway through the little children's book she'd picked up at the airport.

She opened the door and held on to it for support as Gavin, looking lean and dark and dangerous, strode inside. It was all she could do to keep from throwing herself into his arms.

"Well?" she asked uncertainly.

He threw a look at the sleeping boy, his harsh features relaxing slightly. "Teresa's a bitch in the highest order," he said flatly.

"She's Tucker's mother," Callie murmured, though she couldn't help but agree.

"Not for long. She's giving up custody."

Callie lifted her brows. "Really?"

"She's determined to sell him to the highest bidder, if you get my meaning," Gavin muttered dryly. "It'll be hell paying her, but apart from murder, there's not a lot of alternatives."

"Paying her?" Callie grasped the one comment that made sense. "Are *you* getting custody?" she asked eagerly.

Gavin sighed and pulled her into the adjoining room, her bedroom. He softly closed the door behind them. "It's a maybe," he admitted.

"Oh, Gavin." Callie couldn't stand the restraint. She touched him, her hands light on his shoulders.

She felt his hesitation and she dropped her arms, turning so he wouldn't see how much the merest hint of rejection hurt her.

But he saw how she felt and it cut deep. "Callie..." he groaned, his arms tightening around her waist.

She was limp in his arms, needing him so much. Her breath escaped in a fluttery sigh, and she lay her head on his shoulder, praying with all her might that he would give in and love her. She pressed her face to the warm skin of his neck, tasting him with her tongue, and it was the final straw for Gavin.

He twisted her around, his needs overriding his conscience. No matter how hard he tried to keep Callie out of his screwed-up life, he couldn't do it. One look at Teresa—seeing her hardened face, her grasping ways—had let him clearly see the woman Callie was. There was no greed in her eyes, just a soft sort of sadness that disappeared every time she looked at Tucker. Her beauty was different from Teresa's; it was more than skin-deep.

"Damn it, Callie. You should tell me to leave," he muttered grimly.

"No." She shook her head, devouring his face with soft, misty eyes.

"You don't know what problems there are."

"I have this crazy feeling things are going to work out," Callie whispered near his ear, her breath warm and soft. "Hold me, Gavin. Please."

"Callie..."

His protests were weak. Changes were already happening within him, but still he resisted.

She pulled back to regard him with troubled eyes. "Why don't you want me here? Because of Teresa?" A sound of regret issued from her lips. "I suppose she wanted to kill me for taking Tucker away."

"She doesn't give a damn about that boy," Gavin disabused her. "All I had to do was meet her price and you were forgotten. It's Victoria who's the real problem."

"Why?"

Her breasts were pressed against his shirt and he felt the curve of her thigh as it gently brushed his leg. With difficulty, Gavin pulled his mind back to the conversation. "She wants Tucker for herself."

Callie's mouth opened in surprise. "What does that mean?"

Gavin shifted, trying to put more space between them, but the movement only brought her body in more direct contact with his. Almost reluctantly he brought his hand down to her waist, resting on the swell of her hips. "Victoria likes to control, and she wants to control Tucker," he said distractedly.

"You're beyond her control, though, aren't you?" she said, smiling a little.

"Oh, I don't know. She got me to go after Tucker."

Callie's face was close to his, so close he could see the gradients of blue in her eyes. It would be unfair to her, he knew, to continue this; he had nothing to offer her, not even Tucker. But his body had a will of its own and with a groan he lowered his lips to hers, tasting the blossoming fullness of her mouth.

"I want you," he said thickly, heeding the desire thundering in his ears.

Her arms tightened, her breasts flattening to him, her body trembling with an eagerness that brought him to instant, full arousal. Convulsively, his fingers slid to the hollow of her spine, and he strained against her, condemning himself for being so weak.

"I've been so afraid..." Callie murmured brokenly. "All this time, since you found out Teresa was in Denver...you've been different...."

He sighed, wishing he could explain. "I know."

Callie sighed softly, her breath expelling against his cheek. "Just love me," she whispered.

He scooped her up into his arms, half turned to lock the door, then lay her on the wide, four-poster bed, her hair splaying richly against the jade satin coverlet. Callie's eyes were warm and languid, her mouth a curve of soft desire.

Gavin sighed in submission as her hands undid the buttons on his shirt and the zipper of his pants. His own fingers were fevered as he stripped off her dress. Then his leg insinuated itself between hers, one hand slipping sensuously along her inner thigh.

"I'm sorry," he muttered.

"For what?" Her own hands had begun an exploration that made his breath catch.

"For taking more than I can give," he ground out.

She would have answered but his mouth prevented her, his tongue twisting and demanding. The blood was flowing wildly through his veins and Gavin was beyond thinking. He thrust himself into her, feeling her open to him with the full power of her love, and for an instant he was consumed in self-hate. But then she surged toward him and his thoughts splintered. All he could hear were her small, throat-catching sounds of pleasure. All he could feel was a flooding tide of sensation that broke over his head, drowning him, pouring through him, sending a shudder of emotion down his lean frame that left him weak and utterly in her power.

It was with a feeling of complete contentment that she lifted her lids and stretched sensuously on the coverlet, aware that Gavin was propped on one elbow, looking down at her. He drew his hand across her sweat-dampened forehead and murmured, "Callie, Callie..."

She laughed and tugged him closer until he fell across her with a groan of surrender. "I love you," she said softly, unknowingly feeding his own self-disgust.

"You don't know what you're saying." He pulled himself away to contemplate her soberly.

Her regret was instant and total. "Don't spoil the moment, Gavin," she whispered.

"Damn it all, Callie. You're too trusting!"

"Of you?" she asked, her eyes serious. "What are you trying to tell me?"

Swearing under his breath, Gavin rolled to his side. "You don't know anything about me. I'm not who you think I am. I've got debt, my dear. A ton of it. And if I don't hit oil soon this whole deal with Teresa is just talk, nothing else.'' He raked his hands through his black hair, squeezing his neck as if he found the whole situation intolerable, as indeed he did. ''Martinique is over, Callie. That was then—this is now.''

She sat up, her hair falling in bewitching beauty over her breasts. Gavin turned away from the appealing picture she made, but her hand lightly touched his shoulder.

''If it's money you need, I've got it.''

''No.''

''I don't even want it, but it's there.''

''No!'' He wrenched around and bore her back against the wrinkled coverlet, his eyes blazing.

Callie licked her lips. ''Don't be a fool, Gavin. I can finance this deal with Teresa, and I can even finance your oil operation if it's in trouble.''

''Damn you!'' With a smothered curse he left her trembling on the bed, snatching up his clothes with an inner fury that Callie found almost frightening.

''Well, what do you want then?'' she demanded shakily.

''God knows!''

He was at the door, his head bent, shoulders slumped. Callie's eyes were eloquent with feeling, which made it doubly hard—and absolutely necessary—for Gavin to have her understand. ''You'd better go back to San Francisco,'' he said bleakly. ''Before I decide to accept your offer and end up hating myself for life.''

There wasn't a lot Callie could do to change his mind. She tried, by every means she possessed, to make him listen to her, but he wouldn't. She knew now what had been eating at him, but it certainly didn't help the situation. He was bound and determined to push her out of his life because she was a wealthy woman.

She thought about his oblique references to the Cantrell money and knew that he'd been subtly warning her against him all along. If she'd thought Jonathan's inheritance was a millstone around her neck before, she'd had no idea what the future could hold. The man she loved didn't want her because she had too much money. Good Lord, could anything be more ironic?

It didn't matter what he thought, Callie decided. She refused to leave Denver—for Tucker's sake, if nothing else. The boy was totally overwhelmed by the Rutledges and on a collision course with Teresa, who seemed determined to play her role of mother to the hilt whether Tucker wanted her to or not.

Gavin, who most of the time was either locked behind closed doors with Victoria or on the telephone, had tried to give Callie a wide berth, but she'd tried equally hard to catch him alone. She sensed the tearing ambivalence of his feelings, and though she sympathized, it angered her that he should feel so compelled to thrust her away. She was old enough to make her own decisions, and she'd certainly had more than enough experience in weathering life's worst trials.

Only Victoria seemed to take an active role in Callie's life. The older woman was intrigued with her, and for all her imperiousness, she recognized and appreciated the closeness between Callie and Tucker.

"You love him, don't you?" she said one afternoon, while rain streaked down the diamond-shaped panes in the dining room.

Callie was uncertain who exactly she meant but she answered yes, anyway, figuring it didn't matter.

"What do you expect to gain by staying around him?"

"What do you mean?" she asked, selecting one of the flakey rolls from the silver serving dish.

Victoria sipped her tea, studying Callie across the table. There were only the two of them home. Gavin had taken Tucker into Denver, and Teresa was back at her hotel.

"I mean, how do you expect to figure into things? Has Gavin asked you to marry him?"

Callie nearly choked. "Heavens—no!"

"Why do you say it like that? Are you telling me the thought hasn't crossed your mind? You and Gavin could do far worse than get married and try for custody of Stephen. After all, he's going to inherit from the Rutledges. I've already taken steps to ensure he's in my will."

The woman's audacity amazed and inflamed Callie. With a deliberation that was a warning in itself, she carefully set down her roll and dusted off her fingers with one of the rose-colored napkins. Five days with the Rutledges had been more than enough time to convince her they were as cruel and uncaring as Gavin had made them out.

"I don't know what you're fishing for, Victoria," she said coldly, "but you're way off base where I'm concerned."

The old woman craftily raised her eyebrows. "The money isn't an issue with you, then?"

Callie could have laughed in disbelief. "If Gavin hasn't told you about me, I'm not about to, either. But no, the money isn't an issue. Thank you for breakfast."

She left before her temper forced her to say something unforgivably rude. What was she doing here? she asked herself. William was undoubtedly desperate by now, and she wasn't accomplishing anything in Denver apart from spinning her wheels and making herself miserable in the process.

The phone rang as Callie made for the stairway, and before she got to the first landing Laurene appeared at the foot of the stairs. "It's for you Miss Cantrell," she said stiffly.

"Thanks. I'll take it in my room," Callie answered, not correcting the woman's mistake. The Rutledges knew nothing about her and she preferred it that way. Let them think she was a gold digger fantasizing after Gavin, or even Tucker. Their preoccupation with money was worse than the Cantrells'!

"Hello?"

She knew that only one person could be calling her, William, so she was unprepared when Derek Cantrell's pompous tones came over the wire. "Callie?" he said stiffly. "Well, it's about time I tracked you down!"

"How did you find me?" she asked, sinking onto her bed, more amazed than angry.

Derek gave an undignified snort. "William hasn't exactly been a wealth of information, if that's what you mean. But when I found out what you were doing, I had to contact you."

Callie's eyes narrowed. She knew William hadn't talked to Derek, and knowing Jonathan's brother, she was certain he'd found out where she was by other, probably unscrupulous, means. The man wasn't above raiding William's office.

"What do you want?" she asked.

"Catherine and I want you back in San Francisco. Now. This gallivanting off to the ends of the earth won't stop the lawsuit, Callie. You're just giving us more ammunition."

"Are you actually warning me, Derek?" she asked with a trace of amusement.

Derek's tone was noticeably cooler when he said, "You've changed a lot, haven't you? What's been happening?"

How could she explain to Derek that she'd finally pulled herself together? No longer was she the tremulous widow, dazed by her husband's and son's deaths. She'd learned to accept fate. Sighing, she said, "I'll be back in San Francisco soon. Is that good enough?"

"No." Derek was positive. "Not while you're squandering your money on Gavin Rutledge."

"What?"

"Oh, come off it, Callie. I've done some research. Gavin Rutledge is the black sheep of his family. He doesn't have a dime. I don't know what game he's playing with you, but you can bet he's after our money. If you don't get back here soon, I'm coming there!"

Her hand was gripped so tightly around the receiver it ached. "Derek, so help me, stay out of my life! If I want your advice, I'll ask for it, but don't hold your breath. For the moment 'our' money is fine," she added tersely. "But I'll be sure to let you know when I sign on the dotted line!"

She slammed down the phone, then was instantly flooded with regret at her hasty words. She shouldn't have challenged him, she thought with painful hindsight. But it was just too much! The Rutledges and the Cantrells were cut from the same cloth, and she was sick to death with all of them.

Except for Tucker and Gavin.

She was pacing the parlor room when she heard the engine of Gavin's rental car. Fighting back an urgency she didn't quite understand, Callie hurried to the entryway, ignoring the questioning glance Laurene sent her way as she hovered by the front door.

When Tucker came through the door she gave him an extra hard hug, and he squirmed under the unexpected embrace. "Let go! I got new clothes. Look!"

Gavin came in with several large sacks and Tucker began tearing into them with his usual unbridled exuberance. A lift of Gavin's dark brows sent Laurene back to the kitchen, her mouth pressed together in defiance.

Callie was incensed all over again. Couldn't they be just a little nicer to him? Being the family bastard was a fate worse than death.

"What's the matter?" he asked her as Tucker bounded up the stairs, precariously holding one of the sacks.

"They're terrible," she said, her lips suddenly quivering.

"Who?"

"Everyone!" She swept an arm around to include the whole house. "I hate the way they treat you."

Gavin shrugged. "It'll all be over soon."

"Will it?" She lifted uncertain eyes to his.

"I've come to a tentative agreement with Victoria. I'm leaving Denver and going back to Wyoming. She wants some time alone with Tucker."

"What about Teresa?"

"As far as I know, she's packed and ready to go wherever the wind takes her. She doesn't care who gets custody of Tucker as long as she gets her money. God! What a woman!"

Gavin's sentiments were an echo of her own, but her heart felt lighter knowing that Teresa, at least, was an obstacle already hurdled. But Victoria was another matter.

"You can't leave Tucker here alone," she said. "You can't."

His lips tightened. "I need Victoria on my side, Callie. It's the only way. I've told Tucker how it is, and he's willing to stay here with her for a while."

"I don't believe it. He wouldn't allow you to leave him, unless—"

She realized belatedly there was no room in his plans for her. Her breath caught and she looked at him through wounded eyes. "What about me?"

"I want you to come with me," he said tautly. "You and I need to get some things straight."

"Oh?" she said with a bitterness she couldn't quite contain. "Maybe if I go with you, I'll smarten up and leave you alone?"

"You know that's not it!" he said impatiently.

"Do I?" Callie understood far more about him than he gave her credit for. "It's to be a lesson, isn't it? In the rugged life of a roughneck. What do you think I'm going to do? Turn tail and run?"

He grabbed her arm when she would have walked away, and they dueled silently with their eyes. All Callie wanted was a little reassurance and a lot of love, and she knew it was more than Gavin was willing to give.

"Come with me," he urged. "Please."

"I don't like the idea of leaving Tucker here."

"Neither do I, but I have to get to Wyoming now. Things are happening."

Callie blinked, aware there was more to this trip than she'd originally imagined. This was the first real information she'd gleaned about his wildcatting business. She hadn't thought much about it, but there had to be other people involved. Gavin wasn't running the drilling wells all by himself.

She felt petty for squabbling with him. "What can I do?" she asked, spreading her hands.

"Be with me. Stay with me."

She let his strong arms draw her against him, felt the sensuous touch of his fingers at the back of her neck and his breath fanning her cheek. She thought of Derek, frantic to have her back, and William's continual pleas for the same. She thought of Tucker, so innocent and trusting, believing he was destined to be with Gavin—and even herself. And she thought of Gavin, how much she loved him.

There was too much at stake for her to give up now.

"I'll go to Wyoming," she said.

If she'd thought the Denver skies were threatening, they were nothing compared to the black-lined clouds rolling across the Wyoming desert. Gavin's wells were to the southwest, near Rock Springs, and as Callie bumped along beside him in the pickup she realized anew how much of Gavin was still a mystery. He'd been right, she mused with an inner grimace, to make her see his life first hand. His reasons didn't matter. If she was seriously contemplating holding on to him—and she was—she had to understand everything about him. This was the kind of man he was. This was where he lived and worked. This rugged terrain, where plants and animals eked out a living, was a big part of the rough, uncut and determined man she loved.

The road they traveled was barely a road, more like twin ruts across naked dirt and rock. She saw the drilling rig long before they pulled up in front of a dust-covered trailer. When she stepped from the cab the wind cut through her jacket and whistled past her ears.

"What are you thinking about?" Gavin asked as he came to stand beside her. They were both dressed warmly in boots, jeans, sweaters and jackets, but still Callie shivered.

"You were right. Martinique's over."

"So I've been telling you," he drawled, but there was no animosity in his tone and for that she was grateful.

Heads bent, hands deep inside warm pockets, they walked together to the trailer. Gavin held the door for her, helping her inside. It was small and cramped and the pervasive dust had sneaked in with the wind; she suspected it was impossible to keep out.

There were two men seated at a narrow table, who straightened, hiding their looks of surprise upon seeing Callie. Gavin sent a smile of understanding their way.

"George, Kent, this is Callie."

One of the men, big and bearded, stood and wiped his hands on his soiled trousers before shaking Callie's hand. "I'm George. Sa'pleasure," he mumbled, and she smiled and told him the same. The other man looked as if a strong gust would blow him over. His hair was thinned to near baldness and he wore wire-rimmed glasses. He glanced questioningly from Callie to Gavin, then back to Callie.

"Kent's my geologist," Gavin explained. "He's also a partner and nervous as hell."

"With good reason!" he exploded temperamentally. "I don't mind telling you we're at the end of the line here. The next time you decide to take a powder buy me out first!"

"Don't get panicky," Gavin drawled. "We have more than enough time to panic later."

"What's happening?" Callie asked, enthralled by this peek into another of Gavin's facets. She gave him a grateful smile as he drew out a stool for her.

"Kent got excited over the last soil sample," he explained. "The formation structure is showing holes in the rock and signs of friction."

"What's that mean, exactly?"

"Maybe nothing, maybe everything. It's too early to tell."

It was obvious the geologist was still fuming over Gavin's call to honor with the Rutledges. George, however, had no such qualms, and as he began talking to Gavin about the situation, even Kent thawed and tossed some log books under Gavin's nose, jabbing his finger down on the pages for emphasis.

The men had forgotten she was there, Callie realized, but she didn't particularly mind. She could watch Gavin this way, without having to feel embarrassed about it, or worried that he might catch her.

His broad back was to her and his jacket gapped at the waist, showing a stretch of plaid shirt above his low-riding jeans. There was something totally male about Gavin that she'd rarely encountered before, and it overloaded her senses, made her think crazy thoughts.

"We're out of money." Kent sighed, stretching his back. "There's nothing we can do."

Callie pretended not to see Gavin's swift look her way. She frowned down at her fingernails.

"We'll figure something out," she heard him say under his breath.

"Better do it soon," was George's advice.

As if the men finally made the connection between Callie and Gavin, one of them, George, cleared his throat. "Kent and I have been doing double duty for a time out here. S'pose we could sneak into town for a while?''

"Sure. Go ahead."

Callie wondered, as they left, if Gavin even realized the touching reason for their request. They'd wanted to give them time alone.

His head was bent, once again, over the soil samples, as Callie came up behind him. "If I wasn't afraid of getting my head bitten off I'd offer you another stake," she said.

"Don't."

"How about a loan, then?"

"No."

"You must have made money in the past, Gavin, or you wouldn't be the man you are, live the way you do."

He slid a look over his shoulder, eyeing her through narrowed lids. "What's that supposed to mean?"

"It means, I understand enough about oil to know it's an up and down business. You make money, you lose it, you make it again. I don't think you're such a bad risk."

"I'm a terrible risk."

"Let me be the judge."

His jaw tightened and that dangerous side of him she kept glimpsing showed through again. "This isn't San Francisco, Callie. It's not Martinique, and it's not even Denver. You understand?"

"More than you know."

He turned with one lithe movement, catching her off guard. "I don't know how to treat you anymore."

"That's obvious. But I'm still the same woman you met in Martinique, and you were pretty clear about your feelings then."

"Well, I didn't know things were going to turn out this way," he muttered as he attempted to turn around, but she slid her arms beneath his jacket.

"What way, Gavin? What way?"

Her breathless tone was more effective than any argument and he groaned as her hands moved down his taut hips. "*This* way," he growled, sweeping her to him with a hunger that surprised Callie even as she welcomed it. Why couldn't it be this simple? she wondered, kissing him, feeling the velvety warmth of his tongue tasting hers, responding to his urgency. "Don't let me go," she whispered.

"I won't." The words were dragged from him. "I can't."

"Hold me."

He did more than hold her. He made love to her with his hands and his mouth, mining deep needs within her that had her groping for him, unbuttoning his shirt, her breathing as wild and uneven as his. Then he backed her into the adjoining room, and Callie heard springs squeak as she fell gently on a narrow bed.

"I've been living out of motels for months. My other wells have turned up dry, and all the money I've made is down that hole," he muttered, his weight pushing her down. "It's cold and hard out here and there's no margin for error."

"If you're trying to warn me against you, save your breath." Callie pressed soft kisses down the lean curve of his jaw. "I'm not as fragile as you think."

"You're not as tough, either."

"Neither," she said, winding her hands behind his nape and pulling his mouth down to hers, "are you..."

* * *

What crossed Callie's mind as she entered the hushed foyer of the Rutledge manor two days later was that within these walls nothing would ever change. She and Gavin could dream and plan and conspire but nothing would ever truly change. Victoria would still be the matriarch, Laurene would still silently dream of what she would do with her pitiful inheritance, and Tucker would grow old with no one to love him.

But she was bound to change that.

"Gavin . . ." she whispered, plucking at his sleeve before he could alert the rest of the household that they had returned. "I need to talk to you. There's something I've got to say."

In their time together in Wyoming they hadn't actually sat down and planned. Gavin was mostly involved with his partners, drilling for oil, and there hadn't been time to really discuss Tucker and the future.

She hadn't worried much about it, either, because Gavin had given up trying to talk her out of his life and had even grown accustomed to her being in Wyoming with him. But now, back at the imposing Rutledge manor, she berated herself for not pushing the issue harder.

"What?" he asked distractedly. Though his blue eyes swept over her face she could tell he was miles away. Like herself, he felt the chilly atmosphere, and the remote part of his nature she'd come to loath and expect, the part that invariably emerged when he was around his family, was settling over him.

"Victoria's only objection to your having custody of Tucker is that she thinks you're a risk taker and that you have no money."

"It's one of her objections. I wouldn't say it's her only," he answered dryly.

Callie thought about her earlier discussion with his grandmother and she bit her lip, aware she was trying to make the woman's prophecy come true—but for different reasons. "I know you have to get back to the oil rig, but you want to clear this issue up with Tucker. So do I. Do you trust me, Gavin?"

Her urgency penetrated his distant senses. He frowned down at her. "I thought we settled that on Martinique."

"You know I love Tucker, don't you?"

"Of course."

"And I've told you enough times that I love you, too. Do you believe me? Well, do you?" she demanded impatiently as he continued to stare at her.

"What has this got to do—"

"Do you believe me?" she hissed in a low tone. "Yes, or no?"

"Yes."

Callie exhaled slowly. Now came the hard part. She tried several times to form the exact words but nothing sounded right.

She heard footsteps coming from the direction of the kitchen. Laurene. There was no time left. Even now Gavin's head was beginning to turn to greet the newcomer.

"Marry me, Gavin," she whispered before her courage could desert her. "Marry me for Tucker."

His jaw slackened and she never knew what he would have said, because at that moment Laurene appeared, looking distinctly harried.

"You have a visitor," she said in scathing tones. Callie, whose eyes were still appealing to Gavin, took a long time in realizing the woman was talking to her.

"A visitor?" she repeated blankly as Laurene inclined her head toward the parlor doors.

But she needn't have bothered. The doors opened as if on cue, and with the kind of drama she was used to from him, Derek Cantrell stepped into the foyer, smoothing down his dark blond hair with a careful palm.

"Hello, Callie," he said, his smile not quite reaching his eyes. "I've been waiting for you."

Chapter Eleven

It took a full three seconds for Callie to respond. Derek's sudden appearance drove all thought from her mind. She was stunned, yet at the same time she was aware of Gavin's harsh intake of breath. But was his response because of Derek, or because of her unexpected proposal? She didn't know.

"Derek..." she murmured unsteadily. "What are you doing here?"

"Putting action to words," he said pleasantly enough, but she saw him sizing up Gavin as a worthy adversary.

Gavin returned Derek's appraisal with his own narrow-eyed suspicion, but he didn't move. He was waiting, Callie realized, for her to give him some clue as to what her relationship really was to this man.

"Derek Cantrell, meet Gavin Rutledge," she said. "Gavin, Derek."

They shook hands like two dogs circling one another. Seeing Laurene's avid interest, Callie stared pointedly at the woman, glad when she melted back into the shadows.

"Could we talk? Alone?" Derek asked Callie. He coughed lightly. "We have some unfinished business I'd really like to get taken care of."

"The Cantrell inheritance. I know." Her smile was brittle.

"I'm trying to save us all a lot of heartache over this thing. Let's not let it get nasty."

Derek's attempt to make his interests sound altruistic was the wrong way to go. Before Callie could answer, Gavin drawled, "No let's not let it get nasty. By all means, let's keep it civilized."

Derek shot Gavin a glance just short of hostile then he flicked back his sleeve, checking the thin gold watch on his wrist. "Could we have that talk, Callie? I really don't have that much time."

"You shouldn't have bothered coming to Denver at all," she told him succinctly.

"Well, I didn't have a lot of choice seeing as you weren't exactly rushing back to San Francisco." Moving, he positioned himself in front of Gavin, his shoulder a pointed barrier. At the same time his hand grasped Callie's elbow in a hard, persuasive grip. He discreetly tried to nudge her toward the parlor doors, but Gavin shifted his weight.

"Take your hand off her if you don't want it broken," he said without emotion, and Derek, more out of surprise than fear, dropped his arm.

"I beg your pardon."

"I said take your hand off her," Gavin reiterated, though the deed had already been done.

Derek blinked, his mouth curving in wry disbelief.

Oh, Derek, don't, Callie moaned to herself. He had no idea what he was inviting.

"It's okay, Gavin," she said quickly. "I'll talk to Derek."

"I'm coming with you."

"Now, look, Rutledge." Derek adjusted his tie and let mockery curl his upper lip. "Callie was my brother's wife and she and I have known each other a long time. You just happened to walk into the picture during the last act. You don't know what's already gone on."

"Then I'll be enlightened," Gavin said, smiling, holding open the door. He gestured for Derek to go first, and there wasn't anything Derek could do but comply. With lifted eyebrows meant for Callie, he preceded Gavin into the room.

Callie, sensing another bloody battle was about to unfold, squared her shoulders and followed them. Inwardly sighing, she watched as Gavin leaned indolently against a bookcase, arms folded across his chest, and Derek arranged himself on the rose and cream love seat, a slim leather briefcase placed by his side.

"You should have told us you'd be gone so long," Derek admonished.

Callie smiled uncertainly and went to stand in front of the fire. "I didn't know I had to report to you."

"You don't. But let's be frank, you've got my family's money at your disposal—at least until we go to court—and it plays havoc with my nerves."

His surety and arrogance had always gotten under her skin. "Think I'm going to squander it, Derek?"

He couldn't help throwing a look in Gavin's direction, a knowing gleam entering his eyes.

"I told you not to come here," Callie stated, growing angry. "I don't know what you expected to gain by this visit, but it's all wasted effort. I'll be back in San Francisco soon enough."

"I think we could settle this outside a lawsuit, Callie. You've said yourself you feel the Cantrell money doesn't belong to you. It doesn't." He moved his shoulders negligently, keeping Gavin in careful peripheral view. "I don't know why we're even quarreling."

"Because you're not being honest, Cantrell," Gavin answered grimly.

Derek dropped his head and straightened the crease on his slacks with his fingers. He waited for several seconds, his mouth tightening by degrees. "I resent your interference," he told Gavin coldly. "As far as I'm concerned, this is none of your affair. What's between you and Callie doesn't affect my business relations with her."

"Derek . . ." Callie raised her hands.

"No, look." He stood up sharply, his lips a thin line. "I don't have time to argue. You know how Catherine and I feel, Callie. We know you deserve part of the inheritance. We've always told you so. Come back with me now and we'll settle the whole thing amicably."

The last thing she wanted was another fight. Though she neither liked nor trusted Derek, she was as anxious for the battle to be over as he was.

Sensing his first advantage, Derek pressed, "I can make a plane reservation for two. Otherwise it'll be up to our attorneys."

She remembered that William had told her Derek and Catherine had new counsel, and the idea of a hairy court scene made her shudder. Drawing in a long breath, Callie glanced at Jonathan's brother, seeing the eagerness written on his face. Derek had shown admirable re-

straint considering how anxious he was for her to relin-
quish the Cantrell fortune. She almost pitied him, and
pity made her want to let him know how little she wanted
the money.

She knew she should go back to San Francisco—she
had to at some point—but now was such an inoppor-
tune time.

Gavin's eyes were on her. She could feel them. He'd
also been a model of propriety, especially considering
Derek's oblique comments on his character. Without realizing it, she threw him an appealing look.

His mouth hardened. "You got your audience, Cantrell," he said deliberately. "Now give Callie some time
to think it over."

Derek's neck suffused with color. "She's had time."

"Not enough."

There was nothing worse than bare civility, Callie
thought with a wrench. And Derek was a master at the
game.

"Back off, Rutledge," he warned coolly. "I've toler-
ated you because I've had to, but you haven't got your
hands on my money yet."

"Derek!" Callie was appalled.

But Gavin was also learned in the ways of cruelty
handed out with a smile. He straightened in direct response to Derek's challenge, a cold flame of anger burning in his eyes. "Be careful what you say, or you may find
it to be the truth."

"Callie." Derek swung his gaze to her. "For God's
sake, come back to San Francisco. You're in way over
your head."

Her prime interest had been in defusing the situation,
but Derek's high-handedness piqued her anger once

again. "I'll take my chances," she said coldly. "But thanks for the advice."

His jaw sagged. For a moment he looked as if he didn't know what to do. Then he snatched up his briefcase and strode to the door, grating out, "Very well. Then I guess the next time I'll see you is in court."

The door whispered shut behind him.

"Just your regular kind of guy," Gavin drawled, looking thoughtfully after him.

Callie's head throbbed. She pressed her fingers to her temple and tried to muster up the strength to go on.

"Callie . . . ?"

"I almost hate them," she said, swallowing. "I would have given back the money if you'd let me."

"I know."

"Why didn't you let me?"

Gavin's gaze darkened ominously. "Because you were being railroaded. That miserable leech plans to steal your inheritance and expects you to thank him for it."

"But I don't want the money. You won't let me spend it on you, so they might as well take it back."

"Is that how you really feel?"

"Yes!"

He would have argued more but her white face finally penetrated his conscience. Realizing how undone she was, he went to her, enfolding her in his arms. "Do whatever you want," he assured her roughly. "Just don't let them take you."

Her fingers were entangled in the hair at his nape. Did that mean he was reconsidering her offer? she wondered. "You never answered my question," she reminded him a bit shyly.

"Which question?"

"You know."

She felt him squeeze the bridge of his nose, and she knew then, with a sinking heart, that he'd hoped she wouldn't ask again. Still, she was in too far to give up now. "Marry me," she repeated. "What objections could Victoria have then? I—love you," she faltered, dying a little inside as she put her heart on the line. "We both love Tucker. He'd have two parents who love him."

"It's the answer to everything, right?"

His pride spoke for him; hostility simmering beneath the words.

"Yes," she said simply. "It is."

"And if there were no Tucker—just you and me—would you have brought this up?"

"No." Callie swallowed hard. "I would have waited, hoping you would."

To her relief, she felt his silent laughter. "I've never had a woman ask me to marry her before," he mused.

She ducked her head to his shoulder, embarrassed. "I've never asked a man."

"You must be desperate."

"I am." She chanced a direct look into his eyes. "Desperate."

A soft rap on the door prevented him from answering.

"Mrs. Cantrell," Laurene said, sticking her head inside the door.

"Yes?" She felt impatient by the woman's poor timing.

"A Mr. William Lister is on the phone and he insists on speaking to you," she said primly, as Callie slid from Gavin's arms. "He's been calling at least twice a day ever since you left, but since I didn't know the number..." She tossed a meaningful look in Gavin's direction.

"Thank you." She realized belatedly that Laurene had apparently learned she'd been married before. Had Derek related that information? Probably. He would have felt compelled to give some reason for wanting to see her.

"Has Mr. Cantrell gone?" Laurene inquired.

"Yes."

Satisfied, the older woman softly closed the door once more.

"Looks like things are coming to a head in San Francisco," Gavin observed dryly. "You can take the phone in here."

"You're not going to stay?"

Callie was surprised and unhappy to see him walk toward the door. She'd been so certain he was on the verge of agreeing with her.

"William Lister's on our side, isn't he? Don't worry. If Derek shows up again I'll be more than happy to…take care of him." He paused on the way out, the quirk of humor around his mouth making him appear more sexy than any man had a right to. "In fact," he drawled, "I can't think of anything I'd like better."

Her pride wouldn't let her call after him. He knew where she stood; it was up to him now. Disappointment weighing heavily upon her, she picked up the receiver and answered William's call.

The November rain was mixed with snow as Callie gazed unseeingly out the window. She was in a quandary. After Derek's visit she'd just about decided to meet the Cantrells in court, but William's recent call had changed everything.

"It'll be terrible for you, Callie," he'd stated flatly. "Derek and Catherine didn't wangle their way into my office and search through my private papers because they want to be *fair*! They're out for blood. Your blood."

It had been all she could do to calm the normally staid attorney down. She wasn't surprised that Derek had used his considerable charms and influence to get himself into William's office—the poor secretary had thought he was a member of the family William was representing!—and it certainly explained how Derek had found out about Gavin and the other Rutledges as well.

But William had been beside himself. "He's threatening to come after you, Callie!"

"He's been here already," she'd answered in a subdued tone.

"What?"

"Derek's already given me his pitch about settling amicably. He wanted me to return with him today. God, how did I get into such a mess?"

"Oh, Callie. He'll make a case of this business with Rutledge and the boy," William had bemoaned. "Come home and defend yourself."

While he had continued to fume over Derek's tactics, Callie had tried to convince herself that she'd made the right decision. But she'd never been able to fool herself for long and she realized, rather painfully, that she had run away from the situation for far too long. It was time to go home... at least for a little while.

"Okay," she'd said on a sigh. "I'll come back. I'll try to be there early tomorrow morning."

"You mean it?" William had been surprised. "What about the little boy?"

Her heart had twisted painfully as she'd realized she was going to have to say goodbye to Tucker before she'd hardly said hello. But she'd put off her duties long enough. When the mess over the Cantrell fortune was finally straightened out and Derek and Catherine were just an unpleasant memory, *then* she could come back to Denver and see him again. "I'll be there, William," she'd assured him. "You can count on it."

And I hope that Gavin waits for me.

Now, as her eye followed the incessant drip of snow and rain, she had the distinct impression she was being watched. Squaring her shoulders, figuring she might as well face the issue now as later, she turned around. But the blue eyes scrutinizing her so carefully weren't Gavin's; they were Victoria's. She stood in the doorway, straight and proud, her only concession to age the smooth, ivory-handled cane gripped in her right hand.

"Did I overhear that you're leaving again?" she asked in her pointed way.

Too inured to her autocratic manner by now, Callie wasn't even angry that she'd eavesdropped. Victoria was Victoria. She wasn't about to change. "I have some business to take care of in San Francisco."

"And then...?"

"And then...and then, I'm coming back," Callie said with more conviction than she felt. But she would return. For Tucker...and for Gavin.

Her snowy white brows drawn pensively together, Victoria slowly walked toward the fireplace, staring into its dying embers. "You seem like a level-headed young woman, Mrs. Cantrell. I've enjoyed having you here."

"Thank you." Callie attempted to hide her surprise.

"It never ceases to amaze me how women like yourself fall for my grandson."

The hidden barb beneath the velvet. It was always the same. Grinding her teeth together, Callie let her facade of graciousness toward Gavin's family crack wide open.

Queenlike, she drew herself up and said evenly, "You mean, Gavin?"

"I think it's his refreshing honesty that does it," Victoria mused, ignoring, or oblivious to, Callie's rising anger. "He has a way of telling the truth and making it appear romantic, somehow. But make no mistake: he isn't in line for an inheritance unless he steals it away from Stephen."

"Mrs. Rutledge, I think it's fair to say, I don't give a damn."

Victoria was not deterred. "My advice is for you not to capitalize his wildcatting venture. You'll waste your money."

Something inside Callie snapped. She thought of Gavin growing up under the cold specter of the Rutledge money, never being able to share, never being loved or wanted. For that she hated Victoria Rutledge and she hated her daughter, Gavin's mother, as well.

She lifted her chin. "It's my money to waste," she stated flatly. "And I wouldn't call Gavin 'down for the count' yet."

"Just so you understand the facts," Victoria murmured.

"I understand more than you could ever guess." Callie swept across the room, furious and reckless. "Don't you realize you've lost something beautiful? Your money has kept you from loving Gavin. You're his family. All he's got. Yet you act as if his illegitimacy is *his* fault! What a backward—sorry—thing to do."

Victoria's eyes glittered in surprise. "You shock me."

"Do I? Good. Because you shock me, too."

Confrontation had never been Callie's strong suit and she'd already suffered through more than a lifetime's worth. Her bravado slipping, she turned blindly to the door, knowing in her heart she hadn't helped. She'd just angered Gavin's grandmother and possibly ruined his fight to win custody of Tucker.

In the hallway she searched for Gavin but he was nowhere to be seen. Climbing the stairs she felt a weariness invade her legs that was bone deep. Exhaustion was overtaking her. When Tucker suddenly careened around the balustrade, gleefully throwing his arms around her, it was too much. Tears threatened the corners of her eyes.

"Ahh, sweetheart, it's so good to see you," she said, hugging him back.

"You are not leaving again," he said, tuning into the truth with that rare gift children alone seemed to possess.

Seeing Gavin standing behind him, Callie's heart flooded with more feelings. He was so unconsciously sensual, so elementally male. Loving them both so much it hurt, she said reluctantly, "I have to go back to San Francisco for a while. Just a while."

"I see." Gavin sounded grim.

Her eyes were on Tucker's anxious face but every nerve was attuned to Gavin. Sweeping back a lock of the boy's overgrown hair, she said haltingly, "I have to go. Do you understand?"

Tucker emphatically shook his head. "No."

"It won't be forever. There are people waiting there for me."

"That man?" he demanded suspiciously.

"Derek? Did you meet him?"

"He is taking you away."

Callie's breath caught at his resentful tone. Feeling way out of her depth, her words stumbling over one another, she said, "That's not—you don't understand. Derek was my husband's brother and I—"

Tucker didn't wait for her to clarify what she meant. He twisted his neck to make sure Gavin was still behind him and said something fast and low in French.

Shaking a finger in front of his nose, Callie said, "That's not fair! I'm telling you the truth. Do you know what shirking your responsibilities means?" She didn't wait for an answer as she swept on, "Well, I'll tell you. It means not doing what you should. I can't shirk my responsibilities any more, Tucker. I've got to face up to them."

"Where is San Francisco?" he mumbled miserably.

"Only two or three hours on a plane. I'll be back. I promise," Callie said urgently, squatting down to meet him eye to eye.

Giving in, Tucker's arms squeezed her neck and Callie's lids fluttered closed in relief. But upon opening them again she found Gavin's gaze fastened pensively on her face.

"When you're ready, I'll take you to the airport," he said unemotionally.

"Tomorrow." Callie managed a faint smile of thanks, and the issue was, at least on the surface, settled.

She seemed to have a knack for leaving a situation just before it reached crisis level, Callie thought tiredly as she set her bags on the veined marble entryhall floor of the Cantrell home. She'd taken off for Martinique right before the legal battle with Jonathan's sister and brother had heated up, and now she'd left Denver when her relationship with Gavin was at its most critical point so far.

Sighing, she stepped up the half flight of stairs to the main floor, walked down the cream-carpeted hallway, and switched up the thermostat. Though the house was huge and had been a holding of the Cantrells for several generations, she'd tried her best to make it a home—refusing servants and converting one of the rooms into a playroom. Still, for all that, it didn't feel like a home. The house, she thought ruefully, like everything else, really belonged to Derek and Catherine.

She flung herself down on the sofa, kicked off her shoes, and leaned her head back on the cushions. All she could see were Tucker's tear-filled eyes and Gavin's lean, sensual face. She'd left them at Stapleton airport, unable to look back as she'd boarded the plane, for fear that she, too, would break down and cry.

Why? she asked herself now. It wasn't as if she were leaving forever. This was just a temporary separation, she reminded herself firmly. Temporary.

So why did she feel so miserable?

There was only one way to combat this depression, she decided, resolutely rising to her feet. She would call William and have him contact Derek and Catherine right away—today, if possible—and get this show on the road.

And what are you going to do about the money? a voice inside her head taunted her.

Padding to the telephone in her stockinged feet, Callie bit into her lower lip. As much as she wanted to be rid of the Cantrell inheritance and all its incumbent headaches, she hadn't forgotten about Gavin's need for financing. He might not want her money, but he needed it.

As she dialed William's number, a dreadful, insidious thought crept into her mind. What if she gave up the money and then lost Gavin and Tucker, too—maybe as a byproduct of her actions?

The new secretary answered her call and asked if she could hold. Callie said yes and gave her name, her brain on a tortuous path of its own. She knew in her heart that Gavin's feelings for her were far removed from any monetary concerns, but she also knew he thought she should keep the inheritance. Being deprived on his own self-worth and portion of the Rutledge fortune had made him careful to hang on to what was his. Yet, this money wasn't really hers.

And Gavin needed it. What if, after she'd given back the money, he cut her out of her life anyway because he was in financial chaos and wouldn't take her down with him? What if Victoria ended up with Tucker? What if they were all losers because she made the critical error of giving up their only security. What if... what if... She could drown herself in "what ifs."

Callie sighed. The truth of the matter was that it didn't really matter. In the back of her mind, all along, she'd known the right, best and only thing to do. No amount of soul-searching could change one indisputable fact: the money wasn't hers.

"William, it's Callie," she said after he came on the line. "I'm back. Do you think Derek and Catherine would be willing to meet with me this afternoon?"

"Are you kidding? They'd miss their mother's funeral for the chance!"

The faintest of smiles touched her lips. "Then tell them I've made a decision. Let's meet in your office around four o'clock..."

Chapter Twelve

William's office was in one of the high-rise buildings off Union Square. Callie weaved her way through the heavy sidewalk traffic, feeling an unexpectedly warm wind sweep over her. A pale wintery sun rode high in the sky, and a fine, unseen mist hung just out of reach, coalescing unexpectedly on the crowns of passing pedestrians.

She pushed through the revolving door and stopped to get her bearings. Brushing nonexistent dirt from the cream-colored pleats of her wool suit, Callie then nervously touched the neckline of her aquamarine silk blouse. She was dressed for battle, her hair plaited around her head in a fiery coronet. No more soft, fragile vision of grieving femininity; Derek and Catherine were going to know this was their last and final meeting.

The elevator doors whirred open on the twelfth floor. Callie crossed to William's office and let herself inside.

"I'm here to see Mr. Lister," she said to the receptionist, and had to swallow a smile at the woman's quick assessment of her appearance. Callie had never come so prepared before.

"Go right in, Mrs. Cantrell. They're expecting you."

It always helped to make an entrance, Callie concluded later, when she had walked through the double doors into William's office. Derek and Catherine were already seated in two of the client chairs grouped around William's desk, but upon seeing Callie, Derek half rose, his expression eloquently revealing his consternation. Catherine, blond and impeccable as ever, regarded Callie through cool, unforgiving eyes, then threw her brother a scathing look, whereupon Derek slowly sat back down.

Murmurs of welcome were exchanged but it was William who came around his desk to shake her hand, his own eyes filled with surprise and delight at her composure. "Sit down, sit down. We've all been breathlessly waiting for you."

"There's no point in prolonging this," Callie said, as soon as William was reseated. "I'm giving up the fortune. Now. Without a court battle."

There was an instant of stunned amazement, then everyone had something to say.

"Why, Callie, I must say you've surprised me." Derek stroked his upper lip with a slightly trembling hand.

"I don't believe you," Catherine said flatly.

William peered at her closely. "Are you certain this is what you want?"

"I'm going to keep a small amount for myself. Enough to live on for one year, while I pick up on my teaching career again. But the bulk of it is yours," she said, glancing from Derek to Catherine. "There are, however, a few stipulations."

No one actually groaned but the walls seemed to echo the sentiment anyway. "Jonathan made money on the inheritance—a small fortune of his own. I want his earnings to go to charity, and the money that's invested in these stocks, bonds and companies—" Callie pulled out a folder from her purse, flipping to an earmarked page "—should be left there for the next twenty years, all profits also given to charity. I have a list of charitable organizations on the next page. William can handle that.

"At the end of twenty years," Callie said, taking a deep breath, "the initial funds revert back to you. All of the rest of the inheritance is yours to do with as you wish. Are there any questions?"

She'd bowled them over. Derek, for once in his life, was at a total loss for words, and Catherine looked on in horror, as if Callie had just done something unspeakable.

William cleared his throat. "Ah, I think it's all fairly clear, Callie."

"You really expect us to go along with this?" Catherine demanded chillingly.

"You'll have no choice."

Callie met Catherine's tight-lipped censure with a determination she hadn't felt in years. *Go ahead,* she silently challenged. *See if you'll win.*

Two years older than her brother, Catherine Cantrell wasn't used to being defied. She straightened her spine and had actually opened her mouth to speak when Derek's palm touched her arm.

"Let's think about it," he suggested in a low tone.

It was then Callie knew she'd won. Derek wouldn't let Catherine throw it all away for the sake of proving who was superior to whom. They'd got what they wanted—in a manner of speaking—and so had she. The weight off her shoulders was almost a physical relief.

"You sure about all this?" William asked again after Derek and Catherine had made their exit.

"Positive. You have no idea how glad I am to be through with them!" Callie's face was flushed with radiance.

"What now?" William asked her, smiling with fatherly affection. He knew that she'd probably made the best decision for her own self-esteem. "I have this strange feeling I should break out the champagne."

"Do it," she agreed, grinning, then shook her head and said, "No, wait. Let me call Gavin first. I've got to check in and tell him what I've done. Could I use your phone?"

"Sure, go ahead . . ." he said distractedly.

Callie sent him a questioning look as she picked up the receiver. "Is something wrong?"

The attorney ran a slow hand over his balding pate. "I just hadn't realized this Mr. Rutledge was so important to you. He doesn't—know then, that you've relinquished the Cantrell fortune?"

Ignoring the little trill his words sent down her nerves, she said, "No. That's what I'm going to tell him."

"I'll be waiting right outside when—"

"Oh, William, sit down!" Callie waved her hand and glared at him in mock ferocity. "I'm not going to kick you out of your office. I only hope Gavin hasn't left for Wyoming yet. Oh, hello?" she said, her attention diverted by the phone. "Could I speak to Gavin Rutledge, please? It's Callie Cantrell." She paused, every muscle tense. "Thank you. I'll hang on."

"He's coming," she said, her palm over the receiver.

William looked down at his hands, trying not to show his concern. He had done his research on Gavin Rutledge, and knew that it was quite likely that the man's interest in Callie had stemmed from her money.

Looking at her shining, expectant face he suddenly felt very, very old.

"You certainly took your time about answering," Callie said a moment later, her mouth curving with happiness. "No, no, everything's great. Just fine. How are you?" Some of her animation faded as she asked, "So soon? What about Tucker?" Another pause ensued and she plucked nervously at the pleats in her skirt. "Well, when will you be back?"

William grimaced. He hoped Callie was as strong inside as she'd presented herself to the Cantrells earlier.

She was staring out through the office windows, more reserved now. "I met with Derek and Catherine today. I gave them back their money—with a few stipulations. I've decided to go back to teaching."

Silently William slipped out of the office, closing the door behind him. He didn't want to witness her finding out that Gavin Rutledge was only after her money. As he closed the door he overheard Callie's voice saying with false cheer, "Sure. Call me when you get back to Denver. I'll be here...waiting..."

Gavin hung up the phone and tried to pull his thoughts together. She'd done it. She'd given up her inheritance. He felt a bit dazed by the revelation.

Hearing the floor squeak, he whipped around to catch Laurene trying to tiptoe past him.

"If you're interested," he drawled, his voice growing louder as Laurene's footsteps hurried out of range,

"Callie turned all the money back to Derek and Catherine Cantrell and kept none for herself!"

"I'm sure it's none of my business."

Swearing under his breath, Gavin strode out of the room and out of the house. He wasn't going back. He would rather live out of cheap motels for the rest of his life than spend one more minute with any of them. Besides, there was something he had to do and he had to do it now.

With a last, regretful thought of the luxury of Martinique, Gavin left to bargain every cent he had.

It was almost pathetic how minor the arrangements were that had to be made for Callie to sign away everything she owned. Derek, in an eleventh-hour attempt at chivalry, insisted that she keep the house, but Callie only wanted to sell it. An agreement had been made, and Derek and Catherine had purchased the property from her, leaving her with a small fortune after all.

Time passed slowly. She packed her belongings and got them ready to ship but no call came in from Gavin. Little eddies of doubt swirled in her mind, however, and it was with increasing difficulty that she rid herself of them.

It wasn't that he hadn't been glad to hear from her, but he'd definitely been distracted. Things were happening at the drilling site, he'd said, and he was anxious to get back. Why he hadn't left already was a mystery in itself, and after Callie had dropped her bomb about the Cantrell inheritance she'd never had a chance to ask him.

She wasn't sure how he felt about her giving up the money. At first she'd thought his distraction was because his mind was on oil. He was a wildcatter, after all; it practically ran in his blood. But as time went on, her convictions began to erode and she started second guessing herself. It hadn't been an oil strike that had made him seem so distant. It had been something else, something he didn't want to discuss.

Could he have been just the tiniest bit upset that she'd signed it all away?

"You're going stir crazy," she muttered to herself and closed her mind to further disastrous thoughts.

At the end of two weeks, after Derek had called and asked her if she wanted to stay on in the house longer than she'd originally anticipated, Callie took her fate into her own hands. She called the Rutledge house.

"He's not here," Laurene said flatly. "He left over a week ago. I don't know where he is."

Callie asked to speak to Tucker but Laurene informed her he was with Victoria. They'd gone for a chauffeured drive around Denver.

Horrified, Callie hung up, wondering what in the world a child like Tucker could find to enjoy in his current surroundings. Did he get to play with other children? Did he have any toys? What about outdoor sports?

Her thoughts turned naturally to Martinique. Tucker's friendship with Michel had been very important to him, as had the fishing trips he'd either poached from the more easygoing captains or that Gavin had paid for.

But what about now?

Making herself a cup of tea, Callie's eyes drifted over the appointments of her elegant home. She didn't give a damn where she lived, she thought tearfully, as long as it was with Tucker and Gavin.

Why didn't he call her?

She was still asking herself the same thing three days later when her resistance broke down again and she reached for the phone. Her hands were shaking and she felt distinctly weepy, both of which made her angry. She shouldn't have to go through all this pain. She was too *old* for it, for God's sake!

Days earlier, she'd thought her see-sawing emotions might be from a different cause. Even though she'd calculated she probably couldn't be pregnant the idea had hovered in her mind, a beautiful secret she had all to herself. Only after she learned it wasn't true did she remind herself that Gavin might not be terribly excited about fathering an illegitimate child of his own—but even that didn't solve her depression.

She'd had to face facts. She was afraid she might be losing him, and it was tearing her apart.

As the line rang on and on, Callie's nerves stretched tighter and tighter. Her hopes sank when Laurene's stiff voice came over the wire.

"I'd like to speak to Tucker, please," Callie said with a catch in her throat. "It's Callie Cantrell."

"Uh...I'm not sure if he's available. Just a minute..."

Left hanging on the phone, she placed her chin in her palm, feeling miserable. She was going to get nowhere; she knew it already. They weren't going to let her talk to Tucker and she wasn't sure she had the courage to call Gavin at the drilling site.

After an interminable length of time the receiver was picked up again. "Mrs. Cantrell. This is Victoria speaking. You wanted to speak to Stephen?"

"Yes...please," she said humbly.

"I'm sorry, but he's not here. He's been registered in a private kindergarten, and he just started Tuesday."

Callie's lips quivered uncontrollably. What was wrong with her? Why did she want to die? Kindergarten could be wonderful for Tucker. But her mind was filled with images of perfectly groomed little boys in blue shorts and blazers, marching single file into a huge dining hall.

"Mrs. Cantrell . . . ?"

"It's Callie," she said faintly. "Call me Callie. I can't stand formality."

There was a knowing pause on the other end of the line. "All right, Callie," she said with cool emphasis. "Is there anything else I can do for you?"

"What happened over Tucker's custody?" The question came out of the blue; she hadn't even been thinking it. But she had a sudden, urgent need to find out.

"I thought you knew." Victoria sounded vaguely surprised. "Teresa left Stephen with me. I have custody."

Her world collapsed around her. *No!* It was impossible! Gavin wouldn't allow it! "I don't believe you."

"It's quite true. Teresa was willing to give up all rights to the boy as long as she knew he'd be well cared for. You didn't, by any chance, think Gavin would end up with him, did you?"

Overwhelmed, Callie could think of nothing to say. Victoria had beaten her down with a few well-chosen words.

"Gavin has nothing to offer the boy," Victoria went on in a perplexed tone. "I'm the logical choice as his guardian. Why is it so difficult for you both to see?"

Nothing to offer the boy but love.

Her throat ached with the effort of keeping her tears at bay. "Where's—where's Gavin?" she managed to get out.

Victoria sighed and said, not unkindly, "I'm not really sure. Callie, since you obviously care so much about him, why ever did you give up your inheritance? Don't you know that was like slipping his leash? My best guess is that he's on the trail of another heiress. I'm sorry. . . ."

* * *

It wasn't that she didn't trust Gavin, she told herself over and over again, but she'd certainly had her faith rocked. Calling the drilling site had only elicited the terse information from Kent that Gavin had "dropped off the planet just as all hell was breaking loose!" and though she had wanted to ask if that was good news as far as the oil well was concerned, Kent's tone hadn't encouraged further conversation.

Where was Gavin? If anywhere, he should be in Wyoming *now*.

And what about Tucker?

Thinking of the boy, Callie couldn't help feeling sick at heart and totally impotent. She hoped he was happy, but she knew, deep down, that the privileges of being a Rutledge couldn't compare to the carefree life he'd lived on Martinique. The Rouseaus, for all their shortcomings, might have been a better choice of guardian than Tucker's own great-grandmother.

And she was as much at fault as anyone that things had turned out the way they had. Wearily, she wondered how she could face herself in the mirror every morning, knowing what she'd done to Tucker.

Why wasn't Gavin fighting Victoria? *What was happening?*

It was seeing the bracelet again that finally shook Callie out of her despondency and forced her into action. Gavin had never given it back to Aimee and Callie had ended up with it by default. Turning it over in her hands, she thought bitterly of how much trouble her possession of it had caused. How ironic that she'd been left with this valuable heirloom when all she really wanted was love.

Well, the new Callie wasn't going to take it. She tossed the bracelet on her bed in disgust, crossing to the night-

stand and snatching up the phone. She would book a
flight out today, to Denver, and if the Rutledges tried to
give her the cold shoulder she would fight them tooth and
nail. If Gavin wasn't there she would track him down in
Wyoming, or wherever. But she wasn't going to give up.
She was going to fight back.

Her doorbell rang while she was making the reservation. She ignored it and it pealed more insistently.

"I'll take whatever you've got," she assured the
booking agent a trifle impatiently. "The sooner the better."

While the agent keyed in the reservation Callie's doorbell rang again and she uttered a sound of exasperation.
She decided she didn't care who it was. She needed this
flight.

"Thank you," she said hurriedly, as the man was still
reading back the information. "I'll pick up my ticket
when I get there."

She slammed the receiver down before he'd quite finished and hastened down the entryhall steps to the front
door. If Derek was trying to rush her out of the house he
was going to get a piece of her mind. She was spoiling for
a fight!

"Gavin."

Callie was so stunned by his unexpected appearance on
her doorstep she didn't know what else to say.

His jacket was hooked over his thumb, and the lines
beside his mouth were etched more deeply—he looked
tired and worn out and wrinkled, but satisfaction
gleamed between his thick lashes. "Aren't you going to
invite me in?"

Her gaze swept him from head to foot. His hair was
rumpled, his chin dark with another three days of whis-

kers, and he looked suspiciously as if he were in desperate need of a shower.

"Where on earth have you been?" she asked, when her voice came back.

"I've been in negotiations," he said cryptically, following after her, his gaze raking over the lush appointments of her house: the veined marble floor, the ultra-thick carpeting, the gold fixtures and crystal lamps.

"Really." Callie's heart started a dance of its own, her spirits lifting in spite of herself. He was here. He'd come after her! "You look terrible."

"I feel great," he said, a remarkable grin splitting his lean face.

"The oil well . . ." Callie could hardly breathe.

He inclined his head, acknowledging the truth, yet not really saying anything. He rubbed a hand over his jaw. "Think I could get a shower?"

"Not on your life. You're going to talk."

She grabbed his hand and dragged him into the living room. It didn't matter what he said; she was already embarrassed that she'd had even the faintest twinges of doubt about him.

Gavin's blue eyes were lazily affectionate. "Somehow, I expected a less friendly reception."

"You deserve to be tarred, feathered and marinated," she agreed, "but I have more than enough time for that later." With an imperiousness that would have rivaled Victoria's, Callie positioned him on the couch and sat down beside him, smelling his musky male scent that was not at all unpleasant. "I've been waiting for your call."

"I know."

"Well, what took you so long?" she demanded impatiently.

Gavin's eyes were on her face, as if he were rememorizing every plane and angle. "The truth?"

"Of course."

He leaned back tiredly, grimacing. "I wasn't sure I was going to call you again."

"What?" Her voice was faint as she heard her worst fears confirmed.

"You know why," he said condemningly, gesturing with his palm. "Look around you. You'd been living like this for a long time, and whether you know it or not, it's hard to give up. What would life be like with me? Uncertain, hard, probably impossible for most women..." He sighed. "You knew how I felt. I'd told you in enough different ways."

"And I'd told you that I could make my own decisions. Oh, Gavin, don't you know the misery you've put me through?"

His gaze softened and almost unwillingly his hand came up to brush her hair back. "Yes," he admitted huskily. "But it was all for the greater good."

"Was it?" Callie's eyes were serious.

"I thought so."

She wanted to be infuriated with him for playing such silly games with her, but though he'd really said nothing to indicate his feelings now, she already knew he'd come back to her for good. "It was all pride with you," she accused. "You wouldn't marry me because of your pride."

He laughed, a low rumble that sounded wonderful. "You're so wrong, my love. I came this close," he said, pinching his thumb and forefinger together, "to accepting your proposal. And it wasn't entirely for Tucker. I wanted you. For me."

"You should have accepted," she said, sliding him a provocative glance. "We could have been together all this time."

"No."

"No?" He was driving her crazy. Just when she thought she understood him, he threw her a curve. "Then why are you here now?" she demanded, attempting to stand.

Gavin reached his hand out and jerked her down again. "Because I love you, Callie. I have since the first time I saw you—even when I thought you were Teresa. It nearly killed me, but I couldn't stop loving you."

It was all he had to say. Her lips parted, trembling. She hadn't realized how much she'd longed to hear him say those words, just in that exact tone.

"But when I figured it all out—all this," he said, looking round with a grimace. "I couldn't take it away from you by risking it in wildcatting."

His arm was sliding around her waist, and Callie leaned forward, brushing her lips against his, her blue eyes soft and misty. "And now?" she asked a bit tremulously.

"And now..." He groaned and pulled her to him, his hands raking through her hair, his mouth demanding more than just a whispered kiss.

It was Callie's need for more answers that broke their amorous embrace. Breathing a little fast, she said, "The well. You didn't tell me what happened. Did you strike oil?"

"Mmm-hmm." His smile was raffish and self-satisfied. "Enough to encourage bankers to advance money on more ventures. But it's no guarantee, Callie. I can move from prince to pauper in a matter of hours.

Although," he admitted, "even Kent's optimistic on this one and that's saying something."

"Where were you, Gavin? Why weren't you at the drilling site?"

His brows lifted. "You called there?"

"You bet I did. And Kent was beside himself because he thought you'd dropped off the face of the planet."

"Ahh, Callie, there's so much to say."

"Gavin, don't keep me in suspense any longer. I've been miserable, calling the Rutledge house, trying to get them to tell me where you were, attempting to talk to Tucker..." She drew in an unsteady breath. "Victoria told me she has custody? Is that true?"

Her anxious face made him touch her cheek, his fingers gently moving over the downy curve. "No, it's not."

Callie blinked. "She told me...well, she basically said she'd bought Teresa off, along with intimating you were off chasing down another heiress."

Gavin went completely still. "What?"

Shaking her head, sorry she'd mentioned it at all, she said, "It was just a way to make me think you didn't want me after I told you I'd given up the Cantrell money. I didn't believe her, but—my God, Gavin, what's the matter?"

His jaw had hardened with the rigidity that always warned of disaster. "Damn her. I should have known—"

He cut himself off and Callie said, "Who? Victoria?"

"You know where I was?" he demanded. "Chasing down Teresa, *not* another heiress. Good God, when I think about my grandmother I want to slam my fist through a wall!"

Callie knew she was missing something vital. "Teresa? You were after Teresa?"

"I'm ashamed to say it, but Victoria pulled one over on me," Gavin said, relaxing a little, his mouth twisting self-deprecatingly. "She settled with Teresa and led me to believe I had some bargaining power with her. No dice. Once it was all over and Teresa was gone, she told me she had custody and that was that. I'd just found out right before you called."

"That's why you were distracted," Callie said, remembering.

"So I went after Teresa. She wasn't too hard to find. She'd given Victoria a number where she could be reached and I just helped myself to it. I tracked her down in New York, living with a man who seems to like money almost as much as she does." His expression was wry. "At least, they both know how to spend it."

Callie could well imagine. Teresa had made a very definite impression, and though she must care about her son to some degree—it was impossible for Callie to believe any woman couldn't love their own child—cash was certainly a higher priority than Tucker.

"They weren't exactly thrilled to see me at first," Gavin went on sardonically. "But I made my own deal. I offered her all the money I had left for Tucker."

"Gavin!"

He shook his head. "I wasn't as penniless as I made out to you." He gave her a quick look to see how she was reacting, but Callie kept a poker face. "That was just to warn you about the potential I had for losing," he admitted.

"You absolute wretch," she said with feeling.

"Don't get me wrong, Callie. I can lose."

She kissed him, hard. "You can win, too. Go on. We'll discuss your tendency to lie later."

He smiled, his eyes darkening in direct response to her touch. "There's not a lot more to tell. I made a sweeter deal with Teresa and convinced her to work only with me in the future. The custody papers hadn't been filed for Victoria yet, and I breathed down Teresa's neck to make certain things went my way." He sighed. "I went straight from New York, to Wyoming, to here. I still have the dubious pleasure of telling my grandmother."

"You should have stopped me from giving up the fortune," Callie murmured. "I would have helped you."

"It's better this way. I only wanted you to keep that money for you, but you look...happier," he said, scrutinizing her carefully.

"I am. So much." Her lips curved invitingly. She felt curiously light-headed. "So Tucker is truly yours?"

Gavin tightened his arms around her. "I put the fear of God in Teresa. I'll be mighty surprised if she tries to back out now."

"But Victoria...?"

"Oh, that's right." With an endearing kind of reluctance, he pushed her away and got up. "Mind if I use your phone?"

Callie leaned her elbows on the overstuffed arm of the couch, resting her chin on her hands, watching him. "Be my guest."

The connection seemed to take a long time. She realized, as she watched him stretch his tired muscles, how truly weary he was.

"It's Gavin. Get Victoria on the phone," he said rudely, and Callie lifted her brows at the tone. "Laurene and I have an understanding," he said in an aside. "She loathes me and I loathe her. It's a mutually satisfying relationship. Ahhh... Victoria—" he pinched the bridge of his nose "—there's something I have to tell you..."

* * *

Callie waited outside her bathroom door, listening to the shower, a smile hovering at the corners of her mouth. She couldn't believe this was her life. She couldn't believe she could be so lucky as to have a second chance.

Gavin had told Victoria that he had custody, and surprisingly, she'd given in graciously. She'd even wished him luck—an absolute first, Gavin had told Callie later—and then she'd had the audacity and gall to tell him he'd better hang on to Callie if he wanted her blessing. When Gavin had gotten off the phone he'd been so dumbstruck by Victoria's change of heart he'd looked lost. Though she'd kept mum, Callie had a feeling Victoria had somehow finally realized some of the foolishness of her ways. She hoped it was a sign of the future.

Hearing the taps shut off, she twisted the doorknob, and snatched up a towel, holding it out to Gavin as she snapped open the shower door.

Her boldness made his mouth twitch as he wrapped the fluffy peach-colored towel around his lean hips. "I would have invited you in," he said, inclining his head toward the shower.

Looking at him did strange things to her knees. "I love you," Callie whispered, suddenly dry mouthed.

His arms enclosed her, drawing her against his tautly muscled frame. "I'm wet ... I know I'm wet," he murmured, but his hands were fumbling for her clothes, pulling them off with an urgency that left Callie breathless.

There was no room for words. They came together eagerly, Gavin's arms slipping sensuously around her to carry her to the bed. She felt something cold and sharp against her lower back—the bracelet—and when she pulled it out, both she and Gavin looked at it for a silent moment.

Then he set it aside and his mouth searched for hers, his lovemaking intense, a passionate assault on her senses that Callie eagerly welcomed. There was new feeling between them, a powerful unspoken commitment that made her breath catch.

In the aftermath of lovemaking, Gavin kissed her throat, touched her in ways that let her know how much he cared.

She traced her fingers through the hair at his temple, her heart full. "For a while, when I was waiting to hear from you, I thought I might be pregnant," she whispered.

His mouth was still at her throat but the kissing stopped. He didn't say anything.

"I wasn't," she said, her eyes filling with poignant tears.

He looked at her then, and seeing her reaction, his own eyes burned with a long-forgotten sensation. He hadn't known he still possessed the ability to cry. It made him mute with gratitude to this one, remarkable woman. "I'm sorry," was all he could think to say.

Callie shook her head against the satin pillow. "I wasn't sure what you'd think . . . considering we weren't married and after everything you'd gone through . . . the way your family treated you. . . ."

"Well, I would have dragged you to the altar," he said with a return of humor. "You can bet on that."

"Is that what it's going to take? To get you to drag me to the altar?"

Her insecurity was touching. Gavin loved her more than he'd ever loved anyone. "Lady," he growled. "You never give me a chance to ask."

Callie smiled through her tears. "Ask," she begged softly.

"Marry me. Right away. We'll live anywhere you want, do anything you want to do." He squeezed her with powerful arms and added, "We'll be a family. You, me and Tucker, and if you want more children, all the better."

"Wyoming will be fine," she said. "Anywhere will be fine."

"I take it that's a yes."

"Yes."

They looked at each other, reading the other's eyes— love, commitment, desire, trust and respect were there in equal proportions.

"How would you feel about a honeymoon in Martinique?" Gavin suggested in the drawl Callie found so attractive.

"Can we afford it?"

"If the well's going a tenth of what I think it is...yes."

She didn't tell him about the money from the house. She would save that for later. "Then let's go."

"There's one more thing first . . ."

Hearing amusement beneath his voice, Callie squinted up at him, seeing the sparkle in his blue eyes. "What?"

"I don't want to get out of bed yet. I'd like to try out one of your suggestions."

"My suggestions?" She was baffled.

"Uh-huh. Something about marination, I believe."

And he laughed as she tried to hit him, pinning her arms down and kissing her until all she could think about was loving him.

Silhouette Special Edition

COMING NEXT MONTH

FORGIVE AND FORGET—Tracy Sinclair
Rand worked for the one man Dani hated—her grandfather. And though
Dani knew it was just Rand's job to entertain her, she found herself falling
in love with him.

HONEYMOON FOR ONE—Carole Halston
Jack Adams was more than willing to do the imitation bridegroom act, but
he didn't want to stop with an imitation, and Rita wasn't willing
to comply. She wanted someone serious and stable, and Jack was
anything but.

A MATCH FOR ALWAYS—Maralys Wills
Jon was a player without a coach; Lindy was a coach without a player.
They made an unbeatable team so it was only natural they would find each
other. Suddenly tennis wasn't the only game they were playing.

ONE MAN'S LOVE—Lisa Jackson
When Stacey agreed to help Nathan Sloan with his daughter, she didn't
realize that the father would be the biggest puzzle—and cause the
most problems.

SOMETHING WORTH KEEPING—Kathleen Eagle
Brenna was unsure about returning to the Black Hills, but nonetheless she
was excited to compete against Cord O'Brien. She was confident she could
win the horse race, but she might lose her heart in the process.

BETWEEN THE RAINDROPS—Mary Lynn Baxter
Cole Weston was hired to prove that Beth Loring was an unfit mother. But
how could he build a case against this woman when he found himself
falling head over heels in love with her?

AVAILABLE THIS MONTH:

DOUBLE JEOPARDY
Brooke Hastings

SHADOWS IN THE NIGHT
Linda Turner

WILDCATTER'S PROMISE
Margaret Ripy

JUST A KISS AWAY
Natalie Bishop

OUT OF A DREAM
Diana Stuart

WHIMS OF FATE
Ruth Langan

Silhouette Desire

**Available
January 1987**

NEVADA
SILVER

The third book in the exciting
Desire Trilogy by Joan Hohl.

The Sharp brothers are back, along with
sister Kit . . . and Logan McKittrick.

Kit's loved Logan all her life and, with a little
help from the silver glow of a Nevada night,
she must convince the stubborn rancher that
she's a woman who needs a man's love—not
the protection of another brother.

Don't miss *Nevada Silver*—Kit and
Logan's story and the conclusion
of Joan Hohl's acclaimed
Desire Trilogy.

DT-C-1

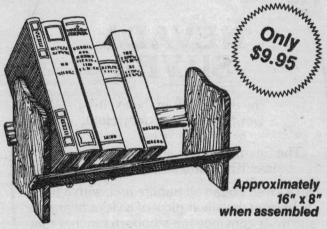